D1522530

Klaus   Rifbjerg

ANNA
(I)
ANNA

translated by Alexander Taylor

An Augustinus/Curbstone Book

The translator wishes to thank
The Augustinus Foundation for support,
Klaus Rifbjerg for many valuable suggestions,
Richard Bethards for his careful commentary
on the English text, and, finally,
the administration, staff and students at
Krogerup Højskole for their generous
aid and support.

This book was   **The Connecticut Commission on the Arts**
published with **The Danish Ministry of Culture**
the support of: **The Danish Government Committee for**
       Cultural Exchange

front cover: Kitte Fennestad

AN AUGUSTINUS/CURBSTONE BOOK

This book was originally published by
Gyldendal Publishers, Copenhagen, Denmark.

LC: 82-5140
ISBN: 0-915306-30-1
Danish ISBN: 87-7456-953-8

distributed in **Vindrose Forlag**
Denmark by: **14 Nybrogade**
    1203 Copenhagen K
    Denmark

CURBSTONE PRESS   321 Jackson Street   Willimantic, CT 06226

ANNA
(I)
ANNA

1

Once again I woke too early and heard my booming name, Anna. Who's calling? Who called? No one. I know where I am, or rather, when I wake up I focus first on crawling back into the room. The name is announced. That's what wakes me. I wake in the echo of my self, and there's no one calling, but my moorings dangle and I can only free my dead-weight in all this weightlessness by finding the way back, crawling in, casting anchor.

I'm in my bed. There is a bed, on a floor, in a room, in a house, on a lot. I'm lying in bed and the taste between my stomach and my mouth and my weightless brain swings the name Anna. It's better to be cheerful, so I say Hi and feel the bit of foundation established in the waking-up process slip. This is wrong. This is really wrong, and panic has already overtaken my ability to choose. Come on then, reality, I'll show you.

If you've never been crazy, then you don't know that reality is the worst insult to the sick. But the words I'm using are too strong and weaken my stand. I have to crawl in and concretize. Anna, bed, adjacent bed. Yesterday the decision was made, and it's a happy day. I'm waking to a happy day, and it's easy to make up your mind about everything, think it through. I can take each thing separately, turn it, observe it, set it aside like a souvenir on a shelf, take the next, smell it, bite, taste, *control*.

It looks like this. Your profile like a cave animal's against the curtain's light, the moon is shining. You are breathing soundlessly, and whatever messages or presentiments there must be in you are either resting or doing gymnastics behind your flickering eyelids. Perhaps in your unconsciousness you still sense me here among the apples and oranges, Anna, in the Biblical bed, drawn by exhausted but proud asses. Perhaps you really know, Tom, that I am lying here ready to be cut up, the main course, brought in under a lid of silver, steaming, breathless, reflecting the hunger and longing of the Roman Legionnaires, ready to fulfill their dreams, who for nights, weeks, months, years have lacerated their feet over the plains of Anatolia, craned their necks out over a well in Judea and screamed their civilized horror into the face of the enemy, whose language sounded like the rasping of a reluctant rubberband. I'm going now, old friend, and it's a desertion.

I'm up for sale. It was yesterday afternoon, and it isn't hard to remember. Reality looked like this: The light machine-bright, the leaves of the plane trees dry, the grass still yellowed and mottled, small shoots in the wreathed topknots of the palms. The house white with tiles, stained wood, the geraniums in bloom, a few withered leaves among them, too. I want to sit down and count them. There you have it: the geraniums are an insult. Their withered leaves an affront. Their lush, pink, newly bloomed, bawling, delicate, defiant petals a threat. There are the flowers, and I fetch the wicker chair. Inside the drawer there's a knife. I fetch the chair and put it down next to the geranium bed. There are a lòt of geraniums. Once they were seeds, then cuttings, now they're here in Anna's garden, it's the month of March and the ocean is a place out back. If one wants to count the geraniums or their petals, one begins with one. Then comes two. One, two. Very simple process. Then three. Three geraniums or three petals. If one closes one's eyes, perhaps the geraniums are gone--someone or other has said that. But if Anna opens her eyes and looks at the geraniums, which a gardener has planted, in the clear daylight, then there they are.

It's amusing to think that he can defend himself. Perhaps, then, the desire is less, too. It's like in the theatre. A shadow bent over a sleeping body in the dark, and isn't it unthinkable that he should be able to go on sleeping after the first stab? The clock is watching me and at quarter past five sticks out its tongue toward the East. But there would be an odd sound in the kitchen when the drawer slid out, and it was the moment and maybe I got ahold of the blade instead of the handle. The blade in my hand! So I'm on the sheet now, lying here among the geraniums and the weightlessness. It's so simple.

I'm thirty-five years old and crazy about geraniums. I feel fine. My existence is simple and enviable. I have a bed and Tom sleeps beside me. Farther down the hall John sleeps in his room and Minna lies with her teddy bear. Even if I took it into my head to go into the kitchen now, it would be impossible to get into the drawer. Our watch-boy would wake up at once and ask if there was something I needed. A glass of water. And he would be surprised, but would open the refrigerator anyway and hand me one of the pitchers, even though he knew there were thermos pitchers set out on the night table for Tom and me. I couldn't ask him for a knife. He would root it out and ask whether Memsahib wanted a large or a small one, and Anna would answer: I'll take the large one, the one with the broad blade at the extreme end, the one that Ahcmat sharpens against the stone outside, the one that gleams in the sun when he turns the blade in his hand, the one that's used for meat in the kitchen, the one that cracks against the carving board when it cuts through. The big knife. And I'd go with it through the butler's pantry and dining room and under the skylight and the big fan, yes I would, I'd open the door, but what about the teddy bear? What happens to the teddy bear? What do you do with the teddy bear afterwards, when it's done? Couldn't I remove

7

the teddy bear first and then cut? But she mustn't feel anything, the darling. Darling little Minna, a child in the trees, my child born in heaven between the blue swans and the minarets. My child of lime and jade and corrugated iron, my warm-hearted pixie, here comes Anna now with the knife and lifts you up so that your neck is exposed and your head falls backwards, while you still sleep. Security, moonshine, twinkling, the old ravens clatter across the roof and the camels, which you love, turn their heads toward each other and smile.

That's the way the French movie would begin and a woman with bowed head is led away while the much too heavy doors slam. The caps are wrong and the tinting old-fashioned, yellowish. It's raining, it's raining in Karachi, but only on celluloid: The child-murderer cries and the firing squad goes through its motions.

It's half-past five, and there's no blood-soaked teddy bear to put on the windowsill. On the other hand there is a bill of lading with my name on it here in the bed under the covers. I am free and free from guilt. Hurdles pop up around me, In the dark under the covers with my flashlight I'm writing a book for young girls: Anna Clears the Hurdles. I turn toward Tom and remember everything. My clever man, my friend. A parti-colored garden fly landed on his right ear, and I looked at it while I heard Anna speak. It's so easy. The process can be described physiologically-anatomically. Air, drawn into the lungs in the respiratory process (a kind of spasm) is thrust out through the windpipe, passes the vocal chords, is shaped by the tongue against the teeth, palate, soft palate, stop, *release*--words. I said to Tom: I'm not feeling too well. I said to Tom: I'm feeling depressed. I don't know what I said to Tom but I'll try again. It has to be right. First I noted my face and said to myself: Anna, you have a tragic expression on your face. So I fought back and changed my tragic expression to a serious-melancholy face, but I couldn't accept that. Then I smiled and said: Tom, I want to kill Minna. No, I said:

8

It's my face you see, but it isn't my face. I don't have anything to say about it. When I want it to look tragic, it giggles. When I ask my face to express anxiety, it looks like it's faking. I don't have a face, but can speak. I said: Why is it Minna and not you or John I want to kill? No, I spoke cleverly, I said to Tom (and the garden fly neared his earlobe): Listen, Tom . . .

it was in the garden and I let it grow around me, but felt no security. I'm still lying, all the same. For the garden was terror-struck. It struck a pose with its most trivial mien. It called to me and I felt my vocal chords grind against each other in drought. Its gravel crunched. The fountain, a faun with flute and a clamshell, which covers and streams over his back--exhibited all its cemented commonness. It was as if the imported yew trees gathered dust from the sheer need to hide their resentment, and in the box tree the privet larvae were bristling from branch to branch, from leaf to leaf, verdigris green and pink, gently swaying, their curved horns quivering phalluses in a crazy joke-and-jest dealer's New Year's display. And I'm still lying, for I didn't see anything. I would have thrown myself down on my knees and shouted with gratitude for even a single sight, but only the buzzard's shadow brushed me for an instant, while it flew low from the garbage heap behind the domestics' quarters down to the river. Everything was quiet, ordinary as water, real. Tom shaded his eyes and we moved into the shade, where under the awning Ben Ali had set out some white garden furniture and a sofa hung under a blue canopy.

But I really saw him. Yes, Tom. It's fun to be able to see you once in a while. How did you look? May I say? You're a handsome man. I can't use words like that, but here they come: You're a handsome man, mature; your age is easy: fifty-two; your clothes are easier: shirt, as always in the tropics, without tie and with short sleeves: shoes brown, openwork. It's easy. In reality everything is easy. There I said it, and it's the easiest lie I've told yet. But when I hear myself speak it ironically or bitterly or with contempt, I simply feel the need to cry, but suddenly a film is drawn over the light of the lunch hour and I turn the words around and say, while I smile at you earnestly:

--Everything is difficult, really.

You sat down on the sofa and crossed your legs. We were in the habit of calling it "the Swing," and you often repeat, even though you know I've heard it before, that it's easier to get things swinging when you're sitting in the "Swing". You looked at me and smiled, and I smiled back, while our mouths became self-contained and wanted to disappear like unnoticed, neutral insects in the heat.

Anna spoke, and I listened to her.

--I'm not too well, Tom. No, no, I'm not sick, I'm all right. I'm just not too well.

And he looked at Anna and said:

--What was that you said before about reality? It sounded so philosophical.

That was a good place to start and I spoke myself:

--Nonsense, Tom. Now listen. Have you ever felt like killing someone?

--Yes, often.

--No, tell me seriously. Have you ever had the nearly uncontrollable desire to kill someone?

--I don't know what you mean.

The buzzard uttered his cry and the garden fly was gone.

Tom bent forward and traced one of the grooves in his shoe with his fingertips.

--During the war I'm sure that I really felt the desire to kill.

--But you didn't.

--It wasn't my job.

Stillness.

10

It will soon be half-past six, and I know one can't hold a conversation this way. You've turned many times in bed and in an hour Mirres will come with tea. Clothes are no uniform, a blanket doesn't change anything. I stare from my auditorium's highest balcony, and you are there like a machine, something that can be demonstrated and dismantled. I lie here in my bed, leave it, float over you and watch your heart's peaceful batonbeat, andante, your blood's gliding rich stream and the shadow of your aorta over your chest. I sew you into your flesh, hook and close up your back and marvel at how quickly we forget. Your sex in my hand hundreds of times, your sex in me innumerable times, but how was it now, and can we speak to each other and with each other in only one way? Good morning, strange man under monogrammed linen, now I know why I want to kill my youngest child. So that she'll never turn out like you, or so that she'll never turn out like anyone but you.

In the course of these days, yesterday and the day before yesterday, I've told you everything, but how could you help but not know it? I talked in one and in two and in three ways, but you answered in only one. You answered in the most loving and most refined way. You talked to me like a comforting minister to the bereaved at the funeral of an unimportant person. Not unctuously, not sentimentally, but warmly and drily at the same time. Good handshake. Farewell. No, you talked properly to me, and I saw you before me like the garden and the geraniums and the children, everybody and everything which irritates me and annoys me and is close at hand, which *is* me, which I suddenly cannot reach. If I don't sharpen the knife, dig it up out of the meadow next to the waterfall, crawl up between the rocks and wrench it out of the ice at the edge of the falls, stop my Berber and disarm him, steal his sabre so that I can finally get to see these sinews, these veins, this yellowish, thin bacon-rind just along the neck of the severed head, where the arteries rise

11

like two whipsnakes and send a shocking double stream out over the pillows and sheets and the yellow teddy bear, which wards off the blows with its paws, but drowns at last in the sluggishness of the thick fluid.

Hi, I'm feeling bad, Tom. I'm not feeling so very terrific. To be honest about it, I'm really feeling fairly rattled. It's not that I want to complain. I'm not trying to bellyache. I don't want anything in particular from you. But here is the lowdown, Mr. Ambassador: I wake up too early each morning and feel black inside like a crushed Negro. I wake every morning and hear my name hammered around in a boiler and know that in a minute, in a second, in a little fraction of a course of time, I will go in to Minna with your pocket knife and thrust it into her until she's no longer alive. I will. And it makes my arteries hurt, and the tiny hairs along my spine freeze, and I can't move and after a little while I cry and wake you and you ask what's the matter, and I don't say a thing, but you think I'm having my period or early menopause or delayed puberty and think that if you just treat me kindly, it'll go away in a little while.

Hi, it's certainly a fine life. It is. That's what I tell myself. I feel down my body and say: First rate. It's all there. Two children didn't knock it out of you. It's all there, your tits are still curved, your stomach's only slightly creased, and that down there never changes. Tom taught me that, and there's a story of Colette's about an eighty-nine year old countess whose stomach, womb and thighs are snow-white whereas the rest of her body decays and her face is so loathsome that when she undressed she had to put a bag over her head before the young lovers could pull themselves together enough to do anything with her. Anyway, they all fell, once they had witnessed her beauty, and perhaps her experience, Tom, had helped a little. Her knowledge, which she had gotten from other men, as I've gotten it from you.

12

That's why I grew quiet and listened while you talked. Things went better after Mirres had set out our afternoon drinks and you sat with the green glass and let soda-pearls jump toward your lip.

--I don't know how I can explain it, I said, and wasn't lying. Still, Tom, I feel like I could just throw myself down and blubber all the time and am afraid because I don't even know myself what I'm going to do next.

--Why do you want to kill Minna? Don't you like her?

He smiled and I didn't need to answer.

Then, too, I was in my clothes, you see, and could get up and walk around in the white slacks and feel the collar of my silk shirt at the back of my neck and the little scarf at my throat and my brassiere, and if anyone asked me, I could name everything, everything in the world and say that it was there: Out back to the right the house, inside it Ben Ali, Ahcmat, Mirres, Nhadrudman, Irtu and his wife, the Sarat girls, Ghali, Parta and Minna. Yes, Minna. Farther back: the city, the sea, the desert, the mountains, and farther still everything else. Yes, ask me. Aren't they there, all of them, put in the right places: de Gaulle, Wilson, Franco, Nixon, Castro, Ho Chi Minh, Bourgiba, Nasser and their wives, blossoming, ailing, confused, jealous, admiring, dying? In place. Anyway, in place. And at home: the king, the queen, the prime minister, the minister of culture, the minister of education, the foreign minister, Mrs. Sonning and the director of the Zoo. Ask me, ask me, and I will name the right foot of Jabal who no longer tramples his bronze across Vestre Boulevard, but assuredly now has been exiled to farthest suburbs, but is there, is there. I call on the world to witness my existence and swear that I shall give it life, every single thing, every screw in Polaris turbines, every catgut-suture in the cicatrices of the whole world, each and every one who shouts: Take this my cup from me.

And I said to Tom:

--I just don't know what I should do. Listen: everything goes very well during the day. It's not so bad during the day, and if it gets bad I just take the car and go for a drive. But the other day at the Beach Club it got bad again. I had Irtu sitting in the car and just wanted to take a dip in the pool. Had to take a drink because they came and asked when I had put on my suit, and when I'd finished swimming, I took the glass with me into the dressing room and don't know whether I dropped it, but suddenly it was there on the floor and was in pieces and I wanted to step in it and pick it up and rub the pieces around in my face, or I wanted to pick up a piece and was afraid I would mash it into my breast or cut my breast off. I ran and the woman came racing after me and stopped me before I got out into the open with the others,

--Were you naked?

I heard Anna answer.

--Yes.

Tom nodded. Yesterday or the day before yesterday. He gazed down at the river. The wind had changed and it smelled less intrusive than before. The river doesn't smell so awful, not awful in the Eastern sense, but in the severe heat the transition between water and air is eradicated, and the river lets its turbidness carry up the hill, across the grass to us. The natives didn't understand our wanting to be outdoors, but Mirres had accepted it. Even though we sat no less than two hundred meters from the water, he asked: You want sit by the river?

He's coming in a little while, and it's the best moment here all year round. The job isn't taxing, but Tom gets up at half-past seven every day anyway. Mirres arrives with tea, draws the curtains, and we sit in bed eating. Mirres touches my shoulder to wake me and the intimacy is not intrusive, but fatherly, natural. Mirres is a sikh and was once a Captain in the Anglo-Afghan army. He's nearly seventy

14

and I'd entrust my fate to him if I dared. If I dared tell him that I want to kill Minna. But I'm afraid that he would do it for me because he believed it was something that I really wanted. He sat in the clinic hallway with his back to the wall, and Tom said that he didn't sleep the night Minna arrived. Mirres wore his uniform jacket, yellow trousers, and his medals while he waited, and when he had heard that the child was sound and Anna safe, he took a star from his epaulet, kissed it, and asked Tom to give it to me. It's in the night table now, and I can stretch out my hand and reach it and no harm can touch us. None.

Said it calmly to myself: Everything will be all right. Tom said the right thing with the right words. Understandable, sensible words. Anna listened, and it helped. Tom turned from the river and looked at me, and while he spoke I didn't need to take note of the buzzard, which moved over onto the corrugated iron roof of the domestics, didn't need to count the petals of the geraniums, which is ridiculous. I listened, tuned in my ears and noted the movements of his mouth.

Sleepless, I speak with myself, and my reassessment is comforting in a way. I'm not alone. There are many of us now who argue the same way in the thin hours. You can sleep when you're dead. You are privileged and can sleep the rest of the day if you can't sleep now. With age one sleeps less. It's better to sleep four hours two times than eight hours at a stretch. Sleep is deeper in a short period than in a longer. Sleep means a great deal to your appearance, but do you want to look like a Wolf Cub all your life? Aren't wrinkles a sign of nobility, the black bags under the eyes witnesses to experience and meditation?

On a foundation of strained, tender muscles, my stiff neck, my ringing, hollow head, I build my existence and remember how I, good and silent, took Minna by the hand and walked with her along the river and our white hats with their broad brims sailed beside us

15

reflected in the water. We wanted to find the water rail, but it was just the buzzards that followed us and circled us in black, and the only other birds were crows, which fly faster than the buzzard and bleat their unashamed perceptiveness of the state of things into the heads of each and every one of us. Caw, caw, caw!

We walked there quietly and chatted and didn't discover the water-bearer until he rose from his squatting position and looked straight at us. I don't know whether he was off-limits, but he kept standing there with his bag like a flayed calf-liver down his back, observing us. The wind lifted his loincloth and stirred the tiny silver bells, which hung from his belt and were his trademark. He had to respond and wouldn't speak--perhaps he was mute--he chose to play the role of a natural part of the scenery (his papers were in order) so he loosened the flat drinking cup and untied the water bag. We were to drink and understood by the wave of his hand that the water didn't cost anything. And no wonder, it'd been taken from our river.

According to all the rules it was unthinkable to drink the water, but I took the cup and drank, and when I had drunk gave it back to the man, who filled it again and held it in front of Minna's mouth while she drank. The water felt lukewarm and grey in your mouth, and if it didn't taste of the river, it had taken on the taste of the innerside of the bag, the dull vibrating of the nap of the gut. As soon as we had drunk I wanted to run, but couldn't take my eyes from the man and from Minna. I kept looking at Minna. How long would it take? And what should I do? It might hit her first. Only four years old. Everything that she had drunk to date had been boiled. I telescoped the terror-process to the maximum--I'm good at that!--saw her already drop with feverish brow, her ruddy face quickly discoloring, jaundice, cramps, death. Imagined her mouth already turned blue while, full‾of trust, she followed the water-bearer, who repaid her attention by taking out three small balls and letting them appear and disappear in and out of his hands. Ah, what a circus, what a show in this afternoon's arena, the innocent child and the Pakistani water-bearer presented in a dazzling, unbridled trained act by the white Anna, the child killer. I snatched Minna to me and raced back to the house while she fussed and protested because I'd interrupted her play; I didn't know what either she or I was feeling when in the bathroom I forced my fingers down her throat and a thin, milky liquid began to gush by fits and starts past her teeth down into the bowl. The sanitary, ritual murder frightened and calmed me so much that I forgot my own need, and I remember how the word justice began to haunt the back of my eyelids when a half a day later I lay shaking in bed with my head bent over the edge and coughed up black gall. Perhaps I am an avenger.

There should be a remedy for that, Tom said. He cleared his throat and stood up on the rostrum beside the blue glider, looked out over the audience (Anna) and announced warmly that she had better go home on the next flight.

Now. Precisely. Two days later. I'm lying here. I look at you, beloved, know each hair on your body, even that one there twisting itself around your right nipple, and I have a twenty-minute respite. But I don't wake you, and I don't go crazy, either. With a smile on my mouth, I have laid all the knives aside from the largest one to the nail file in the medicine chest. I am predestined, I am disarmed, I am off somewhere else, which I discover I have always been. You looked at me from your rostrum and said (warmly, kindly) you've got too much imagination, Anna, and I noticed again how my bowed head giggled instead of crying, cried instead of smiling, screamed while it was silent, locked, shut, the key broken, finished. Perhaps the sleeping float someplace the others do not know of, but I'll tell you one thing, Tom. I'm also flying, I'm off off and away, as it says in the song, and there's no metaphysics in my flight. You've given me wings, old

17

friend, you've turned the key and now I fly away from my undeserved guilt, my never-committed murder, my untouched child, my distant son, my grown man--matter-of-factly, with SAS, first stop Teheran, and I'm taking Anna with me.

2

The passengers in transit are better off. Compared to them you're relegated to coolie-status. They're already sitting there, watching from behind their newspapers the upstarts from intermediate stops. Men from Bangkok, fellow countrymen, Germans destination Frankfort, fat or charcoal-grey anonymous, watch with your night glasses and the taste of the stop-over's Coca-Cola, Anna, who's coming aboard. Here in Karachi Anna gets on and feels a rain of internal comments like a meteor shower. Pussie. Bourgeouis snob. Drip. Washed-out. Good enough piece of ass. The hips. Where will she sit. English. The red hair, the complexion, the high cheekbones. The cunt. Takes her coat off. Maybe here. No.

Anna takes the seat nearest the aisle, experience, no draft. Sets the fur next to her (next to me). It was an easy day, a day of crystal, no an ether day, not stuffy, not bright, but hovering, invulnerable. Your honor, judge me so I can be free. I am free and doomed. Therefore I can use the day to, as in a mirror, tell everything. Mirres came in with the tea and the letters, as I said. I let him touch my shoulder, let on that I slept, and he came back and touched me again. I sat up and smiled at him and remembered the way his fingers look when he is serving. His nails are square and nearly blue, white and blue as the whitewashed light late in the tropical half-year of winter. He stands with his fingers beneath the silver, and he smiles and shakes his head because you don't hear anything while you are serving.

I sent John to school, feeling light-hearted compared to him since school has made him dumb and well-behaved. When all this happens to him some day, it won't strike inwards but outwards. John will be bald. Bald and handsome like Tom. He will meet problems and solve them one by one. It's easier than meccano and more entertaining than mathematics. If things go really badly, maybe he'll get pimples at a totally inappropriate age--no, that's not right, pimples, they're not John; he'll get by with allergies. John Hayfever! Little John Hayfever from Karachi! Naturally. Chronic sinuses. Every time he sees a banyan tree he'll sneeze. I could see it before me while he tied his tie. John walks out in the garden with the Maharaja of Bengor . . . aaahhhh chuuuu! Your excellency must forgive me, but I am allergic, I cannot tolerate pollen, pollen from the banyan tree. And he pulls his huge, snow-white handkerchief out, my old, bald, handsome John and wheezes and sneezes again, and the Maharaja observes him from the corner of his eyes and thinks: These Europeans and their lack of inhibitions. There must be something behind it!

When he's standing in his blazer and with his school tie halfway tied there steals over me the feeling of ads in women's magazines. This aquamarine-blue Vermeer-light, these white beds, the pink babycuffs of the Cannon towels, the grey of his flannels, and I want to pull my skirt up and my pants down and say: There boy, it's from there, from that nastiness that you've sprung. No, not sprung, but been pulled, twisted, slapped. And so it is the silence and the grooming, the coolness, which frees me from him and him from me. Goodbye, John, we'll see each other if we do.

I dressed Minna and Ghali helped. She took each piece of clothing and held it out. It was quite an operation. And great for me. I was Anna, the operating surgeon. I was Anna, the surgeon, the great doctor, the woman who cuts in order to heal! We spoke, but with very few words. Pants. Bow-tie. Shirt. Armband. Comb. I conversed with Anna excitedly at the same time.

Good morning, Mrs. Ambassador, I said. You have everything really under control. If your ship hasn't quite come in, at least you've had easy sailing. Listen now, Mrs. Terlow. Everything is clear. It's morning in Karachi. You're standing in your daughter's bedroom dressing her. Everything's fine. Ghali is standing right beside you. You can smell her. It's light. Night is shoved aside, rolled up like a used tube of toothpaste, squeezed flat, and tossed in the river. Tom is sitting in there already, staring at three dispatches from the foreign ministry that don't mean a blessed thing. You yourself are deathly calm. You cooly notice that when you speak to yourself your old school slang pops out of your mouth. Are you the eternal high school student from Rysenteen? Yes. That's a fact. But everything's gone very well. You've gone far. Who could have read in your stars that you'd end up as an ambassador's wife in Karachi. Who could dream that B.A. candidate Anna Bryl would fall in love with a ministry official and follow him through thick and thin? A lot of people. Fewer would have guessed that Anna would end up as a juggler of knives in Pakistan and a sleepless thirty-five-year-old with compulsive-neurotic fixations.

Dressed Minna in this my gallows humor and smiled wanly. Wanted to sing, heydidilididi, heynoninonino, but chose instead a bone-dry grunting as I turned my back to the child and the nurse and went over to the window. Maybe the birds had some words that should be said. They used to be good to cling to when the ship keels over, and I understand Niels Holgersen not only because he leaped on the goose to get to Lapland, but also because he was locked up, alone, had qualms, wanted to kill his parents, but preferred to flee.

Out here in the East it's only SAS that observes the regulations. No airplane with any self-respect stops at a proper distance from the runway and tests its motors before takeoff. No, they dash right up onto the camel, give it the gas and hurtle off with twitching wing flaps and rivets from the wings showering behind. We others have to go through the checklist first. That's behind us now. We've kept a proper distance, the huge jet turbines have been tested, and our friend

Sigurd Viking slinks down the runway as the blue landing flares are sucked faster and faster past the windows. In the slip stream a back returning to a car.

We agreed back then in the fifties, when the world was whole and round and safe, that we would never say goodbye. No long leave-takings and sentimental patir c'est un peu mourir-talk. We would always see each other again, and if we didn't, that was something-- yes, what is it you call it--fate? has decided. It was a fine time then ten --eighty years ago. It was, really. And that can be said without irony. Many people imagine that the dividing line between past and future, new and old, lies at the end of the Second World War. But they're wrong. It's only now that we're taking leave of the good old days. And it isn't ourselves who are saying goodbye, but the others who are saying goodbye to us. But can you remember, Anna, when a whole bottle of schnapps cost 19 kroner, and the wars that took place were always just and unambiguous and comprehensible? It was a good time. Back then you "went with one another," back then you began to go with Tom and discovered Europe together and lived at home on the weekends, and there was no end of possibilities if you just thought about it and did the right thing. Those were the years of good conscience, for you simply couldn't help doing the right thing, it was so obvious what the right thing was, and it wasn't hard at all. But then everything sped up, listen now, Anna, it all sped up, and now Tom is standing down there and doesn't want to go because you are leaving him and he's heard that maybe fate is a dumb, aggressive bastard and reason in forced retirement in Harzen, and that you (I) travel to Denmark, where we haven't been for three years.

When I looked at him I had to ask: Am I sick? His face showed I was sick. But I'm not sick. I'm well now. Completely well. I'm on my way and my turbines are working fine. We're flying at my speed and I adapt to it quickly, don't I? I look around me and everything is fine.

Then, too, that sort of anxiety is on the decline. Which of these men is afraid? None. Perhaps they do consider, when the stewardess finds time to bring them the flight's third whiskey, that it upsets their ulcers or even accelerates the cancer process, yet also alleviates the strain and strengthens, with its blend of euphorizing and sedative effect, the soon-accomplished addiction. We are the natural fliers, but I don't think we were back then ten years ago. We were pioneers, to be compared with the Wright Brothers, Alcock and Brown and Ellehammer. Tom laughed when I said that Gustav Rasmussen flew all right, but always by propeller. I don't know whether he visualized him with a propeller instead of a nose; anyway, he never sat in a Caravelle or a DC 9 as we all do now--if it isn't a DC 8--and fly home and fly out and fly here and fly there with the sneaking feeling that we're flying too slowly, too, or in the wrong direction.

Good, philosopher, you're on the right track. I know it all right, just need to look once more. What kind of trough is that to sit in? What kind of hysterical trolley, which in minus 50 degrees and at 900 kilometers per hour whisks away headed for Iran? What kind of a generation are we that finds itself in a middle-aged need for comfort? Who says that the oedemas of the leg, the unnatural folding of veins and arteries, the seventeen rich meals from here to Kastrup are not just a compulsion which is ingeniously reconstrued as "service," which goes down with everything else we allow ourselves to be served. Anna, the rebel.

I should tell you some more. I'm wearing different clothes now. There are more, stockings, e.g. A sweater and a skirt. And gloves. It was too hot down there, but it won't be hot much longer. My coat's in the luggage rack. I raise my hand and look at my gloves. All women wear gloves, but perhaps mine are more natural and perhaps a little more elegant than most. My gloves are from Barbados. In reality (ah!) a tortoise had crawled up on the beach at night to spawn. I strolled on the beach and bent down over the trembling animal and a glove crept slowly out of its sex. I put it on in the moonlight, and saltwater and birthwater blended and dripped down onto the beach. I sit with my brood of tortoises and look through my fingers at a person I have seen before. A young man with long hair and strange clothing. He's dressed like an Indian from the mountains, but he's fair and has blue eyes. He sat in Tom's office the other day, and now I know who he is. Maybe I'll talk to him later on.

Can still never be done with my clothes and my rituals. The times are gone when I put on the same clothes every day and bought new ones only once a year. I think of myself in pieces, everything is new. The shoes crocodile skin, the stockings net, dress shantung, the shirt cashmere, the underclothes silk, the rings cat's eye, the polish on my toes silverdust, and when I cry my tears are petroleum. I open the door to the living room on Vibe Road and know that father and mother are to the left and Kjeld to the right; the second door in the hall to my right is mine, and as soon as I open the door the morning light falls in over the bookcase, the preparations in the jars awaken, the tiny foetus turns slowly in the heat from the radiator and the taxidermy-scent is like the drought of the specimen drawers in my own heart.

If only I were free and could do what I wanted. The sentence is pronounced out loud, but not so loud that anyone can hear it. The man with the long hair is sitting next to the man with the short hair. If I were free and could do what I wanted, it would be possible to solve the Minna-problem. The sum of my salt tears could be collected in a jar like that of the foetus back home, but larger, and Minna could be in it after I had cut her up. That would have to take place in the kitchen as usual, but at a time when I could be alone and use more knives and maybe a meataxe. Saturday between two and four. Mirres will have gone home and the others will think that Memsahib is in the kitchen to see whether anyone has been into the sugarjar. It won't

24

be difficult to lure Minna because we always do things together in the afternoon. Come, come, come. I stand behind the door and send up the old prayer to Allah: Wherever you travel, wherever you go, may the bountiful palms of Allah grow. Come, come, come. There's my little darling then and whish, swish cloven in two from crown to crotch by Mummie's meatcleaver. She weighs less when I pick her up in halves, the little Minna, and the rest of it goes easily, even though the joints and thighs are difficult. They have to be twisted and pulled a little and hit and knocked and tugged, but then it's over, and even though she is less decorative as pounded meat, there's something good about Minna's head in golden section. Anna's little folding girl with the charming edge of tissue against the cranium, the roulade of the brain sliced through, the tongue still trembling and the slightly inflamed tonsils, and above all the eye, the eye liberated, stretched, in the sinews' parachute lines, whole and round as a ball, intact and guarded over by the half-case of the nose and the sinuses' little foghorns.

I talked further with Tom, and we discussed *everything*.
I said to him:

--Tom, I said, mornings I wake very early and can't sleep. I lie in the dark, feeling depressed. I wake up when I hear my own name, but no one is calling. It's something inside me. It's like an echo. I'm very unhappy, and I think that I'll never fall asleep again.

--Have you tried taking a pill? asked Tom.

--Yes, I said, I've tried to take a pill.

--Have you talked to Dr. Nariman about it?

--I mentioned it in passing, and he asked if it had anything to do with my period, if I overexerted myself, if there was anything making me unhappy.

--So what did you say?

--I said nothing was making me unhappy. I thought it was

enough to say I felt unhappy.

--Hm, said Tom.

--Now I'm telling you. I wake up early in the morning in the dark and am afraid I'll commit a crime. I have to make myself heavy and black in order to not go out to the kitchen and take the big bread knife and kill Minna.

--How long have you felt like that?

--A long time.

--You wake up early in the morning and want to go out to the kitchen and take the big bread knife and kill Minna?

--Yes.

--But you don't do it.

--I haven't done it yet.

--Do you know why you want to kill Minna?

--No.

--What's wrong with you Anna?

--I don't know.

--Is it something between us?

--What would there be between us?

--I don't know.

--Of course it's nothing between us. You know that. All this I said to Tom while I looked at him and followed an artery that couldn't allow free flow because of his tight watchband.

--I simply can't see your blood because of the watchband.

--What?

--Your watchband's too tight.

--It's the heat, Tom said.

If only I could convince immediately of my tenderness for him. Who? Me? Anna? Yes, since it's true. Back then when there were no uniforms for youth and everything was ugly and safe and patched and poorly cut and too expensive, he came to me, and we lay in beds that were too small and made love badly, and I didn't know I was beautiful, even though he told me. I couldn't believe it. But anyway, I was proud and grateful and totally still when he tossed his politeness to the foot of the rocking bed and stamped himself into me. And I sat at his mother's ghastly table and crocheted my way through her ambitious twaddle and watched the mealworms dance the lancers in her unwashed hair and knew that in a little while Tom and I could leave and be alone together.

In twenty hours I'll be home again and I don't know what that means anymore. It will be wonderful, they say. I think it will be wonderful to get home. Doesn't one miss Denmark after staying for so many years in foreign countries? Yes, naturally one misses Denmark after being away for so long. How long is it, really, that you've been away, Mrs. Ambassador? We've stayed in the Far East for more than three years--with breaks, however. In between we've travelled to Europe and Africa, Japan and Australia, but never to Denmark. How odd. Doesn't one get vacations in the diplomatic service? Yes, and my husband has been to Denmark on official trips, but I've stayed away ... I mean there was no reason for me to go along. I think . . . Yes, what do you think, really? I don't think I've seen enough of other countries . . . yet. But now. Now the trip takes me home. And why only now? Because I have to see the doctor. Denmark has the best doctors. If you're crazy in the head, there's nothing like a Danish doctor. You can do anything you want in a foreign country, buy clothes and catch tortoises and drink poisoned water, but when you wake up in the morning and want to kill your favorite child, then there's nothing to do but get out of the pinch as soon as possible and go home to the beechbright islands and get cured. And yet, Mrs. Ambassador, you feel convinced that it's really possible? Yes, at least I believe it now. And it's not you who should take my hope away. No, no, of course not. In fact, I'm really proud that you show such trust in

27

your country. Not to mention the medical profession. Yes, I am, in fact, a doctor myself, if the truth should be known. And it will, God forbid!

I see this truth around me, and it somewhat resembles my country. None of these men and women are strangers, with perhaps the exception of him I saw through my fingers earlier. And him I've met. But even if the others haven't been in my house personally, still, they've been there. I've given them herring and schnapps, and they've looked at me with their round eyes and their mouths have twisted gratefully. Think, so far away! Charming! Yes, you get a bit sentimental out here. And their hands sweaty, not from the heat, but because everything they do is slimy and shady--the more idealistic it sounds, the larger subsidies they get. But the boy didn't get anything because he got no farther than the front office.

He's strange to look at. The motors are running at cruising speed, and he's leaned back against the head-rest. The man beside him is reading the paper. Here we are. I've chosen him. I've chosen him to look at, and he doesn't know I'm sitting here and won't know who I am, either, when he sees me. I've plenty of time now and am thirsty. I lift my hand and press my left nipple carefully. No light comes on and no stewardess. I lean my head against the seat in front of me and my hair falls forward over my shoulders and hangs along my cheeks, cooly. I sit up and feel my bra tighten and my breasts lift slightly. I reach for the little button over the seat, press it, the light comes on. I smile. Anna smiles her independent smile. We are the only two strangers on the plane--all the rest are known. All the rest have already dropped down and lie with aluminum in their throats, charred wallets, hands blown off, shattered sexual parts. Their suitcases hang gaping in trees and from a bottle hair cream drips slowly and greasily as its scent blends with the rancid smell of desert fox. The stewardess comes, and I ask her for two gin and tonics and point, without saying anything, at the young man's back. She looks at me a little surprised, but nods and smiles her whatever you wish you will get until the permissable boundaries of the rules of civility are overstepped. Then there is nothing to do but wait. And if the button didn't light before, it's lit now. The interlude, my idea, the vibrations of the light alloy, the freedom, the separation for the first time in years, my respite from the crime--I call for the stewardess again and see her seamless stockings on her tight calves as she turns and comes back. Ask her for a blanket and she lifts it down and tucks me in and I help and smile and my hand helps under the blanket and oh glow and smack luxury too among the minarets stockings without fasteners nix groin-elastic and licorice ribbons, but over me still eyes and smile and hair and tiny cap and in between my legs free entrance to all signalling which is welcomed and blinks and comes comes comes. And is extinguished. And drink. At the same time. Dip the fingers of my right hand in viscous cunt juice, smell them--I haven't done that for ten years. Not in an airplane.

But what is it that's happened, and isn't that what Anna is flying home again to find out? Home? I try the word again. Home. Is spelled H-O-M-E, and I don't know what it means. Is it Vibe Road or Karachi? Is it silver nails between your thighs? Is it gin and tonic and cunt juice on two fingers, forefinger and ring finger? Is it stone calm calamity Anna at thirty thousand feet with a series of color slides in her head, which can be taken out, looked at, commented on, laid in boxes and forgotten? Or is it the hippie friend three rows forward to the right with his adventure preserved for me? No, it's Minna with her bonnet tied under her chin and a peacock she is watching with Ahcmat in the souk while he slowly, like a frustrated lead dancer, plucks the feathers from the tail and swallows them one by one. Closed eyes, everything intact, everything calm, blindness.

My operation is interesting to follow. The stewardess,

noncommitally polite, uniformed sex, tries to set down one gin and tonic before one arrested hippie, who'd like to have this present from a stranger, but cannot accept it because of one person sitting next to him who, for five thousand Danish crowns, is supposed to accompany this criminal home. Look, the word came, and came naturally. Now I remember everything. Tom's had that kind of case before. Young people, blown by a chance wind through Karachi-- from where? Blown by a chance wind from Nepal, Thailand, Vietnam, where, holding hands, singing, with a magic stick in their mouths, they have promenaded along the Ho Chi Minh Trail, saying that the world was a flower, a pink geranium and half a pound of mayonnaise.

He sat in the office and waited with his white friend, and walked through and forgot for half a minute my manipulations with the cold steel. I haven't thought of him since. Well, well, he also belongs to the new, which we don't understand. He's a product of progress, as Tom says. Maybe he's produced by machine. I can see it before my eyes: It's home there in Denmark and was built during the years we weren't there. It's a nice big shiny machine with numerous pipes. One of those that Storm P. created to shine shoes with. It's about the size of the K.B. Hall and is produced in cooperation with the government, not the old or the older government which I knew, but by the unfamiliar recent one. First Hedtoft and Hansen had to go and young Krag and then the time was ripe for a fabrication of new times, new people. Putt, putt, putt says the machine and out come all the strangers, putt putt, putt, they say with their mouths and hands are laid cupped behind ears and bowed heads laid out and even more functional ears added and everyone claps their hands and says: Look what we have made, what we and progress and the galloping times have produced, A new generation! Putt, putt, putt and they come biffing out with long pipes and furs like those Mirres' forefathers wore up in the mountains. But then they go too far away from the machine and then suddenly they're sitting in Tom's office and believe that he has a little pocket machine of some sort or other that can free them and get them home. And he raises his eyebrows and doesn't understand a thing, but reads his directives and exchanges glances with the white man and stamps and stamps and stamps papers and then the trip returns to the time machine again.

Now she's standing right in front of me saying something. I listen:

--I'm sorry, but there must be some misunderstanding. The gentleman doesn't wish to (smile) . . . or more precisely: *May* not accept your drink . . .

--Who says?

(Confidentially)--The situation is a little difficult. The gentleman--Perhaps you know him?--the gentleman with the long hair is being transported. You see (whispering) the gentleman sitting next to him is from the police and travels for the Foreign Ministry and the Bureau of Narcotics.

--Yes, yes. But isn't he allowed to have anything to eat?

--Oh, yes, naturally he gets something to eat.

--The same as the rest of us?

--Yes, of course.

--But then why can't he have an aperitif before the meal?

(Smiling, but stiffer)--That's another matter.

--Ahah. But what if you try to offer the gentleman next to him a gin and tonic, don't you think then the man with the hair might be allowed to have one too?

The stewardess stands up. Stands with the glass in her hand. The ice is melting.

--If you really want me to, I'll be glad to try.

She turns and goes. The stockings are too tight for her legs. The stewardess uses groyne holders. Anna sits up in her seat, eager. It's a good flight. It's a fine plane. Just look at it. It's long and has two rows of seats, three in each row on either side of the aisle. It isn't completely full--there has to be room for the people from Teheran. But those who are on board are treated well. Their stomachs are not too full and not too empty. At the bottom of the stomachsack at the exit to the intestine there's a little sea of whiskey & gin & cherry heering & juice & chocolate & choice crackers. Part of it's already absorbed and sits over the brain like a clamshell with light shining through. Anna has one, too. She notices its mother-of-pearl, and in her mouth too, the lemon teases forth the taste of shellfish. Her fingers smell of salt and sugar-- she herself is an oyster with its innards in darkness, but a feeling of light is reflected from the inner side of the now-wide shell. If she opens herself too much, she will die, but she can allow herself to rattle the lid, sneak it ajar, peek out. From her fingers she knows that all is wet and black inside, but living. If one drips lemon on Anna, she stands and looks in all directions, full of expectation.

The stewardess comes back and stops opposite friend hippie and the white man. She has a tray in her hand, and when she leans forward, her breasts are pushed to each side and her blouse gapes slightly at the neck. Her facial-ballet, gestures, and body movements are controlled and well-studied. The little tray disappears and I (Anna) cannot see it. On the other hand, it isn't hard to see what the men are doing. The hippie's shoulders come up, as if he wants to go backwards into the seat. The white man's arms gesticulate up and down. A brief moment passes; then the tray comes into sight again and the glasses are still on it. The stewardess looks this way, and I signal back delightedly. She misunderstands, or doesn't understand and comes closer.

--Now I've tried, she says.

--Yes, I saw you did.

--But I think you'll have to give up your . . . friendliness.

--What did the white man say?

--Who?

--What did the gentleman next to the gentleman with long hair say?

--He's not drinking at all.

--He doesn't drink? But that shouldn't prevent his seatmate from drinking.

(Seriously)--I'm afraid that you'll have to carry out the invitation yourself. Dinner has to be served.

--Yes, of course.

--What shall I do with your drinks?

--Give them to me.

The stewardess looks at me. She's tried everything within the limits of the rules. She has slid down an emergency slide and breathed pure oxygen, she's peeled oranges and emptied diapers, but never killed a child. She sets the little tray in front of me, and I feel proud. My face is tragic, I giggle, feeling it's the right thing to do. I've had a gin and tonic, and now there's a gin and tonic next to a gin and tonic. My face isn't tragic and I don't giggle. I smile and think about my trip. It came about this way: after ten year's marriage with Mr. Tom Terlow, who is seventeen years older than I, but still liked to kick the foot out of my old mahogany bed on Vibe Road, where he felt secure and in good hands, I have, to liberate myself from a compulsive situation, decided to fly home. Many people will call this an escape, and if you asked my old friend the buzzard, he would remove a single solidified piece of goatshit from between the right and left claw of his right foot and say: We who live on rolling corrugated roofs and mainly fly between the garbage heap, the river, and the servants' quarters have on occasion no choice. On the other hand, if you asked my neighbor, the English ambassador's wife, Mrs. Hyst-Appledorn, she'll open and close her lorgnette three times, think about her childhood armadillo, the difficult brombie-trips on motorcycles with lassoes whistling after clay-colored kangaroos, the honey-yellow sundowns over Brisbane and say: You got to stick with it, darling. But I travel because I'm a Dane and remember how Miss Harboe went fluttering through the sleeping quarters one time at camp school and hummed "Wondrous Evening Air" and the painfully melancholy fart-atmosphere was and is and remains my nostalgia, my grudging, warped love for Denmark.

Now she's in her element, the longlegged air hostess. Now she's coming and our little compressed salvation-cart with stale air beneath ice-cold cellophane, steel coffee and tepid bordeaux. And if she pours juice or water for the Danish man and his Nepalese prisoner, I'll scream and be put off the plane.

But no one can do that in these modern times, and if they try, I'll open my red passport, my eyes flashing, and say: I, Anna, I designated child-murderer p.p. appeal to my diplomatic immunity. Tom has signed it here, the foreign minister of the most civilized land with the best doctors has placed his name here, and apart from this you know just as well as I do that if we were outside, everything would look different. In here, out there. In here, warm; out there cold, high speed among the stars, aluminum's-speed, plexiglass, death. But also an enormous singleness of purpose, concealed behind the skin, seeking, sending, accepting apparati, codes, messages, revisions, accounts. Behind the mountains Teheran, a pivoting radar under colored lights. And here I am sending forth three rows to the right my own echo. Wait for an answer. Is there one? Am sitting completely still and spin a transmitting I around in time with the radar, Echo-Anna.

34

3

The stopover at Teheran is always touching. The stop at Teheran brings out my tenderness. Here the oriental arrogance meets its downfall, here sovereign indifference hasn't become second-nature. The airport in Teheran is a misplaced amusement park, a warehouse from Nørrebro dropped into the desert: here the East stops and here the East begins. Here is Europe still and Europe on its way out. In the international flight's conventional single file we walk from the plane to the transit hall, nursery school children again under black umbrellas, and the Shah's variegated lights in the monogram dump their neon over us like ice-cold holy water. Indoors blue quicksilver against whitewashed walls and glass cases with all my friend's regalia on display. Furs, sheepskin peasant coats edged with colored yarn, embroidered hats, Persian ponchos, jewelry of lustreless stone, chests hideously decorated, all demonstrating sovereignty and civilization, but uncertain and vulgar. Everything smells of weak currency and poor conscience, social reforms as sham maneuvering, and tourism in scenes from Potemkin. Here Anna straightens herself up in the ripeness of her creme-scented skin and goes straight to the bar.

She (I) orders a cup of coffee and tries to locate my little comedy team: the devil and the sheep. But they're gone. The sheep has without doubt asked for permission, and is standing out there now, and if one of them can pee, perhaps the other shouldn't, or the one who thought he had to can't while the other fires away. I've always loved men's rooms with their elevated, sacred comedy, these rows of backs in front of the praying wall's tiny niches. Tom doesn't like it when I look at him while he makes water, and I--who've grown up with a brother--don't understand the taboos of the defecation-ritual.

Maybe it's his position--nonsense--I've unbuttoned his trousers during foreign banquets at least five times and held his sex in my hand hidden by rich damask, still he frequently resorts to an American colleague's assertion: Once your wife begins to use the toilet while you're shaving, love is finished. But I enjoy looking at him, I'll never get tired of watching him, and I don't leave him alone even though he turns and stands with his back to me. I'm fascinated by his functions and his apparatus, which belongs to me.

The coffee in the Teheran waiting room is Germany three years after the war. The coffee in my cup is for me April 1947 in a bone-chilling garret in Lübeck, where Rysensteen was quartered for three days, some of us anyway, because we had read *Tonio Kröger* and should have a look for ourselves. But Anna was far from Thomas Mann and Hans' and Tonio's headmaster and his Wotan's hat when I was sitting in the Grössel family's attic and didn't dare go down to ask to use the toilet. At that time I was afraid of my functions myself. The good people had pumped me full of coffee, or what they called coffee, hot water by the bucketful with chicory, the best one could get, and nothing was too good for these victory-rich Dänen from the North with their good conscience and valor and total Ausradierung of the horrid Naziism, which everyone hates and has always hated. I stared at the picture of Grössel senior with his Iron Cross and the double ribbon on the lapel of the characteristic uniform. He stood on the bureau and looked at me and sat at the head of the table and looked at me, and in both positions he had the same friendly, conceited, yet sly-dog look. Es ist eine alte Geschichte, doch bleibt sie immer neu. But maybe it was simply because he didn't know that my woman's bladder, whose capacity is not small, stood like an oil drum over my pubis and threatened to scandalize the great Lübeck author, whose contributions and memory we had come to honor. I said nothing since I didn't know what one should say, and it was only when I sat on the edge of my bed and my sphincter would no longer act like a sphincter, I let out a wail and prayed to Ingeborg and Lisaweta and all my other dead friends to help me. But at the same time I also cursed the educated literature which never told girls in garrets in foreign cities living with foreign people how they should get rid of their water when they need to. Which likes to give good advice in matters of the soul and would tell with cool irony and warm sympathy about ideal conflicts and noble breakdowns, but can't allow itself a single instruction when one is sitting all squeezed up in Lübeck April 47 and has only an empty stove and a high, slanting skylight to pee in. I chose the stove because it appeared watertight and I couldn't reach the window. It wasn't until later that I could visualize it, the impossible, a girl standing with one leg on the bed and the other on a stool, straddled over a low stove with its lid open to the black cold interior. It was only when the cultivation of gymnastic positions in pornography became readily accessible that I've grasped that my own anatomy made it possible for me to make water down into a stove with a certain precision and without rupturing my spinal column, even though the pressure was nearly fifteen atmospheres, maybe it was the pressure itself that was responsible for the fact that only half went to the side, but I'll never forget the draft, the faint, springwet, carbon draft that blew gently up around my thighs and secret parts as the urine began to run out of the ash pan and spread across the Grössel family's ironcrossfloor.

Anna (I) stands at the counter at the end of the terminal in the Teheran airport, and a reassessment is necessary. It must be quick, for I've spotted a man with waiting-room-eyes watching me. I know these incirclers: the movement of their eyes is graphic, follows definite lines, a trivial pattern from breast to legs, brief glance at the face, breast, leg, leg, crotch, waistline, face, direct to the eyes, away, still away, coast is clear, long glance at the breast, gliding down over

37

the whole body, the ankles, back to the crotch again, face quickly, hips, circles, face, away. In a little while he'll be over if he's fresh enough, but then Abbott and Costello may also arrive, and I'll be the one who draws the circle.

But the reassessment: I look back over some thousand kilometers, the whole trail can still be seen in the troposphere, a whirling, rocking gulf-stream of lukewarm exhaust, enough to lift and drop and overturn a five story building if it accidentally came sailing on a transverse course. I look (while the man takes his elbow from the counter and lifts his coffee cup with his right hand) back over some years of my life, whose trail can still be seen, whose trail I tread now and see that the steady heat from a powerful exhaust, an energetic, conformist, resolute yet tame and unself-evident prelude has become lukewarm too. I want to see things, say things, feel dull poverty. Can put the formula this way: All self-evidence leads at the very end to drought. Acceptance is stagnation. At the same time I know that the poverty of this statement denies its meaning at birth. Have difficulty in grasping the obvious in my dilemma: that I should really wish Minna dead because she is the only living thing I have.

Whether I am from Karachi too?

So far as I know it was this question that the mouth under the eyes formulated.

--What do you mean by *too*?

--Yes, that was a silly question. I'm really not from Karachi too. Ha. Ha. I was just sitting behind you on the plane, a little to the right, and when you came on . . .

Anna drinks from her cup and looks past his eyes. She waits for him to continue.

--I'm from Java and really should have flown KLM, but prefer SAS. It's as though you get home more quickly--it's a roundabout way, certainly, but the company pays for it--not the detour, but the ticket by and large, so I have nothing against contributing a little myself. But everything costs money, you know . . .

He looks at me as though he meant that I certainly did, too.

--Yes.

--But maybe you're not from Karachi at all?

--Yes, I am.

--And on your way home?

--That depends on what you mean by "home."

He laughed. Could there be any other place? Could there be any other place where the sun dances the same as in Pile Allé? Where the walks across the grass down the slope to "Carl and Esther" in Søndermarken are greener? Where the little ducks ride on each other among withered leaves and the pike beneath the decayed bridge feels its white heart stop, rises into the air in a painful turning and scrapes its belly against a rusted cycle wheel?

--I mean . . . home to Denmark.

Now my hippie comes.

--No, I'm only going as far as Rome.

The eyes, the man's T.J. Eckleburg eyes, look at me reproachfully at this affront. Have I trampled on the flag before his sight? Spit upon the Danish flag? Said the king was a queer?

--He wasn't allowed to have it, he says, and moves his elbow a little nearer.

I follow the comic scene from the grey door with the blue light and the blue man on it and understand that there will be no talk of any refreshments for the delinquent during this stopover. The detective--whatever a man like that is called--takes his stand in the middle of the floor with the young man beside him. Has he made sure their trousers are buttoned? If not, the ritual hasn't been properly completed. I desire the security which men's essential distraction gives me when they come from the toilet and with a near-ghostly boyish hand feel to see if their trousers are buttoned, whether there isn't something hanging outside, whether it's properly hung up. But Laurel and Hardy just stand there side by side, and the boy takes out a cigarette and receives a sideglance as if he had stuck a water-pipe in his mouth and the scent of Kif were already rolling over toward the money-exchange windows.

--I got a good look at your little comedy with the three drinks. But maybe that was to get them yourself--without attracting attention?

His eyes are tiny, the skin around them black, his complexion bubbled in the brown skin, sallow but suntanned.

You forget once in a while the peculiar Danish leap from amiable intrusion to vindictive aggression. Or maybe it's only me, who's been away from the country so long I've forgotten how Danish humor functions. Maybe eyes is trying to be funny.

--How is it you said Copenhagen when the stewardess asked you about your destination--when you're getting off in Rome?

Oh, Anna, we can be as cold as ice in the diplomatic corps.

--What did you say?

--You heard me fine, didn't you?

--So I answer: When I realized that you were a Dane and would be continuing on to Copenhagen, I immediately decided to get off in Rome.

Anna gets up and leaves. With her little purse of silk she goes to the middle of the hall. From behind she doesn't look tired, but if you looked into her, the blood sugar, with the evaporating alcohol, the weak coffee, the last comments and the obscure prospects, would be dangerously low. I (Anna) am tired.

It's twenty minutes before departure, and the room, after repeated visitors, nearly used up. Above the doors and the small cabinets by the counters there is Persian script she can't understand, either. Her distraction is so great and her energy so little that for a while she doesn't know whether she's outside or inside herself. For all that, she (Anna) can be considered among other things, and the cloud that hung over her like an undeciphered sign is perhaps deciphered.

Anna Terlow (born Bryl) is thirty-five years old. She originally studied zoology and biology, but she became engaged to a head clerk in the foreign ministry and gave up her studies. Her attention has been directed more to the humanities since her undergraduate days, but even when she was a student, she told herself that an exact foundation is a prerequisite for a real understanding of the humanities. Her background was not buried in the dark. She grew up in the home of a metalworker in Nørrebro along with an older brother Kjeld. Her marriage to Tom, who via embassy secretarial posts in Reykjavik, Moscow, Ankara, and Paris, is now Denmark's ambassador in Karachi, has surely distanced her from her original milieu, but her solidarity and love are undiminished. Her marriage to Tom has produced two children, John and Minna. From the beginning of her life with Tom, Anna felt herself co-ordinate with her husband, but perhaps because of the circumstances, has had to suppress her impulsiveness somewhat. Year by year she has become more beautiful. The obligations to entertain and a good deal of money that suddenly fell to Tom, has sharpened her sense for clothing, hair style, and make-up. Residing for years abroad has not changed her view of existence much, but in an inexplicable way existence has changed its view of her. A specialist in psychosomatic disorders would certainly consider her case mild (more about that later). Anna herself feels that in many ways her legs are cut out from under her. Sexually she's been active since her late teens, since her marriage; yes, right from her first acquaintance with the seventeen-year-older Tom, she has preserved the activity, but only with her husband as a partner. When the desire to kill Minna with the help of a knife (knives) became too strong, she followed her husband's advice and began a trip to Denmark to seek a psychiatrist. So far during the trip she has talked with a stewardess, tried to offer a hippie and a policeman a gin and tonic, been insulted by and insulted a Dane living abroad in Java and among other things told him she intended to disembark in Rome instead of Copenhagen. The balloon with the sign over her head hasn't disappeared and hasn't been deciphered, but certain signs have changed, certain kinds of script replaced by clearer, more ordinary characters. Anna is standing with her back to them, but turns around now. She lifts a finger to her left eye as if to feel whether the slight bag that comes when she gets tired has appeared. At the sound of the terminal's loudspeaker, which announces the flight's departure for Rome, she lets her hand drop and approaches the young hippie and his guard. With the feeling of eminent (desired) confrontation, her energy returns, the balloon over her head disappears and her distraction ends.

We (I) are about to get on. It's announced over the loudspeaker that brother Viking is ready for embarkation and my chance for the contact I want lies here. When I got tired before, I was about to miss it. Possibly aggressiveness helps one to survive (it distracts), but at the same time it's exhausting. I've experienced it before: in trolleys, in buses, in shops, people abuse me, people abuse each other, and I'm left in a condition of deathlike fatigue. But high spirits are on their way now because I've made a decision and because I want to have something and have something to know, which I myself decide. Hippie and white man are standing by the exit to the apron, and it's custos who's holding the yellow plastic transit tag in his hand. I want to shout my: sic transit!--but Rysensteen has to stay home, and my rashness turns into a deep breathing and a strong desire to hang myself firmly in his long hair, which I control.

--You must excuse me, I say.

The white man turns and nods.

--I don't want to intrude.

Zombie looks down at the ground.

It's raining in the dark.

--I just thought I knew you.

The white man bows sideways in the dark--perhaps he wants to introduce himself, but the stairs to the cabin are in the way. We go up slantwise, I a little ahead of the others. I feel cold in the light shirt. The press from behind is strong and the pair pass without stopping, but with head sideways, find their way to their seats. The stewardess has her white scarf over her hat so it won't blow off. My hair is wet. I fasten the seatbelt and read the electric signs, my generation's code: No Smoking. Fasten Seatbelt. Java has found another seat. Abbott and Costello disappear behind the tall seats, the blond hair sticks up. I think quite consciously: What are you up to?

During take-off Anna (I) has time to think about this and other things. It's forbidden to move from your seat, forbidden to loosen your seatbelt before the plane has reached a sufficient height. Thoughts begin before your eyes and move slowly to the rear until their route can no longer be followed. I think about my trip, I think about Tom, and what is to come. I talk to Tom, say to him: My darling, there is only good between us. I can describe our path. I can remember the first time that you danced with me and I said to myself: *my* man. I can remember that you drew a line in the gravel when it rained and we walked the tightrope one at a time under your umbrella and had to keep from falling down. I can remember how happy you were that I was ordinary and not high class, as you had to be on occasion, and I can remember that we swore that no diplomatic job, no government post, no assignment would ever change this *ordinariness*. We never used the word, but still there was reference to a magna carta, a democratic contract, that suited our feelings and your attitude and my attitude, and there was no talk of any coolness, but of love and harmony of dispositions, of a mutual temperament that was not without passion. That was not without passion! It wasn't just the kicking board in my Nørrebro-mahogany, Tom, it was also the thought of what we would do together and what we have done together for many years. But on that point, maybe the odds are too great. Yes. For we don't write down fifty now, but seventy, and it's not with a knife that I'll cut up Minna, but with the pieces of my best bottle of Guerlain. And you just sit back, clever and uneasy, and say once more: What are you up to Anna, for you don't believe that Anna is up to anything, you wouldn't dream of it, and even if you thought of it, you would resign yourself and say: Within the diplomatic corps . . . It's more likely that I'd do that, Tom, than you, and the end of it will be that I, Anna, double-Anna, will gather the phrases that I despise more than anything and begin to pronounce them in earnest.

Cloink. We're in the air. Little belts are scraped off. Little nerves are smoothed out. Little eyes aimed at you like dogs' eyes, at the two blue mothers, who'll come in a little while with new napkins, new forks, new glasses, new ice. Tokyo, Bangkok, Teheran, Rome, Frankfort, Copenhagen--the luxurious confirmation dinners and the long caravan trail of chronic constipation. Here the alcoholism of multi-national commerce is established, here double-morality sprints off with a handcuffed hash bum, while their neighbor tosses down one eight-centiliter dry martini after the other. Here Anna is sitting with her new-won, disdained freedom, her civilized desperation, and confectionery lechery. Should she get up and go over or should she just remain sitting as she's supposed to?

I rise and walk up the slightly oblique aisle. Mr. Hippie has closed his eyes, but the white man is reading the *Daily Express*. Maybe I've made a mistake. Maybe they're coming from Rangoon and know about as much Danish as a curlew. Maybe I'm the one who's flipping out and not the young man who sat in Tom's office the other day and was gone the next. Maybe they think I'm crazy.

--It may seem like sheer persecution, I say. But I would like to make it right again if you think I've done something wrong. It was a sudden impulse . . . My name is Terlow, Anna Terlow . . . I'm married to the Ambassador in Karachi . . . I . . .

The white man gets up, but he hasn't unfastened his seatbelt so he just hangs there. He hangs a moment, then he plumps back into his seat. The hippie looks at him, looks at me. His hair nearly covers his eyes. Then custos loosens his belt and puts out his hand.

--My name is Christensen, Karl Christensen.

He puts his hand out and I let it lie on mine and my fingers are inside this cave for a moment, and it's not unpleasant. I haven't seen Karl Livingstone Christensen before, not really, for it was dark outside and rainy. Earlier he was only seen from the back, but he is nice. I hadn't expected that. There's something out of whack when the law has blond hair and brown eyes, is slim, holds your hand not too long nor too briefly, says your name without a hitch and Karl with an assonant, masculine tone. It isn't good that the delinquent, whom I've decided to save (or who should save me) just sits there like a lump and is no Marlon Brando with wig, but a wet dog behind self-growing curtains.

Karl Christensen keeps hanging there in his impossible position with knees crossed, and suddenly Anna is back there in the cool living room with the custom-made, factory-produced furniture from Lysberg, Hansen, & Therp. She (I) says:

--Sit down again, please. The plane is simply not constructed for politeness. And then I can go back and sit down. White flag is waved, white man has sent out good signals. But what I did between Karachi and Teheran was no insult. Maybe it went against common tact and manners, but what can one expect of a crazy person, and if this crazy person is married to the Ambassador? I sat in my seat and felt a sweet itching, obeyed its call, ordered drinks all around and drank them myself. What the Christ should I ask to be excused for?

--What's your name?

My irritation over this mumbo jumbo is suddenly so strong that I feel the impulse to scratch his eyes. Nail against cornea, trumpetcall on the cortex. He looks at me and if he really were a puppy, I'd put a lump of sugar on his nose now.

--I have the right to remain silent, he says.

Christensen: --This is Jørgen Schwer.

--Good day, Herr Schwer, I say.

He grins up at me.

--I would've said it anyway, he says then. But Christensen is so well-bred.

--Perhaps you think this is a peculiar situation?

--Yes, don't you?

--Yes, I respond without saying anything, it's a peculiar situation. With certain modifications, it resembles all the situations in my life. All my ordinary situations have been peculiar situations--I just never knew it before. I've always thought they were natural. Now I'm in an artificial situation and suddenly I feel that this is the one that's natural. I can say whatever I want, even if it's wrong. Thanks, Minna.

--May I sit with you?

Rules to suspend, suspend them.

--There's no special rule to prohibit your sitting with us. But you are aware of our special situation.

--Yes.

--That's what prevented us from accepting your drinks. I admit the refusal could have been made more politely.

I sit next to Jørgen Schwer, who has moved one seat in.

Naturally he doesn't have handcuffs on. His wrists are slightly red and a little thin, but I don't think it's because he's been chained. We are quiet and look straight ahead. I'm not a criminal (yet) and so Christensen can't arrest me. My conscience is clear and while I say this I know that the buzzard back home slowly opens one of his eyes (the skin transparent over the cornea in the bright light) scratches with his claw toward his cornflakes box and belches.

In my freshly-washed voice I say:

--May I offer you a cigarette?

And when that formality is accepted, I begin to speak in earnest.

--In Karachi I've seen many caravans as yours, but I was too shy to butt in, didn't think it was allowed--or good manners. But when I sat in the plane today I came to think of something strange. All those we generally have sitting around our table can afford a meal themselves. And maybe they're not the ones who should always be sitting there.

--That's just a bunch of shit that should be shovelled away, says Jørgen Schwer.

I listen and repeat his sentence.

--That's just a bunch of shit that should be shovelled away.

Christensen turns toward Schwer and says:

--Now, now, Schwer.

--Oh, I get sick of hearing all that jazz, Schwer says.

What about Anna's speech?

Schwer continues, looking straight ahead.

--Obviously, I'm not the one who decides, but as a prisoner I have the right to point out that the lady is welcome to sit here, but then she should keep her trap shut, too.

--Schwer, conduct yourself properly.

Schwer slams his neck into the seat, wants to come out on the other side. I turn toward him, thinking that my red hair, which falls along my ears over my shoulders, my green eyes, my damned cashmere and deafening, discreet scent of affluence should appease him. But he's in under his hair.

--What is it you're so angry about, Anna asks.

And he says immediately:

--By god, I'm not angry about a thing. I just don't understand what this whole game is all about. And you clearly don't either.

--What game?

--You know as well as I do that I'm on my way home because I've had my fingers in one thing or another and because I don't have any money and because I've skipped out on a sentence that's waiting for me back home, and so you came rushing over, talking about dinner tables, and I don't know what kind of an affectation that is. Why do you want to sit next to me? Because it's exciting? Why don't you go back to your own seat and sleep. It's a long trip. And I'm not a bit exciting.

--But I think you're exciting. Or more correctly: I've decided to think you're exciting.

--Argh, clam up. I thought you just wanted to buy a drink to get rid of the surplus.

--The surplus?

--Because you've seen the Prisoner of Zenda go through the room with his hands tied behind him, do you absolutely have to pay six kroner for three drinks--a kind of absolution, isn't that what it's called?

--That's partly right--perhaps . . .

Schwer holds his breath, then he says.

--By god, it sits the same way on all of them.

Karl Christensen turns toward him, red.

--That's enough now, Schwer!

And I (Anna) think about it. Does it really sit the same way on all of us? Is it really so trivial? In any case, perhaps it sits a *little* differently on me. I've never thought about it before. On sows it must sit really strangely when you think of the boar's corkscrew. But maybe they say the same in the pigsty among the boars: by god it sits the same on all of them! I wonder if the Java man thinks that too, or does he hope to find one day in all the waiting halls among the earth's trading posts one that sits obliquely. Perhaps I should have been nicer to him, perhaps I should have thought that it's all the others which sit obliquely and mine the only one in the world that sits upright. And Tom couldn't have helped me since he knows so few.

There is something obviously delightful in talking with a man whom you can't talk with at all. It's easier than anything else because it is real, and I make my plan. In a little while I'll speak again, but first I'll enjoy my role as Florence Nightingale reversed on horseback. Now listen you little bastard.

First, officially:

--May I have permission to whisper something to Mr. Schwer?

--What?

--I asked if I might have permission to whisper something to Mr. Schwer.

Karl Christensen wrinkles his handsome forehead and squints his eyes.

--You can certainly understand that you've put me in a predicament, but because of your particular position, and considering the relationship we have to each other now, I don't see how I can prevent it. You may whisper briefly.

--Yes, Sir.

Jørgen Schwer stares at me.

--I don't want her whispering.

--How much is waiting for you there back home? I ask.

Schwer looks at Christensen, who looks back at him with

49

downdrawn upperlip.

--Three years, says Christensen.

--I wonder if that isn't the maximum, Schwer says.

--Yes, but anyway, I say and lean over to his ear. Thereafter whispering, wetly:

--Even if you don't have a passport yourself, and even if you think it idiotic beforehand, listen anyway. I'm travelling on a red passport, that is, diplomatic passport. That opens certain possibilities. When we land in Fiumicino try to get away from Christensen for a moment. I'll distract him. When he discovers you're gone, I'll say that you went to the men's room. It's in the opposite direction from the transit hall to Rome. But you won't be in the men's room, you'll be standing by the exit waiting for me. It'll take exactly half a minute to explain to the official that you'r travelling with me and that together we will get a new passport in Rome.

--Agh, shut up now, Jørgen Schwer says.

--Yes, I say, I'll do that, too.

--Why are you getting off in Rome?

--Because I've promised the Java-man.

Christensen is looking out at the dark through his window, and in a little while Hazel will be coming with the food so we can be armed for the descent into the Italian.

4

It was so easy it wasn't until later that I thought of how ridiculous the situation was. While camera one held Christensen and me in a nice medium shot, camera two was busy following Schwer's little maneuvers. Camera one moved in for a medium-close shot while I intensified my flirtation with the chief detective and at last made a spring-zoom as horror was painted on Karl's face, and he undertook an intricate dollie-shot, which only ended at the exit to Rome, where the lens calmly observed the tense situation and only shifted to a medium shot when I came within its view and with bosom thrust forward as far as possible and in my best Italian explained to the respectful customs official what our errand was all about and why the longhaired one didn't have any passport. Two minutes later we sat in a taxi on the way down Via Ostia Antica to Rome, and there was no Christensen. But there was one known Anna and one unknown, antagonistic, indifferent, aggressive Jørgen Schwer.

Since distractions are the only thing that keep people from committing suicide, I said to myself while he puffed away on a Nazionale which he'd already gotten ahold of, god knows where, I must have undertaken this maneuver to save my skin. Anna Terlow, thirty-five years old, Ambassador's wife from Karachi on her way in a taxi with a wild man, maybe criminal, narcotic, psycho-infantile, and with unwashed hair. It was like winning a soap contest arranged by the madman's laundry in Charenton.

But outside I see my beloved Rome in the dark. The yellow-red sodium lamps and the hour-glass lights' la-Morgue colors. In there, twenty kilometers ahead, it lies, all of it--huge stone animals resting in the dark, bats hung up under the lofts until the approaching summer, the hollow-trees sleeping, Romulus and Remus swinging pygmies under the great wolf's teats, the gem-studded Christ child in his crib of marble and long-since consumed days in natural intimacy is matter-of-fact and therefore abstract. Better to hear what Mr. Heavy has to say, he, who along with the Java-man, has gotten a new respite. I (Anna) begin a little stupidly:

--Is there someplace you used to live in Rome?

He glares at me from under his long hair, and I think of John, my son John, and his grey flannels and his tie with the three diagonal stripes and his nannies, both the dark and the light, his shirts with detachable collars after the English fashion, his loving kisses in the morning and his distant gaze when he leaves me and is driven off to let himself be taught and be qualified as an adult.

--I've never been in Rome before.

I notice that he doesn't swear in his sentence and that it's spoken without real aggression.

--I usually stay at Hotel Barberini, but if Christensen calls the embassy, they'll certainly tell him to call there.

--Christensen?

--Yes, you didn't think he'd go on to Copenhagen as if nothing happened? He's probably on his way now. I suggest we stay in Trastevere.

--Haven't the faintest idea where it is.

--I do. I've lived there before. I'll show it to you.

--Hn.

Suddenly I'm very happy about my little boy. Not him back home, but him here beside me. Glad in a way I'd hoped I'd be. He's so primitive and so awkward. He's really so ugly and uncharming that he reminds me of every seedy juvenile delinquent. I've never tried to show Rome to someone like that. And it's wrong, too, to say I feel happy in a way I'd expected. I'm happy in an entirely different way. He, this guy, for whom I had willfully laid my net and made a fool of myself, was the last person in the world I could, for example, *kill*. If I were sitting with the biggest, sharpest, most perverse Hitlerjugend knife, I'd be as peaceful as a Zen monk. I'd hand it to him and say: Jørgen, have you seen my cutlass? Isn't it beautiful? You didn't have anything like that in Nepal, did you? Did you, darling? Isn't everything just nonsense and bad food and cold feet out there in the wild desert? Isn't it Nirvana with a draft and far too many skeletons and contagious hepatitis you've found for yourselves there? Isn't it better, after all, on Nikolaj Square, where you can come around the corner in a hurry and down into the cellar and get a beer and a hot compress and a box of aspirin in "The Little Drugstore" pub.

--Couldn't we use "du" with each other? Anna asks.

He looks at me and nods. Turns around again and stares into the neck of the driver who, per definition, is completely indifferent to both him and our talk and the whole escapade, as if he knew that Inspector Christensen is breathing down our necks and that both Jørgen and I stand to be sentenced and condemned if my diplomatic immunity didn't for some ridiculous reason or other protect me in this situation, too.

I bend toward the tiny back before me and ask the man on its front side to drive to Trastevere, to a hotel, to someplace. It's four in the morning and the March rain clings to the underside of the black branches of the trees, blinks in the light and drops, and I know that the swallows arrive in Rome on the twenty-third. But *we* are here now, in migration from someplace or other, on the way to someplace or other, and we'll stay on the wrong side of the river until tomorrow or until we're found.

The sound of the idling motor wakes my attention to the fact that all my luggage is on the way to Frankfort and that over a double door there is a sign: "Hotel Busoni." I feel down my skirt and notice

53

the cold across my shoulder-blades as I ease my body from the plastic seatcover. And this is how Anna looks now.

She is sitting in an Italian taxi at four in the morning with a Danish hippie or something like that. She's cold even though she was clever enough to take along an extra jersey when she left the plane at Leonardo da Vinci airport. She's done several things she would not have thought possible twelve hours ago. On the other hand, back then there were other possibilities. In Karachi she had faced the apparently inevitable compulsion that she had to murder her only daughter with an axe. To avoid this absurd and repulsive action, the action she'd certainly hate most in her life to carry out, Anna is, at her husband's sensible and urgent request, on her way to Denmark to see a specialist and get these problems cleared up. An immediate relief at the steadily increasing distance from the object of her conflict (conflicts) has started a kind of euphoric process, which, on the surface, may look absurd. Anna hasn't reached Denmark, though she has valid travel documents all the way. Because of circumstances, but mostly because she is following her own impulses, she's in Trastevere, while a very unconventional person--Jørgen Schwer-- waits to see what her next step will be and a fairly conventional person, Chief Detective Karl Christensen, upset that he's let himself be led by the nose so easily and wondering how he could have been, drives at top speed toward police headquarters in Rome. His luggage is also on the way to Frankfort.

While I (Anna) pay with (too many) dollars, Jørgen Schwer sits leaning back with closed eyes. Maybe he won't even get out. Maybe he won't even go with me into this "Hotel Busoni," where a man is sleeping behind the desk or someone else is lying in bed without knowing that the bell will ring in a moment and there'll be a knocking at his door. The taxi driver raises the bills up to the light to see whether it's the hippie or I who've made them, but his protests grow weaker as he eventually gets George Washington's cranium x-rayed and sees that it's empty, as it should be on all the greenbacks.

--Shall we try here? I ask.

Schwer nods and looks at me.

--Why not? he says.

Fired by his generous enthusiasm, I open the door to the rain and step out in front of the "Hotel Busoni," a four-story building, narrow, with shuttered windows facing the street and a garden on the right side, where an acacia with naked branches bangs steadily against the wall. I don't know whether the hippie is used to something better; to me the place looks like hundreds I slept in back then and which I'd sworn I'd never live in again. Why? Oh, because everything has its time, doesn't it?

When he won't knock or ring (apparently) Anna puts her lady-knuckles to the glass of the double door and begins to knock, and at each knock she beats a new consciousness into her head. The picture begins to grow clear--anything is possible--you pay the price for what you don't want to do, either. But it's difficult in the middle of it all to decide if what you're doing is right. This cold morning's tender knuckles, anyway, are a part of a different game and Anna feels relieved that it's still less fatal than the old one.

--Why don't you try the bell? Schwer asks.

--I didn't know there was a bell.

While the taxi disappears (the driver rolls his window up as he pulls away from the curb) hippie steps out into the cone of light, reaches out his right arm and hauls a brass bellpull out of the wall. Somewhere in "Hotel Busoni" a bell clatters. The great Scandinavian confirmation dinner is left far behind, and I feel the vanished gin and coffee like a sharpness in the mouth of my stomach. Apparently nothing is happening in the invoked consciousnesses--if there are any--and again I feel what my sisters before have felt and what generations will feel, that in the cold we become skeletons, that where the intestines should be lies a cold snake, and the column that holds the cadaver up has become a tambourine stick and makes the chin clatter up and down, to and fro. I come from the tropics, Jørgen Schwer, I'm a tiny, delicate woman, a little sophisticated upperclass goose, a spoiled little diplomat-piece, who'd like to be stroked and stroke herself when it's warm and good and one is locked in, who loves stockings that stay on by themselves, but just now I'd give my right arm for a garterbelt, a pair of stockings, my furs and a box of Epsom salts in warm water for my flying-feet.

But in spite of everything the bellpull strikes a papa-san conscious in the Italian March and shortly after a light is lit and half a door opens and the world's smallest, grimiest, nightcowl-clad mannikin peers at us. What do we want? I don't give him a chance to guess, but walk past him and stand shaking in the entryway, which is supposed to simulate a reception desk. A Lei una camera, per una notte? We can handle it, and he unbundles himself from his cigarette cramp by striking up a new one, coughs down into a clenched fist and shoots a book over at us and two small scraps of paper, which I pass on to the hippie-man. Domani, domani. And Cerberus also begins to shake, and while the grey smoke filters by fits and starts out of his mouth and he presses his lips to his hands, he watches with small spasms in his eyes my son, my lover, my fellow conspirator, my criminal, my what?

I let myself into my room, a grave-cold, high-ceilinged, over-stuffed, drawer-like elevator-room with earthcolored portieres and the light swinging high up on a braided string, but before I can decide whether I should go out and find the toilet, there's a knock on my door.

--Yes, I say.

--It's me, says Jørgen Schwer.

I move from the door, take a step backwards, and let him come in. He stands facing me, and the light from the hall, which is behind his neck, makes his face black. He looks like the bear in the story of the three bears. The youngest of the bears, who's been out in windy weather and gotten his hair disheveled.

--What are you really up to, Mrs. Terlow.

Oh, at last, I think, these are the words I had waited for.

--I thought we'd become "du's."

--Yeah, sure.

--You'd better come in. There's a draft.

Jørgen Schwer just stands there.

I take his arm and pull him in. I notice his arm is thin. One blow would be enough, as with Minna.

--Now let me tell you something.

He speaks the words and his voice cracks a little. He speaks like a state official, but has flowers on his pants.

--We have to have a talk.

I nod and sit down on the bed, we really have to talk. I wait. Then he begins:

--I don't know why you've gotten me into this. The other was easier. This will just be harder. I'll end up back home anyway. It's not routine for Christensen anymore. Now he's mad. Can't you see it? Can't you see that everything was cool? I was all finished out there anyway. I can't do a thing. The others had shut me out--they didn't want anything to do with someone who was wanted back home. I'm really not right.

--What do you mean "you're not right"?

--I'm not what you think I am.

--What is it I think you are?

--Oh, shut up. Do you think I don't know? Women who see long hair and go wild and hope for something. What is it you want from me? What is it you're after?

Anna (I) can't fathom him. It's difficult to follow him. Verbally, too, one moment the official-sounding cliches, the next jargon. I ask straight out:

--What kind of game are you playing now? Can I try a guess?

--Go ahead.

--You aren't as insipid as you pretend to be, are you? You're aggressive and ill-tempered, but you're not as dumb as you make out.

--I just want to know what's expected of me.

--Expected of you? Right now you're not on your way to Horsens and Kragskovhede or wherever they send someone like you. I've snuggled you off in Rome. And now we're in a hotel in Trastevere west of Rome. Isn't that good enough? Or would it be better if we were at the Hassler or the Barberini, so we could have eaten breakfast with Christensen? Why not give it another try?

He leans against the wall and if I had been the buzzard on the tin roof, I'd have shaken my head, yet kissed him on the cheek as well. On the other hand, my English neighbor would never have come here. It would soon be five and I realize it's been two nights now since I last awakened too early and whetted my knives.

--Who accepted my invitation?

He doesn't say anything.

--Did I carry you out of the airport?

Still not a word.

--Is there anyone holding you?

He shakes his head.

Then he says:

--I'm going now.

The three words came plodding out of his mouth and settle in a hard ring around my heart. I can't answer. I can only feel the long suction that draws the blood out of my face and has the same speed and temperature as the tidal bore when depression comes on.

--It's better anyway, says Jørgen Schwer.

I straighten up and am still strong enough not to say too much nor too little. My choice is accidental, but it has been made.

--Don't you think we should sleep now?

He nods and walks toward the door.

--Yes, that's best.

The door closes behind him, and I notice my hands need washing. There's no soap in the room so I let the water in the basin run over my fingers and hear the high sound in the pipes which the old system makes. Shortly a new tone rings in over mine. He's washing up, too. We're doing the same thing, and I feel more calm. He turns off the water, the tone disappears, and I shut my faucet, too. It's quiet. Then, carefully, I turn on the water, but the tone comes only when the pressure has grown. I open the faucet wider and the pipes begin to sing. Shortly after his pipe sings, too.

When I'm lying under the blanket in much too thin underclothes, I hear his bedsprings creak. I lie very still, seeing the contours of the room dimly in the glow from the streetlight through the venetian blinds. Well, then, Tom, now Anna is going to sleep. The young man next door turns a few times, then the building grows quiet. Anna thinks of the distance between decision and action, but her notions are vague. There's nothing threatening in the room, even though it's cold and she's a little chilly. She pulls the blanket up under her chin, tries to cover the back of her head against the draft, rolls up her long hair so that it creates a barrier. Sits up suddenly in bed with sparks before her eyes and a sound in her mouth which cannot be heard. The water is running in the next room, the pipes are singing. She sits rigid a moment, then lies back slowly and smiles. There was something he'd forgotten, something one forgets when one is young and has to stay overnight in strange places. I (Anna)

59

close my eyes and sleep.

I wake the next morning and there's been no call. By the gold watch on the chain I see that it's twenty minutes to ten. I've slept four and a half hours. The room is still cold; outside the sun shines. I look over my underclothes but there's no possibility of changing. Then think as I wash my arms and neck and face a little, what will happen now? There's no reason for panic. No matter what I do, it can be excused by pleading mental instability: Naturally, it's not flattering, either to my husband or to the foreign ministry, that a crazy ambassador's wife takes off with a prisoner in Rome's airport, but it can be excused, and if Christensen has been smart enough not to involve too many carabinieri in the case, the publicity can be held to a minimum. But naturally he's had to call home, and of course he has to make certain contacts. Most of my makeup is in my handbag so my mask is in order when I leave the room. I walk bouncy and long-legged down the stumble rug in the hall. If one can't get a caffé-latte there in this exclusive place, I can probably get one around the corner. My young friend isn't awake yet and I like to take it easy in the morning. I'm in Rome, it's strange. Last night's heffalump has disappeared, and beyond the door into something that resembles a dining room I can see a woman who is certainly la patrona, a greyhaired, thin woman, maybe the heffalump's mother or wife or sister, but there's the smell of coffee. She greets me with her back half-turned while she removes a cup and wipes the crumbs from the table. Then I sit down, obviously making up one third of the pensioners present. She doesn't ask me what I want and once again I feel I've arrived in Europe. A back half-turned, no cloth on the table, coffee with milk and a hard roll--or go elsewhere. It could have always been that way for me, but it's not. While she's serving, I notice my heart is beating in loud strokes, not quickly, but regularly and booming, fills the room, comes from a strange place. And when I try to locate it, I remember the night's acacia and realize that the wind is still blowing, that it's cold outside, or at least chilly. There's enough money in my purse to buy warm clothes--for him, too. But so what?

The reassessments begin to get complicated. When he asked Anna last night what it all meant, "what she was up to," self-assured she became ironic about the question. On the other hand, she became more than weak-kneed when he said he was leaving. But have they come a step further, and if they have, what will the next step be? Will Anna be able to claim with any justice that she's in love with the young man, and in that case: on what grounds? Is it a matter of irrational confluence of accidental circumstances, or of the special form of disharmony of the disposition which creates opposite signs, turns minus into plus and vice versa? Compared to Tom, yes, compared to any other man in her circle, Jørgen Schwer is a pitiful outsider, not even interesting or pathetic or stimulating enough to want to read about in a weekly. He's ill-mannered, snivelling, slovenly, scrawny and untrustworthy. He is, in short, a person who should have been taken into custody by the authorities, not just the judicial but the social, too, the National Health Service, for example. But when everything's said, is everything said? And can Anna use Tom or any man whomever she knows as a yardstick for Schwer's person and his potential meaning for Anna? If you, for example, compared him to Anna's brother Kjeld or to Anna's father, would the harmony or positive qualities be more apparent? Most likely Anna would immediately say no to this question, but since it hasn't occurred to her to make comparisons because, among other things, her fixations are bent in an entirely different direction, there's no reason to go deeper into the problem now. There are others more immediately pressing, and they're primarily practical. When she's drunk her coffee, something must be done. Anna hasn't thrown so much overboard that she feels no duty to inform her husband about what has happened--or at least part of it, but at the same time she feels a kind of responsibility for Jørgen and his fate. For even though she rejected his accusation she can't deny she was the most important instrument when Jørgen Schwer's defection was transformed from idea (dream) to fact.

The she-heffalump comes in and puts a bill in front of me (Anna). It isn't out of line considering the time of year, the nature of the rooms, the location of the district, and the quality of the breakfast. The only thing that makes me react is the arrogance with which both his and my breakfast are put on the bill. But of course he could have eaten in his room. Or perhaps here earlier? She looks at me and I open my purse again and think about the exchange confusion. Hey, Rysensteen, hey girls, what about a paper money factory? What about a little press room around the size they always use in banks, no, not press rooms, dummy, but the kind of whirligig gadget that says dikkedidikkedidikkedidik and you get 1,000,000 lire from the teller. Wouldn't that be an idea? Wouldn't it be something we could cash in on? The she-heffalump stares at my dollars, and I explain to her that if it's too complicated for the hotel to change them, I could certainly take the trouble to go around the corner and get lire for dollars. But George Washington shows his true face once again, or is it Abe Lincoln, as she tugs at the money a little, the wife asks wryly whether I want to keep the room or whether it can be readied for the next guest. "There wasn't very much luggage." I say politely that as a rule one has permission to use the rooms undisturbed until noon, and she answers: I just thought.

"I just thought." The fake periods after this statement sprinkle down into my empty coffee cup, and something I must have known all along begins to dawn. But I ask anway, in order to make the process slower, better (worse?). What does she mean by "just thought"? Yeah, she just thought that when the boy (il ragazzo) had left so early, then the lady (la signora) would be leaving now, too. As soon as possible, perhaps? One never knows. One never knows anything. We simple hotel folk don't know so much about life. Particularly not out here in Trastevere in March, do we?

It was, of course, something I should have known. Hadn't Tom told me hundreds of times: If you're on the run, it's a matter of spreading out. Every man for himself. It doubles the chances and the responsibility is lessened. The moral problems of a relationship to others is eliminated. It's perfectly true that no man is an island, but there are times when pretty assertions are superseded by practical considerations.

Ever since I was a little girl people have deserted me. Once we had been at the zoo and walked out through Frederiksberg Gardens to the trolley and stopped at a bench to sit a while because the wind was blowing hard and against us. I was watching two ducks that were snapping at each other on the grass and were often about to be blown away even though they took cover and nipped each other's feathers, and when I turned around my mother and father were gone. The asphalt path bent around a corner and they were probably just on the other side where I couldn't see them, and if nothing else had happened, maybe the experience wouldn't have become so fixed. But in that moment all the terrible possibilities came marching in front of my inner eye: you'll never find your way home, you don't know which trolley to take, whether you have to change or not, whether you have enough money, perhaps they hate you and abandoned you on purpose--an unbelievable noise sounded near me, next to me, over me; the ducks suddenly stretched out there wings and the webs between their feet shone orange, I moved a hand to my throat and at the same moment the tree ten meters to the left of the bench crashed to earth, my mother and father appeared in the curve of the path and I saw their white faces like two Pierrots looking in on the scene. They hadn't forgotten me, but they had left me.

I leave the table and go up to the room without any real reason. I do what one does when one leaves a hotel. Open the door to the shaft and see the bed. During my short sleep I hadn't moved very much--the blanket and bedspread lie about as they were before I turned in. My shape is gone and I don't feel like thinking it now, because it's cold and I have only a coat to cover me when I go out. My furs are in Kastrup, lie bristling, purposelessly electric in a fortuitous office. I go into the room and over to the sink, turn the water on hard and the singing sound is there right away. I feel the accumulated urine from yesterday, from last night, and from the morning press its way forward now. It's probably ghastly out in the privy. And there's certainly less draft from a washbasin's outlet than from an empty stove. My underpants are too thin but easy to take off and I've shot my rear end up over the porcelain and let go, I feel both cool and warm and put my left hand on one of the faucets both to support myself and to regulate the stream which, as it was, started all this. Gradually, as I emptied, satisfaction comes and a desire to sleep. But I have to go on, don't know exactly where.

At the sight of the scooter drivers, overtly backfire-lecherous Italian roadboys in the Roman morning, a kind of euphoria appears in Anna. She doesn't lean back in the taxi, but sits straight up, moves her head and eyes when something catches her attention, turns when she wants to follow a vehicle passing in a definitely hazardous, fantastic manner, turns toward the sound when a strange untraditional, colorful three-tone horn strikes up.

Whenever something new--desired or undesired--distracts her from the thing she herself perceives as the most immediate problem, she feels better. Now it's a matter of very simple things. She's decided to drive to the embassy to report that she's still alive, that she isn't dangerous to her surroundings, that she can certainly continue on her own by plane to Copenhagen. If they connect her with Schwer's disappearance, she'll deny everything. There are no particular grounds to couple her with this person's disappearance. Even if Karl Christensen maintains that she had a whispered conversation with him on the plane between Teheran and Rome, there's no proof that this conversation with Jørgen Schwer was about his escape. The chief detective will also be able to state that Anna led him on a wild goose chase when she said that Schwer had gone in the direction of the toilet and not toward the exit. But she could have made a mistake like anyone else and no one could demand that she should pay particular attention to a young delinquent like Schwer. All in all it looks like the delays and obstructions that could lie between Anna and her reunion with her native city and meeting with the doctor, which will relieve her situation, are not hard to sweep aside.

On the way to the center of the city, she (I) stops the taxi in Via Condotti and asks that it wait. I've been here before with Tom and know what I can get. No one will wonder whether my dollars are counterfeit or not when I buy a spring coat, gloves, shoes, pantyhose, jerseys, a scarf, a hat, two slips, a skirt, a belt, six handkerchiefs and position myself in such a way that I can observe the display window in the mirror, where people's contours and faces are reproduced darkly when they walk by or stop, are transmitted to my silver surface and leap toward my eyes. A lot of people walk by, many stop and stand there. I watch them closely, shift my glance from my new clothes to the mirror's and window's people, but there is no one I know. Yet.

5

I come out of the Via Condotti thinking about my background and origins in a clumsy, conventional way. So I dismiss the taxi. Maybe the sequence is different but the consequence is the same. I have numerous packages to carry, the sun has come out and white clouds move between the blue and the tile color over the houses in the narrow street. At puberty I was too tall and too thin. My mother once said that I "was awkward." When one added to my "awkwardness" red hair, freckles, and immunity to suntan--I burned like a ship's side painted with red lead rather than turning brown--it's only fair that since then and even today I conpensate. Beautiful Anna has bought clothes on Via Condotti a lot, the sun is shining (in Rome), her head is full of half-decisions and unformulated hope, her problems are transformed from the spectral to something concrete, and they're not big. It's a long way to Vibe Road, and Anna allóws herself a moment to enjoy the distance. It's also a long way to Karachi and Pakistan, where Mirres is perhaps sitting on the floor of his kraal now, staring at the hundreds of kroner he must cut up into fractions to get food, medicine, pleasures(!) and entertainment for his six children and one wife. This distance Anna enjoys too. She feels comfortably immoral and sovereign--she can walk if she doesn't want to take a taxi, she can take a taxi if she doesn't want to walk.

Turns in on Via Veneto and everything is like it used to be. In those places where the tables and chairs haven't yet been set out, they're being set out now. People are sweeping and watering, and there is a special freshness in the air which you don't find in the summer or spring. It's the first time I've been in Rome in the early spring, and even though maybe my hair needs setting, I'd also like to

66

sit here, in the orchestra, in order to see and be seen. I pretend that my packages are small dogs, and I stick my fingers in under their strings as if I were very quietly scratching my pug on the neck. They walk by as if they'd been ordered, every one, these grey-clad, grizzled Romans with fine olive light on their faces, brushed mustaches, and a familiar arm on their companion's. They walk by, many of them on business but most of them have time to talk, to converse and send small glances to left and right. The women bear themselves forward like ships, but in their noble bearing there's a new impudence, trumpetshaped trousers, immense ornaments and loose mermaid's hair like my own, swung to both sides. When glances and smiles are sent and received, a laughter shoots up like coral in a sudden wave.

I order a capucino to drown out the memory of the she-heffa-lump's coffee, and escape is impossible when my brother-in-law Morton steers straight at me. His lips move and I hear the noise of the cars and the phones in the offices ring, the thin flicking of the lines attached to the facades. I hear Minna's little heart beat in a cup of oil on the kitchen table, and then the first sound of his voice reaches me. He's a friendly old gossip, dumb, but he paints.

--Anna! Just the sound of your Italian name and I'm done, darling. Where've you been so long and where's Tom--have you left him and at last realized what's good for you and me and the world?

I touch Morten's hands, which lie over mine and slowly loosen my forefinger from the string around the package with the sweater.

--How can you be in Rome when you're in Karachi? How is it possible?

I smile at him, calmly, and tell him how I flew from Pakistan and felt the cold in Teheran, but spring, too, when we approached Italy, and so I got off because I thought I owed it to myself, and now here I am on Via Veneto.

--How can you feel spring on an airplane?

--And you ask that, romantic Morten.

He laughs with his round head and is a little bit embarrassed to be sitting here alone with me in spite of all the palaver. We're nearly the same age.

--Why are you going home?

--I need a change of air.

--But there's nothing wrong, is there?

I shake my head, as I've learned one should. Many years of training have taught me what one talks about and what one doesn't talk about, and not only that, but whom one speaks with about what and whom one doesn't speak with and about what. I would really like to tell him about it now, but I can't. It would be good to say: remote Morten, in the last few months I've had in Karachi somewhat of a bad depression, which came about because I felt I was no longer able to control my own actions. It's a feeling which--as far as I know--afflicts different people from time to time. Some people can handle it better than others, though I couldn't control it. Particularly when it manifested itself in a strong desire to take Minna's life. Therefore, Tom thought it would be better if I went to Copenhagen to get psychiatric help, but when I arrived in Rome I already felt so recovered that I felt like getting off the plane and going into the city and sitting in the sun on the Via Veneto and talking with you. Then I would have told him everything, and it would have been easier between us.

But I haven't told him everything. Even when I decided I couldn't tell him everything, couldn't tell him anything and repeat everything I'd like to tell him but couldn't, I omitted something. And it amazes me now because a short time ago I'd decided that the Christensen-Schwer problem didn't rank on the same level or have the same degree of difficulty as my relationship to Minna and--Tom?

--You're all well, aren't you? he asks.

--Yes, we're very well, thank you.

--At home they talk of nothing but third world problems, but what do they know about them? They want to give charity, but they don't understand that it's investment it's all about. I'm on the way to Tanzania myself. There must be something for a capable man to do.

--What about the factory back home?

--It runs by itself, Morten says.

It runs just like himself by itself.

--So we should do Rome together, you and I. How long are you staying?

--I haven't decided yet.

--Fine. Then Alfredo can take out the gold spoon.

And I'll put my magic stick in my mouth and fly somewhere else. But why, really? What is there to keep me from spending the day and the evening--and the night?--with this nice sweetscented man. Isn't it the very dream, without obligations, with money in your pocket, new clothes on your back, freedom from responsibility, to surrender yourself to what the travel brochures and literature call the Eternal City? But can a sick woman do that? Won't it increase the burdens she already bears? Or put it another way: does she bear any burden at all? What about the man on the corner, the knee man, who's removed by the police time after time and comes back just as quickly again to play a few lire together on a cracked tin violin? Isn't his simple problem weightier, more tangible, more *real* than Anna's? She has every chance now. She can get up and take Morten Terlow by the arm. They can promenade together, well-dressed, well-protected, well-heeled away arm in arm like the other tourists and the other Romans. They can stop in front of Magli's and look at shoes, they can push open the door to Ritz's deluxe cafeteria and fill up on snacks and drink Orvieto, they can take a fiacre on a tour up the boulevard to Borghese, drive through the wall and the gate, continue on to Villa

69

Giulia, turn around, place themselves before the bust of Caesar and be silent for two minutes while they imbibe its expressive distance and think about all the damned, many, beautiful, indifferent, historic years that have passed since the emperor lived and let himself be portrayed, they can leave the museum and gulp down Capitolium and Forum Romanum and Colosseum and Vita Tritone and Quattro Fontane and Fontana di Trevi in a mouthful, but Anna says straight out:

--The only thing I want to do is sit a little while at Rosati's.

--I don't know it, Morten says and looks both disappointed and eager. His ideal is a gold spoon up to its neck in spaghetti, but mention the name of an unknown restaurant to him and he can be consoled.

We get up and he takes me by the arm. He carries some of my packages, while I have a finger under the string of one and feel a little tightening which tells me my stockings fit like they should, the little tightening which is a clamp on that part of the brain where everything is kept that mustn't slip out. Now. I hold his sleeve's tweed by the hand and on the left the mirror-windows drive past with their reeking piles of plastic-packed, flower-garnished, perfumed, leather-creaking, garlic-scenting, intoxicating luxury. To the right the kiosk, where there isn't yet anything about me, neither in Corriere della Sera, Il Messagero, Times, Frankfurter Allgemeine, The Christian Science Monitor, Berlinske Tidende, ABC or The Guardian and to the right, too, at the corner again knee man on his little anti-capitalistic, four wheeled demonstration cart, where he sits with a rose behind his ear and plays the violin for us so the muscles on the inner sides of my thighs tighten and everything I wear of nylon and elastic and silk rustles and exists. And around my finger a little message tightens forth, a bubble sprouts up and over my head, and I carry it like a balloon above me on Via Veneto, and inside it sits

70

Jørgen Schwer, obscure, fake hippie, vanished foundling, accused of diverse crimes, awaited not with joy, but with lukewarm vindictiveness, momentarily vanished runaway but certainly not in high spirits, arrived at an unknown destination, sitting at the right hand of the jukebox, from where he (perhaps) will come and judge me living or dead.

Pass by the Pension Dinesen, go along the wall on the right hand, round Monte Pincio, climb through difficult streets, which become unreal and unrecognizable because Morten is talking, telling me about 1) Denmark is in peril 2) not because of the present conservative-liberal regime 3) but because of dangerous tendencies of disintegration 4) which manifest themselves in 1) much too much attention to immaterial phenomena such as a) flower children b) so-called activists c) random pressure groups and 2) distract attention from the real problems x) the economic balance y) intensity of investing z) the possibility of competition and profit.

But there is Piazza del Popolo, and Anna feels she doesn't need to say anything more or think about what she's heard. She would have said something but can't because she's said the same things so many times before, and in the second place she isn't quite sure what she wants to say. Her relationship to Denmark is very distant. She hasn't been home in many years, and when she left, she felt free. Not because she hated her relatives or her country or her king--she herself represented all the above-mentioned institutions in foreign countries--but because she suffered, or thought she suffered, from spiritual monoxide poisoning. Now she can see Rosati's in front of her and knows that the intellectual's raft is also an oxygen-deficient fringe under clouds far too low, but she isn't a participant: she's an observor, a neck-reclining coffee drinker, reticent, sphinx-like, beautiful Scandinavian witness, who attracts attention, but is without obligations, who radiates curiosity, but doesn't require correct, true (trivial) answers.

In front of the table and the small hedge the piazza is humming wildly, fuel-farting, red, grey, classic. And Morten turns to Anna and says:

--Why did we come here?

--They have the best Campari. Rosati's Campari is famous.

--Does it come from somewhere else then?

--No it comes out of the usual bottle. But it's poured with care-- just like good draft beer--it's filled up beautifully and the ice is shaped like children's hands, infant hands from Jerusalem.

He looks at me.

--No, no, I hurriedly say, but you know very well how crucial the relationship is between alcohol and that which thins it, don't you? You know very well how important it is that a drink isn't too strong and not too weak.

--Yes, yes, he says, with his eager acceptance of every banality,-- it's just like marriage, too little and too much--it isn't good, it can ruin everything, salt and pepper, yes, yes, wonderful, but if one uses too much seasoning it doesn't work.

--And there shouldn't be too many cooks, either, I say, flirting, a bit thickly, and he looks confused and sets one of my packages down while he hunts for a cigarette.

--Cooks?

--Yes, in marriage, I mean.

--Ah, no, he says, no, certainly. He's still confused, and my sense of time as with Caesar is stretched out and I only see the table in front of me as a flowing, dangling mass, the hedge melting into spinach along the sidewalk, and there my life (just like theirs) tramples somewhere else, I here, he there, I here, strangers who crowd in, shouting: that's my table, our table, he, she, her, it, its table, it's the first day of school after the summer vacation and we're on the way in through the door to the new class and the smell of varnish, the slight stickiness under our flats, the pictures in the classroom different from last year, the desks higher, the inkwells not yet filled, the curtains translucent, without spots, outside peaceful August, hope not a subject for discussion, but a fact and the loud rapid voices: my desk, my desk, we came first, you're cheating, home free for this one, no, home free for this, I want to sit by the window, I don't want the front row, I'll tell on you if you don't let me in, shhh, here she comes, here she comes, she who has her own desk, her desk, her desk, which will go on sitting there until she falls and is carried out, whereas we can go, go soon and never come back.

Home in Pakistan we speak slowly, and it's rare for anyone to raise his voice. The loudest voice is Minna's. When I'm sitting in the huge living room with the pillows along the wall, I can hear her down by the river. I have myself screamed twice--when I saw the flagellants in Kinambur (Mirres stepped forward and grasped my hand) and when a scorpion came out of John's polo boot.

Ah. And here we are speaking too loud, to hear each other over the noise of the scooters, and it's natural because many things are crowding in demanding to be said.

--You two really must have problems with the life out there, Morten says.

For a moment I'm nervous, but then it occurs to me that it's not my problems he refers to, but others'. And I answer, reassured, that to a large degree that was true. Our Campari arrives. It's as it should be and Morten begins a long speech about how unusual it is and how good. I find myself longing for something I can't define, and suddenly understand how miserably I'm treating Morten. Has he deserved it? Isn't he, too, a product, and in a way innocent? That's just what he is: innocent. And isn't the reason for my anger and distraction that he's outside my sphere of influence? It's different with Tom, who came to me and said (or so I interpreted it): Oh, you Rysensteen's rose, you lunchroom Maureen O'Hara, let me step into your sphere and become another. In exchange I'll bestow on you riches, career, foreign countries, jewels, children, dogs, camels, buzzards, and English neighbors with hyphenated names and upper lips of asbestos, but so that I myself can bear the burdens which are necessary for all this to become a *reality*, you must lend me your strength, let me take a seat in the withe basket of your sound reason, on the unfailing and weatherproof suspension bridge of your womanliness and your sex. Let me enter Vibe Road, which is as far from the Terlow Mansion as one could imagine, let me sit at your and your parents' dinner table, hear their beautiful, hoarse plain voices, let me smell your simple kitchen odors and smile when your father recites from the newspaper and laughs or swears, let me pretend to be interested in your brother's problems with soccer blisters and measurements of inclinations, your mother's bronchitis, and let it all debauch in a long sigh, where I lie with my bare feet against your rose-colored rump, observe your mist-back, which is planted in your hips like a vase, while the foetus, your pale, anonymous, inarticulate, democractic prize and symbol is turning in its alcohol.

He was allowed to enter. Who's ever heard of a prince who'd a need or a wish that wasn't fulfilled? He entered and all the wishes-- mine and his--were fulfilled. He sits today with the tropic sun on his neck and the king's stamp is all over him, and am I not sitting here myself in my new clothes, the emperor's wife in exile? To top it off, with a slave from my husband's family before my feet in the old fashion, pursued and attended, simultaneously wanted, sought after, and fled from all in the same day. Maybe that's what rankles me the most, that he whom I chose to flee with is himself fleeing from me.

Good. Morten Rabbit, I'll try again then.

--Have you ever considered that when you're out there--when

we're out there, that then you can't do anything?

--What do you mean that we can't do anything?

--I remember what I said when I gave up my studies when I married Tom. I said: There won't be any change in my attitude. I'll develop and become different, but my basic attitude will be the same. It's often a strain--in spite of all its charm--to enter the Terlow family, and I've seen enough frightening examples in his circle never to become like them, even if we advance from here to the moon. I said, when we were going abroad for the first time: you have to get to know the customs of the country, you have to know as much as possible about it in advance. Not because you're afraid to make a fool of yourself--on the contrary--but because in any event you shouldn't try to impose your views which the natives (there you have it!) don't have a natural basis for aguing against and refuting. I don't want to be a colonist. The next time we went abroad or moved I had no time to get acquainted with anything but household problems and how I should get enough servants. And what am I today: colonist.

--No you're not. You represent--or more correctly: you and Tom represent Denmark abroad. Certain practical problems have to be solved, you solve your part. It's a realistic attitude and there's nothing wrong with it.

--I'll tell you one thing, Morten. There isn't anything you get accustomed to more quickly in the whole world than the bad customs of other countries. There's nothing in your whole life that happens as quickly as getting used to a place where the master-slave relationship is as recognized and cherished as our own health service. Just as long as it's yourself who's the master and the others who're the slaves.

--Aren't you good to your "slaves"?

--Yes, I'm good to Tom.

--What did you say?

--I say: just your formulation of the question--even though you hesitate at the word "slaves"--is enough to make me want another Campari. Yes, I'm good to my slaves. And I even love some of them. They're doing all right, and I don't belong to that type that collapses with universal compassion and can't get a bite down as long as others are hungry. I just couldn't keep it up.

--Was that why you left?

--No, I didn't leave for any particular reason.

--But in a way your attitude hasn't changed at all, even though you say it has.

--The question is simply whether you can have one attitude and be something else, Anna says and watches a loudspeaker-car drive into Piazza del Popolo, where it opens its mouth and calls toward the walls and the adjacent streets and down toward the river something she takes to be her own name. She rises halfway out of her seat and stares at the grey car, which drives first on the right side of the obelisk and now swings around to the left while it belches its corkpopping echo, and when the funnel turns right at her, she automatically covers her ears with her hands and opens her mouth. Morten watches her, but mistakes the direction of her stare and looks toward the sidewalk to the oblique right of Anna, where a man in a cotton coat and brown, soft hat is approaching in the direction of their table.

La principessa dell'arena, la grande Anastasia Aurora bellows the car right in front of them, and the sound is thrown back and the a's fall against them like lumps of earth and leap up from the asphalt and the stone bridge. The car breathes wheezily and the funnel turns slowly toward the left; sounds begin again but return from the back wall of the square sharper, the vowels smaller, the consonants lisping . . . una senzatione straordinaria . . . sera . . . sera . . . questa sera . . . questa Anna . . . senzatione . . .

The man in the brown hat and cotton coat stops on the other side of the hedge in front of Morten and Anna's table. There are many people at Rosati's at noon, always people arriving by car, parking their scooters on the sidewalk, talking a moment, driving on, laughing, picking someone up, throwing cigarettes over the hedge, arranging a date. The loudspeaker-car leaves and Anna slowly turns and looks at the man. Morten watches them both. He's surprised at Anna's reaction, but he's been brought up to not interfere more than absolutely necessary. In the family's heraldry there is interlaced an invisible credo: Keep safe, keep out.

Karl Christensen has also gotten new Roman clothes. Maybe they don't become him nearly so well as Anna's new clothes do her, but he's a nice man and a young man, he has broad shoulders, the brown eyes match the hat, he's just the thing to clip out and place up on a horse or stick a guitar in his hand, and Anna (I) can't help smiling at him both because the loud voice has disappeared and because Karl Christensen couldn't hide a tiny, satisfied smile under the professional deadpan.

--Livingston, is it really you? What are you doing at Rosati's?

Christensen keeps on standing there for a moment, and the wind from the river makes his right lapel flutter. Then he feels awkward (and unprofessional) having to talk over a hedge that's planted in green pots and is piled up in the middle of the city. He walks with strides suitable to a policeman over to the entrance, turns the corner and edges his way toward us between the tables, where no one takes notice of him. Only Morten leans toward Anna and asks:

--Who the hell is the Robert Hall man?

--From the police, Anna says.

Karl Christensen stands in front of them, and Anna turns and looks at him. It's time that she (I) say something sensible to him.

--Would you like a chair, Mr. Christensen?

Which perhaps isn't very sensible, but expedient, when one feels overtaken and wants to gain time. The game quickens, and no

77

loudspeaker-car could frighten me now. If Morten had that kind of eyes, he'd now see an empty bubble over Anna's head, yes, perhaps no bubble at all. He looks at Anna, who with new color in her cheeks is leaning toward Christensen, who meanwhile has taken a seat and says:

--I have great difficulty grasping just why you should be interested in a person like Schwer.

--Schwer?

--Yes. I could imagine others, a number of people both at home, in the East, and possibly here, too, who'd want to be in touch with him, but your interest escapes me.

--I'm afraid I don't quite follow you.

Morten (sweet) inserts:

--You know you're under no obligation to say anything at all, don't you?

I nod and look at my two cavaliers. The only thing missing is a Dave Hemmings, a camera, an enlarger, and we're equal to "Petra" or "Marie Claire."

--You speak as though Schwer and I were buddies, or on a fairly intimate footing . . . but to be completely honest, I didn't even know his name was Schwer . . . if we're talking about the same person.

Karl Christensen looks tired. He has a nice way of looking tired. He reminds me of my biology teacher in Tietgens Street, who could also get that disappointed expression when you'd promised him a Sarah Bernhardt cake for his coffee break between the double classes and came with chocolate beans instead.

Christensen takes a deep breath and I watch his arteries oxidize and redden.

--Will you tell me what you whispered to Jørgen Schwer on the plane?

I look at him as honestly as possible and say:

--Yes.

A little color returns to Karl Christensen's cheeks. Morten has leaned back in the brown wicker chair.

--What did you whisper, then?

--Do you want to know all of it?

The chief detective nods.

--Yes, preferably.

Anna (I) takes a deep breath and says in an uninterrupted sentence:

--I whispered to him that since the first moment I saw him in the embassy in Karachi my heart hadn't been at peace and asked him to follow me out to the toilet where without attracting any attention he could satisfy my hunger.

Morten:

--Anna!

Christensen:

--I don't believe that.

Anna:

--Good.

Anna:

--I whispered to him that since the first moment I saw him in the embassy in Karachi I had but one thought in my head and that was the thirty pounds of *Cannabis sativa* that we had collected during our three year stay in Pakistan. Would he buy it on the spot, or would I have to force him with bribery to get it through customs in Kastrup and distributed in Copenhagen?

Morten looks at me and his eyelids begin to flicker. Christensen is extremely calm. Then he says:

--Why do you insist on playing games?

--I'm not insisting on anything whatsoever, but it seems you don't believe what I say.

--No, I don't.

--In other words, you think I'm lying.

Christensen, who's used to handling the concepts lie and truth with care, shrugs his shoulders.

--May I try to review the case?

I nod, and Morten, who doesn't know anything, nods too. Before Karl Christensen begins his elucidation, I say:

--Since it appears I've taken over the role of criminal for a while, perhaps I may be permitted to offer you a refreshment? Or is that against the rules, too?

Christensen's smile is fine. He says:

--Since at this moment the only one charged isn't here, and since this involves only an informal conversation in connection with Schwer's disappearance, I won't oppose your friendly offer.

Somewhere or other a series of brittle bells break forth in chime. So the way is paved and the chief detective steps forward.

--When I first saw Mrs. Terlow, it was in the Danish Embassy in Karachi. I had travelled to Pakistan on official business to get and bring home Jørgen Schwer, who'd been on Interpol's list for a long time for, among other things, international drug traffic, embezzlement, violence, petty theft, bad checks, forgery, and smuggling. Schwer had been seized by the Pakistani authorities a week before, and, as an intermediate stop on the way home and because there were papers to be signed and delivered, we stayed--I and the accused--in the Danish Embassy. The second time I met Mrs. Terlow was on the plane from Karachi to Teheran, where she kindly offered me and the prisoner drinks, which I, on official and ethical grounds, refused to accept. During the stop in Teheran, and on our way out to the plane, Mrs. Terlow tried to make contact with me-- perhaps to apologize for any intrusion, which really wasn't an intrusion. If anything it was I who should have apologized because my manner of refusing the invitation was more than clumsy. When after that Mrs. Terlow approached me and Jørgen Schwer on the plane, I invited her to sit down after she had delivered her unnecessary though friendly apology. It appeared as if she wanted to sit with . . . countrymen, and even though she seemed--I hope you'll excuse me--a little over-excited, I saw no reason to deny her wish. When a little later Schwer conducted himself ill-manneredly toward the Ambassador's wife, I protested against it, and perhaps it was because of his insults I later agreed to a conversation between Mrs. Terlow and Schwer, to be conducted in whispers. It was Mrs. Terlow, who displayed great friendliness and seemed to be a little calmer, and it escaped my notice, therefore, that at some point Jørgen Schwer left our company. He wasn't handcuffed. Mrs. Terlow thought he'd gone in the direction of the toilet, but when I looked for him there, he had vanished. A search of the whole transit hall yielded no results, and when Mrs. Terlow had also vanished, I had to assume that she was the prisoner's accomplice. I called a taxi and drove straight to Rome.

--And Jørgen . . . Jørgen Schwer, have you found him? Anna asks.

--No, Karl Christensen says.

--Oh, says Anna.

6

My telephone rings and someone says my name quite naturally, Anna. It's light, and the sounds from the street and the square outside are like a fountain, rising and falling. I am up high and descend from a great height, return from the milder stratum where dreams have approached and vanished, where those familiar and unfamiliar to me have spoken, and I have answered or watched myself answer. Even in sleep I've known all along that I was Anna, and the word in the receiver I now hold to my ear, is a confirmation. Anna. The voice pronouncing my name is familiar and unfamiliar as with the voices I've been hearing all along, and I sit up in bed to make it all clearer, come closer, wake.

The voice repeats my name, and I answer yes. The voice in the receiver is far away, but the sounds in the room around the speaker give me the feeling he's nearby. It's a man, and before I can assign him a face and shape, he says: Jørgen Schwer. In dreams, early morning dreams, I leave my bed and rise into space, strenuously hovering, as if I had to lift myself by the hair to carry out the process. The height isn't great, about half a meter from the floor and the strain of holding myself up considerable. I move slowly, think hard about what I'm doing and formulate my wishes one by one. I'd like to go up higher, but the greater heights are reserved for another kind of sleep, one more liberated or narcotic. Right now I can't tell, and even though I pull the blanket aside and get up with the phone to my ear, the effort is enormous and I want to return, go inwards and upwards. But my desire cannot overcome the restraints. If I can make the windowsill, wrest myself up to the edge, just raise an arm, twist a knee into place, there's a chance to descend in an accelerated dive, gain speed, return to the height, at the height, brush the nearest rooftops and the power lines, see a house in front of me and with a final effort go over it and shift myself into gear where new possibilities appear and the strain, the effort can be reduced.

The telephone cord is long and when I stand by the curtains and draw them aside, I'm connected accoustically with an invisible room and at the same time see Piazza Barberini, the street leading to Victor Emmanuel and Santa Maria Maggiore straight ahead, Via Veneto's curve to the right and the square itself deep down there, a slide under the lens of a microscope with the cells and lymphocytes and the bloodstream in tiny gymnastic spasms, stopping and flowing, irritable and decisive.

--Are you there? the voice asks.

And I laugh because I've been raised to answer all questions truthfully but don't know what to say without lying. But when Anna has taken the receiver and has said her yes once, I answer again and confirm our expectations.

--Yes, I say.

--I'm coming up then, Schwer says.

Before I can answer, he's hung up, and I guess and realize that if he says "come up" it must be that he's in the lobby of the hotel. It's a cool challenge and my heaviness disappears. The lengthy morning's washing and care contract--I look from my watch to the mirror, eight-fifteen, choose to camouflage the dark circles under my eyes, go into the bathroom and put on the white terrycloth robe that's hanging there, turn on the water. Through the spout the stream is wide and mildly seething, the heated floor reminds me I have feet. I hold both hands under the soundless, nearly soundless, water and watch the flattened bubbles against my skin. The water glances off my nightcream, but its heat reaches me, its texture. I ask myself: Is there a connection? Anna (I) leaves my home in Karachi as arranged with my husband. A compulsion made living with my family impossible, but since we don't live in the dark ages but in the twentieth century there's a cure for that, too. No problem is so great it can't be solved. Still we feel (Tom and I) for either clearly sensible or maybe sentimental chauvinistic reasons, that a cure in Denmark is preferable, yes, is of vital importance. Begin therefore on the long journey, but don't get any farther than Teheran before the compass begins to deviate from the course and on arrival at Rome there is no course. Or is there? Yesterday evening I thought everything was decided. I ate dinner with my brother-in-law Morten after giving my explanation to chief detective Christensen. To be sure, my explanation wasn't satisfactory. I didn't divulge that I was the one who helped Jørgen Schwer escape, less to protect myself against eventual unpleasant consequences than to protect him. Or did I think about my motives at all? And aren't there questions approaching from another quarter? What was it I decided with Morten and promised the white man from the police? That I will continue my journey as planned and report to Karl Christensen immediately if I come in contact with Schwer at all? Yes. And isn't my story really completely discredited if the chief detective knows that Schwer could only pass through customs because I insisted and came up with an improbable explanation which the Italian in an improbable way accepted? Yes. But, so *what*? What is it then that's really wrong?

The water's running into Anna's basin and she should turn it off for she no longer has any use for it. She stands in front of the mirror and has dried off the cream and water with a pink towel. She's putting her face on in a primitive way. When she has put on the mascara, she starts to brush her hair. She observes herself closely in the mirror. She asks the same question again:

--What is it then that's really wrong?

84

But before she gets to answer it, the buzzer sounds at the door to her room. For a moment she stands with her arm raised over her head and the brush against her red hair, then drops her arm, lays the brush down on the glass shelf and turns off the water. Aside from the faint sounds of traffic, rising and falling, it's quiet in the hotel room and you don't hear her footsteps to the door because she walks from bathmat to bathmat and then on the thick carpet in the bedroom. She opens the door almost the same moment she unlocks it and the lock makes a rattling that echoes in the long corridor outside. Even though she doesn't immediately recognize the person standing before her, since Jørgen Schwer has had his long hair cut, she (I) says immediately:

--Hello, dear friend, come in!

He stares at her, and perhaps the unexpected welcome intensifies his suspicion that she is really crazy. He steps inside, both because he had wanted to meet her and because it would be laughable to go back now. He closes the door behind him and turns.

--Why did you come back? I say.

He walks over to the bed and stands there as if he'd rather sit there than one of the two easy chairs.

--You can sit on the bed if you want.

He stares from the bed at me and goes over and sits in the easy chair to the right of the window.

--I need some money, he says.

--How did you know you'd find me here?

--You said it yourself, he says sullenly.

--And don't you think it's dangerous?

--What?

--To visit me at the Barberini?

--Have I any choice?

--I thought you had contacts everywhere.

He gives me his fresh air kid look, ill-fed and aggressive.

--Who says so?

--Karl Christensen gave me a lecture yesterday. About you.

--Is he here?

--You said so yourself.

The dreams were tiring, the oxygen too thin up there, the morning gliding too strenuous. I want to sleep.

--Why did you get your hair cut?

--There aren't so many people with long hair in Rome.

--You mean there are none besides you. Why did you have long hair at all?

--It's better--in the East--then they just think you're an idiot, simple idiot or hash-bum.

--And you're not.

--No.

He turns sideways and rocks on one of his feet. A child who has done something and won't admit it.

--What is it you want?

--I've already told you.

--And if I say no?

--You won't.

He turns again and looks at me. Now everything is very easy. Now I'll take three steps over to the phone, lift the receiver and call Morten. He's staying at the Hassler, wanted to move here yesterday, but I said it wasn't necessary. Everything's decided. I fly home via Zurich today 3:15, arrive Copenhagen 7:45. As soon as I get home I'll visit the doctor, a certificate will be written out attesting to my mental incompetence, it will be forwarded in numerous copies--one to the foreign ministry, one to the police, one to the psychiatric ward, one to my teacher, one to Minna, who is saved, one to Tom, one to the press, who must have the story by now, one to Karl Christensen (as a souvenir), one to the buzzard to sharpen its beak with and one to dear old Dad and Mom, which they can show to my brother. I pass Schwer on the way to the phone and he follows me with his eyes. When I lift the receiver, he looks away. The static humming hangs like a spring between the receiver and my ear. And to boot, there are two recipients, two possibilities, handsome, white Karl and lovable Morten.

--Who are you calling? Jørgen Schwer asks.

--Christensen.

He doesn't know what to say. Would like to say: No, you're not, or You're not that stupid, but he just sits there pouting. I keep holding the receiver and then I say:

--Why did you run off on me?

--It was too dangerous.

--To be with me?

--Yes.

I put the receiver down, wanting to hear him say more, say something further about it.

--Go on.

He looks at me again and thinks he can see madness behind my freckles. He sits there knowing a lot, he feels like he himself was fat superior knowledge, lead solidifying in water.

--I don't have time.

Again a plop.

--I have to move on.

Look at his slum complexion and say to myself: Finished, finished, finished and never again. I lift the phone off the hook once more and hit the call-button. Jørgen Schwer turns toward me and leans forward. I tap more anxiously to get ahold of the receptionist or operator, but remember that you should dial after there's a dial-tone. Or should you first dial the operator at the dial-tone, or should the switchboard make the call. I look around for the books or the little instructions on the table, as his head follows me in tiny jerks and his eyes blink. Remember that both numbers are in my purse, but that doesn't help. Remember gym class where for the first time a fierce sound came out of my sex during a difficult exercise and Miss Schmidt shouted: Keep it together! Squeeze! And I heard it roar even louder. Continence, that's the word, squeeze both ends together and compose yourself, only roar when you're alone with the one you love. But can I do it? The switchboard announces itself with its Pronto! Pronto! And I don't know what to answer. But the boy says:

--Stop that.

He begins to rummage in his pocket like a man who suddenly can't find his wallet in a restaurant and a moment later I'm calm and feel like laughing. He sits holding the largest and blackest revolver I've ever seen in his hand and it strikes me he shouldn't have cut his hair, for if he'd left it alone he'd now resemble Buffalo Bill in late puberty.

--Jørgen, I say, what kind of apparatus are you sitting there with?

He answers my rhetorical, giggling question by pointing the revolver straight at me. Then he says:

--You've told Christensen where you live, and he hasn't put an immediate guard on you or moved in himself because he's dead certain I'd never find you here or look you up. On the other hand he's also damned sure that if he's going to get the chance to take me here in the city, he has to use you as bait for as long as possible and tail you from place to place. Or is he already standing downstairs aware that I'm here or staying in the next room?

I shake my head. He isn't in the next room.

I shake my head, because I don't know what else to do. His explanation doesn't make sense and I don't understand Christensen, either. I don't understand the vagueness around them. They should, according to their professions, be deliberate, rational, logical, but everything they do is just as erratic as what I do. Maybe you could speak directly to him sentence by sentence, but can you talk sense with a man on the run, and would the opinion of a mentally deranged person hold any water? I say to him:

--To be completely honest, I don't understand much of this. I haven't told Karl Christensen I was the one who got you into Italy yesterday. I think he's guessed his way to this connection but somehow he doesn't want to hold me responsible. Together we've arranged the continuation of my journey, the tickets are ordered, and I thought I'd never see you again. I don't know why I've done what I've done, but was disappointed when you left me in Trastevere. Now you want money from me and you'll probably be arrested shortly either by the carabinieri or by Christensen. So why do you want money? And why shouldn't I be permitted to report you now so we can end the whole thing? I didn't *mean* anything by it. I didn't mean anything.

He sits with the revolver in his lap and says:

--What do you mean you didn't mean anything by it?

Anna, naked under her nightgown under her bathrobe under her skin, Anna, exposed shellfish out of water, winces and says:

--You get my money if I can come along.

He stares incomprehensibly at me and the mealy skin around the wings of his nose contracts. The lower edge of his front teeth is visible.

--Why the hell do you want to go along?

--I don't know.

I get up and go over to him. The phone is on the night table and the cord is long and thin.

--You've no idea where I'm going, for Christ's sake!

He moves violently and the revolver slides around in his lap.

--Aren't you going home?

--Home where?

--To Denmark.

--Yes, as a matter of fact.

He looks offended again, and I want to know more of what's going on. Anna Terlow and the criminal mealworm. He gets halfway up and slams the black telephone back on its hook. The sound disappears. The Pronto-animal has given up. It's twenty minutes to nine.

--I can't have you along, he snaps.

--How do you plan to get home?

--Through Switzerland, Switzerland and Germany.

--Without a passport?

--Maybe you think we can get through on *yours*?

He's already scoffing at my red passport, which has at least gotten him this far.

--Clod, I say.

--What? he says.

I'm surprised that he's not in a greater hurry, that he's not more nervous. That he doesn't shoot me with his big, black play revolver. That he comes and wrecks my game, which was so simple. Up in the morning with Mirres' hand on my shoulder, the huge tray in bed with Tom in the other bed, glasses on my forehead, the morning mail, senseless dispatches, ink, seals, stampings. The dressing room after the bath, the walk through the rooms, across the lawn, the river, the heat already as dense as water, Minna, who's brought out, is accompanied down, let loose. The walk under the willow tree that I'd had sent from home, grown like a broadwinged rocket in three years and the control that hasn't failed, hasn't failed, hasn't failed yet except the day with the waterbearer, the man who came out of my zodiac and held out his small black bowl. And John gets his morning kiss, bears my lips away, no, not them but the red color, a shadow of it, bought, sold and paid for, each time with the same feeling of respite: you perform an act, even a betrayal, and it involves forgiveness and oblivion. The act excludes reality, reality excludes the act.

--What about your husband?

I'm not prepared for this ethical question now, and it occurs to me that I myself haven't asked it before.

--He's already worried.

--Why? You mean he knows about it?

--Yes, because of that, too.

Jørgen Schwer gets up and walks around the hotel room forty meters above Piazza Barberini with his gun in his hand. He stops by the door to the bathroom, turns and walks straight toward me.

--I don't know what you're up to and I'd rather not have anything to do with it. But I don't want to hit you. You can just give me the money, it won't matter, you'll be home by evening.

He comes a step nearer and I can smell the cheap aftershave and hair cream some Figaro or other has rubbed into his head. A pimple shines furtively on his neck just above his collar. His costume's different, too. It must have been what he spent his money on, that and the gun. Apparently everyone gets new clothes in Rome. When Morten shows up, it'll probably be as a hippie or big game hunter.

--It's in my purse.

He looks around the room and can't locate it.

--It's in the bathroom.

--So get it.

I smile at him and see my brother before me: You'll have to get it. It was you who threw it into the other yard. It was *you*. Anyway, I'm not getting it!

He turns and goes to the bathroom door again. Stands with his back to me and stares at the phone. Then he lifts the gun and aims at my heart. The skin under my left breast contracts.

--Go get it.

And I little girl (Anna) don't know anything, I don't know anything about dum-dum bullets and the boy from vocational class who's here in Rome, in the middle of the city, in the morning; it's light, the sun is shining, spring is coming, they didn't teach us anything about this in Tietgens Street, not a word. We got innoculated with everything about the production of lead, by roasting and reduction, we even touched on the formula for the production of ordinary gunpowder (sulphur, charcoal and saltpeter), but they didn't tell us anything about calibers, explosive force, recoil, ballistics, yes, and even at the university--and this is perhaps more important--we heard nothing about reaction patterns, context of action, chance statistics, and sudden madness. Not for others and not for ourselves. We heard something about life, its rise and its course, but who discussed slot machines?

Without his hearing my little inward "Bow-wow" I run across the floor past him, fling open the door to the bathroom while he steps aside, look through my right eye's very corner into the weapon's black eye, which follows me, and slam the door behind me. But not even here, where I used to be alone, can I hide now--my two new friends--one of whom previously ran *away* from me as quickly as he could--force their way in, and under their three-eyed surveillance I look around in the bathroom for my purse, which holds my most valued possessions: mirror, make-up, comb, passport, money. He keeps me covered, while I go over to the large mirror above the sink, where his arm, hand, weapon, are reflected behind my shoulder, and my own face shines transparently. I pick up the purse with both hands, close it with a snap (the weapon doesn't move) turn and approach the criminal again. I pass him, and he lets me go into the

92

room without saying a word. The neighbor beyond my headboard has gotten up--a rattling toothglass announces him, an optimistic fart and nearly the same moment the sound of an electric razor or toothbrush. An ever-so-minimal knowledge of guns and the sound they make cannot prevent me from an absolute certainty that former hippie will hardly blast away now. Therefore, Anna, clever Anna, stops at the foot of her bed and nods to him as if she wants to say: If you want money, you can come get it yourself. And as if he understands both this and the neighbor's blastings, he walks quickly across the floor with the gun lowered, shifts it to his left hand and reaches the right out to me with an urgent, imperative gesture. And I notice the contempt settle in my throat like gall, I see these poorly-lit, upturned faces with their pinched eyes examining my bills, sniffing, scrutinizing, munching, follow Mirres while he bows with dignity, accepting the envelope from Tom with his "salary," see this asocial, unappetizing individual approach, this *young delinquent* from Hvidore, Vibe Road, Honduras, Chieng Mei, The School by the Sound and gather all my conscious energy in my right leg, which under the right pressure, released, suddenly fired from the floor, can lift sixteen stone, split a half cubic meter of stump wood and stop a Sherman tank. He stands above me, and I release the brake. In his natural reaction Jørgen Schwer doubles up, convulsively drops the pistol and tumbles against me, tumbles over the foot of the bed, and sends both of us tumbling down onto the mattress, which still retains a little of my body-warmth. At that moment, the phone rings.

I could talk a lot about Rysensteen now and the deficiencies of a girls' school education at the end of the forties and the beginning of the fifties. I certainly had the suspicion it was wicked to kick a man in the groin, but I didn't know--didn't know from either Tom or any of the other men I'd known--how long it can hinder normal breathing, yes, any breathing at all. I've seen men in real life and on television who'd been hit in the testicles, seen them suffer and double up, too, but I didn't know they could be transformed into balls themselves, tiny compressed thunderballs, tiny, raw, Brussels sprouts, that shrink more and more around themselves, seem to shrivel, contract in order somehow or other to return to a bearable condition and survive.

The phone rings a second time and I try to squeeze my way toward it under the little stone man, but am suddenly afraid that his breathing--when it comes--will expose us. Expose us?

It's Christensen on the wire, and I don't say a thing when I pick up the phone. He speaks.

--It's nine o'clock, and I just wanted to wake you as I promised. Did you sleep well?

When I don't answer, he continues.

--I spoke with staff back home, and they've promised me that you'll be kept out of the case as much as possible. I was glad you told me the reason for your trip home, but also I want to let you know that you're brother-in-law is worried.

--Worried?

--He's reluctant to send you to Denmark alone.

Jørgen Schwer opens one of his eyes halfway; and I see the color in his face change suddenly from putty to desert grey and then blossom into scarlet, billowing up from his collar toward his temples. His pupil is invisible, his eye is white.

--I think . . . I think I've worked it off, I say.

--That was my impression last night, and I don't want to press you further, even though I know you haven't told me what you whispered to Schwer on the plane.

Lay my hand on Jørgen's hair, feel the oil.

--Why are you protecting me?

--I'm not protecting you. Have you seen any sign of Schwer?

Turn my head and look at him two centimeters from me. His

legs lie over mine, bent. A spasm moves from his lowest stomach muscle up over his waist toward his breastbone, it stops a second, is repeated quick as lightning, goes deeper and suddenly he opens his mouth. And a sound that doesn't belong anywhere in the world and probably can't be kept in it, either, breaks over me. I hold my hand over the mouthpiece and press so hard to shield it that the plastic bites into the palm of my hand. What have I done?

When the scream, the scream of the damned in hell, ebbs out, there remains the sound of the neighbor's little apparatus and Christensen's voice continues its Danish hallo, hallo, hallo more demanding and suspicious each time. Jørgen Schwer is breathing in gasps and I uncover the mouthpiece and say:

--Yes?

Christensen shouts.

--What's going on there, is anything wrong? Aren't you alone?

--Yes, yes, I say, I'm alone.

--Yes, but what kind of a sound was that?

--What sound?

--The sound . . . that scream I heard before?

--No one screamed.

While we are saying these things to each other, it occurs to me that I'm about to learn something about my own tension and reaction. I want to free myself from something and so attach myself to something. People speak to me in a definite tone of voice and I react with a different tone of voice. People want me to do one thing and I do another. Is this innate pampering or habituation? Am I normal, crazy or evil? Or am I nothing? Schwer takes a pillow with his left hand and bores his face down into it to dampen his breathing. He presses his right hand to his groin. The mirror on the wall across from the foot of the bed shows the revolver in slanting perspective.

--I have a feeling, Karl Christensen says, that you're . . . not telling the truth . . . just like yesterday.

--Yesterday I told the truth.

--Are we going to start that all over again?

--I don't know what you mean.

His voice is changed; he casts in a new direction, with the wind.

--Aren't you feeling well?

--Yes, I feel fine.

I look at Schwer.

--Perhaps a little sleepy.

--When you get home you can rest.

--Yes.

It's true. When I get home I can rest. I can sleep when I'm dead, too. In the past two nights I haven't had any trouble sleeping. The man on the bed woke me up, but I don't hate him for it. He's made me aware that I can sleep. He woke me and I said to myself: You could have slept longer. It's a fine day.

--What was that?

--What?

--There was someone groaning!

--I didn't hear anything.

And as if to punish me, he says:

--You're aware the newspapers have the story?

I don't answer but look at the young man next to me with the freshly cut hair and awful clothes. He's opened his eyes and is watching me. I smile at him. Christensen repeats:

--Hallo?

I don't answer.

Very loudly, but as if at the same time he's already hanging up, the chief detective says:

--I'm coming over right away.

The click and the static hum is once more the only connection between me and the telephone. On the switchboard the wires move out in all directions, the possibilities are enumerated in plugs and jacks, combinations, constituents, local, non-local, inter-urban, long distance, transatlantic conversations per cable and wireless, but right now they're cut off. I place the receiver on the hook and say to the man on the bed:

--He's on his way over.

The man on the bed looks at me.

--Where's he staying.

--At the Termini.

--Is it far?

--Ten minutes.

He turns his face away.

I (Anna) bend down and kiss him on the ear.

7

A common failing in the upbringing of the generation I belong to (one would call it the fifties) is that no one ever called our attention to the fact that praise isn't necessarily and always a matter of course, when we've done something good or have exceeded what we ourselves consider our limitations. We who have roots in the thirties are accustomed to being cheered and cherished for all our performances from the first poo-poo in the pot to the last swallow we've forced down our throats on our deathbed without vomiting. I don't know if I'd expected that Jørgen, just because I'd planted my carmoisin-red lips on his ear (which is in fact cute) should have sprung up and shouted a hallelujah and been grateful. No, I don't think he should have done that, and I think too that maybe there's something unjust--towards myself--in describing a spontaneous act that sprang from sudden tenderness, as a "good deed." But I must admit that I (Anna) had difficulty putting up with his constant sulkiness.

Maybe my upbringing's oldfashioned, but neither on Vibe Road, at Rysensteen, in Paris, London, Budapest, Rome, Reykjavik, Istanbul and the other places I've been alone, with Tom, with my children, with my father and mother and Kjeld, have I been sulky for more than ten minutes at a time. That's probably the reason people have trouble taking my depressions, my sickness, seriously, and that's probably why I have trouble accepting it myself. At the edge of the (train) tracks, on which I often want to lie down as the express is approaching, I feel a kind of absurd, obscure elation. And when I've conquered the crisis and so still have the possibility of being cheerful or at least not sulky,

I'm not sulky. It's self-contradictory that such a destructive urge, as I feel once in a while and will soon be treated by the best doctors in the world--the Danish--is often accompanied by giddiness. In the sleepless morning hours when the buzzard has buried his face under his wing and the white film is stretched out over my whole existence, I catch myself making strange noises with my mouth, little whistles, poppings, smackings. And so I got insulted, too, when Jørgen, as we stood in the back of a clothing store north of Borghese and tried to find a pair of pants and a sweater that fit me, rushed me and chewed me out because I giggled and spoke my best Italian with the Madame, who was enormous and whose hair smelled of burnt shoe polish. I really couldn't bring myself to walk in these coarse, hideous, pre-cut, far too short worker's pants, and the boy went crazy when I accepted the woman's offer to go get a pair of dungarees from a store around the corner while I stayed there waiting in my shift. We'll be caught anyhow, and probably have to pay less bail while we're still in Rome. He kept looking gruff and couldn't manage to be at all happy about how beautifully everything had gone up to now, our quick exit from the Barberini, the terrific close call and glimpse of Christensen as we turned up Veneto and he entered the piazzo from the south.

In the taxi to the store he began to bawl me out because I was still with him--which he'd forgotten when I quickly got him to his feet, got my clothes on, picked up the revolver, and got out of the hotel before Christensen's arrival. I pointed out to him that I was no longer only under suspicion, but had to be considered an accomplice, and even if some of it could be blamed on my alleged insanity, there was no longer any chance of giving the police the slip. He grumbled, chose instead to talk about my ridiculous clothes, about my ladyness, about the insanity of my trying to thumb my way to Denmark with the police on my tail dressed in, dressed in . . . (I helped him, said: Schiaparelli coat) . . . "high-heeled shoes," and was about to ask him to shut his trap, but suggested instead some purchases, which could correct the mentioned deficiencies.

And now here we are, I and the melancholy Jøgen staring out over Lago di Bracciano, where we're accidentally landed because the first person to give us a lift was a local potato dealer who just drove and drove until we both realized that the main highway was no longer there. The weather at mid-day is good, a breeze tugs the tail of the balloon, slight cumulus out over the lake and the rushes bend and straighten and bend as if distinguished visitors were constantly passing by. And I think of Morten and Tom, my noble friends, brother-in-law and husband, both left in the lurch and back there, and if you ask me why, I can't answer. If this is a break with my milieu, or a flight into action from stagnation, it should be considered at best primitive at worst infantile. Now Morten is getting up from his anxious rest (if Christensen hasn't dragged him from bed already) and now the wires are red-hot, transcontinentally, occidentally, and levantly so that Tom and the family on Vibe Road and my little children can set their faces in worried creases and think of their poor crazy or kidnapped, depressed, compulsive-neurotic mother. And in a little while my lovable travelling companion says: Jesus, do you think you're sightseeing?

There was a time many years ago when I came down the road here toward the west. It was near sundown and the light spread backwards out over the lake. We had been in Cerveteri saying hello to the Etruscans, who sat in their brown tombs and were painted and had heads like lions and eyes like saucers from the Royal Danish Porcelain factory. But before that we'd been in La Dispoli and swam and everyone thought we were crazy, because it was

100

October and only idiots go into the water at that time of year, not because it's too cold but because it's not fashionable or because anyone with an ounce of sense in his head and any thought for the future is in Rome working. We hadn't really figured on swimming either; in any case we didn't even have our bathing suits with us. That opened a special possibility, for just as soon as we'd seen the graves of the old ones, and listened to the faint throbbing of the ancient insects scratched in clay, we came down into the coastal city's long since winter-stocked warehouses and saw what there was of discolored, shrunken, discarded, old-fashioned, washed-out bikinis and bathing trunks. We dressed with a couple of delayed Germans in a bathing house, who by chance had left open a few cubicles, and when we ran hand in hand out into the waves with the sun already reflecting intensely, and dark red on the water, a helicopter flew in from the north and we threw back our heads and and yelled Fellini, Fellini! while it compelled our faces toward it and made us crouch under the noise, and the pressure of the rotors raised the water around us in tiny wisps.

After that it was Lago di Bracciano and the dark came quickly. The October dark and the moon that shot up as soon as the sun had fallen. We sat under the plane trees at a restaurant with a cement terrace facing the lake and down below children ran playing. They should have been in bed long ago, we said with Nordic rationality, and it never ocurred to us that it was only half past six. You ordered a glass of wine, and I quoted Petrarch elegantly in Italian and translated afterwards my scattered rhymes and we were very fifties and literary. Everything had found it's course, and there was no reason to be nervous, and the strange thing is I'm not nervous now, either, not in the least, am in a way a little proud and couldn't help but enjoy the fact that anyway I've seen Bracciano in March. I hadn't figured on that the day before

101

yesterday.

We walk along the macadam road and I don't want to ask Jørgen about the things I want to ask him. I'm a little behind compared to him, both here on the road and in every other respect. What do I know about Jørgen Schwer and how much is worth knowing? Should I know more or just follow along like small change. For the first time since the wheels left the cement in Karachi, I feel a melancholy overtake me. Maybe there are too many ghosts in Bracciano after all. Maybe I walk here only because I've been disloyal. Whoever counts up our successes and fiascos, they're not recorded anywhere. We're not like the artists, the actors, the poets and painters who are followed with attention by people who've nothing more sensible to attend to themselves. We aren't given grades and we don't get noted on the stock exchange, up or down. We've no defined fiascos that can be turned to our advantage or repressed, be damned or lamented as necessary. Two kites hover out over the lake and I join forces with them and their gravitational lines to earth, not a cable, but a mobile hawser in constant contact. I feel all the birds are my messengers and benefactors. They don't fly too high, never leave our sphere, but are up high anyway, observe, hover on the wind, migrate and come back. The kites continue eastward and will perhaps pass by my Minna, now, in a little while sometime, or never, but other birds are flying including the one I like the most with the broad, serrated wings, the serene sense of thermals and balanced movements. I see her walking there at home and she's probably forgotten me or I only exist as a sudden impulse every once in a while, a miniscule distraction in her play or a question to Nanny: Where's Mommy?--and when she runs down across the lawn the buzzard circles her in its royal garbageman confidence, and I'm in the vague sighing of the wings, in the feather-muffled yet porous

102

flapping against the tin roof.

A Citröen 2CV with a load of rushes passes us. He doesn't even turn his head to see if we're likely, and we trudge on.

Here's Anna trudging along with her new man. She feels a kind of tenderness in her breast, maybe a great tenderness at that, but she herself isn't fully aware why it's precisely Minna, her daughter, Minna's life, security, welfare, happiness that's the background for everything she's doing. When she woke too early in the whitewashed room and felt that something, something one could not argue with, wanted to force her to kill her child, she had to ask herself what it meant. Over her bed like a knotty pergola was the word *Why?* And there was no answer. And the more she thought about it, the more unreasonable her state of mind seemed. Didn't she have everything a person could desire? A good life, a good husband, beautiful and healthy children, a loving mother, a strict though just father and a clever brother? Yes.

But here's Anna, walking with her Schiaparelli coat (crumpled) over her shoulders, her dungarees, her red hair beneath her scarf, her basketball sneakers and her unsuitable purse.

She (I) remembers when Minna was born. We had John before, one birth, boy, dues rendered, Caesar got his, but here came number two, and I felt that perhaps it was *my* child this time. There were no particular obligations attached, no demands with respect to sex, appearance, behavior, temperature, hair-and-eye color. That was in Karachi, too. Home, I thought, really home perhaps for the first time, and I couldn't say to anyone, not openly anyway, that the attachment I felt for the very way of life, the aloofness, the dignity, the rash, treacherous matter of course with which people came and went, stood in back of my chair, waited on me, despised and loved me, went right into my blood. I raised myself on the sheet and tore away the mask when she came out and it hurt the most and I cried and cried and cried when I saw her red hair and heard it was a girl. My girl, I said, my little Anna, my little Anna, and they smiled back at me and were amazed that someone in such a great and awe-inspiring moment could speak such a bizarre language.

I can be seen here from above now, even though I'm not recognizable because my hair's covered. I walk six steps behind Jørgen, and if we keep this pace up we can probably be in Denmark sometime around Christmas. He hasn't told me yet why it's so important for him to go home. But I assume that things are like that in the underworld and among criminals. You cannot talk to everyone about your plans, least of all to associates you haven't even wanted, but whose money can well be used in a pinch. His standoffishness waves like a flag, and my strange mood returns. I'm all right, I'm calm and the thought of Minna makes me feel safe. I've done a number of things and am doing one of them now. It's a great way to spend your life, doing things. At the moment I'm only followed by the police of two nations, the Italian and the Danish. But maybe there'll be more. I imagine the Pakistani will be interested when they hear about my connection with Schwer. He's done something or other out there even if he claims that he was only travelling through. Why not take out the bullhorn and ask Robin Hood himself. I quicken my pace and catch up with my travelling companion.

--Jørgen?

--Yes.

--Can't you tell me a little about what it is you're really doing?

--Like what?

--Yes, as . . . a criminal?

--Why?

--Because it seems we'll be together for a while and I'd like to have a little background so I can initiate a conversation on subjects which interest you, too.

--Why can't you talk right?

--Now is there something wrong with the way I talk, too?

--Yes.

I walk a while beside him, he stares straight ahead. He has scratched a hole in his pimple.

--Christensen said alot.

--To hell with Christensen.

--He said you've been involved in all sorts of things.

--Can't we talk about something else?

--Why are you always so surly?

--So what?

--So cross.

--I'm not cross, I'm thinking.

--About what?

--About how in Christ we're going to get back to the main highway and whether we'll ever get back to it. And that my balls hurt.

My stomach sinks a little at this linguistic openness, which I'm not used to with Tom. But remember from back then. Hey, girls!

--Why do you want to go home to Denmark? Why wouldn't you rather stay here or go somewhere else?

--It's my country.

--Your *what*?

--You heard me all right.

--Yes, but the only thing they're waiting for back home is to put you in jail.

--I have to talk to my connections. Then I can travel again. Haven't any money.

--He tramps on and in a little while we'll turn off, away from the lake; I had difficulty keeping up and am glad when I hear the sound of a car. I turn and am ready to get in position to wave, but don't even get my arm up before I feel his arms from behind and am dragged into the two-meter high rushes by the shore. His hand tastes of zinc. The rushes close behind us, but even squatting we can see out. The car that comes around the corner is green, has a folding top and looks like a jeep. On the driver's side there's a blue light that's not on. We're right at the water's edge and I notice that my pants are getting wet behind. Try to rise up a little between his legs, but he squeezes them together around me, his thighs against my hips. As soon as the jeep has passed he helps me up and without saying a word goes back to the road and trudges along in the same direction as the car. I'm not so dumb I can't see it was a police car, but I say anyway:

--Who was it?

--Cops.

--Yes, but they didn't look like usual ones.

--It was the highway patrol. It's O.K. to keep walking. If only you didn't have that coat on.

--What's wrong with my coat?

--I've already told you: No broads go walking around on the highway with long pants and then a . . . coat like that.

--How could you tell they were police?

--They're the only ones who drive Land Rovers.

--And you could hear that it was a Land Rover?

--Yes.

That's the way a man talks. We can busy ourselves with a great deal here in life, and try to understand it, too, but a man who can recognize a Land Rover by the sound of its motor, that's worth more than ever so much philosophy and spiritual discussion. Isn't it, Jørgen, old sling-shot? Damned if one doesn't get bumptious when one's just been nervous, but it helps your mood, too, although it hurts your feet and the thought about *choice* is so comic. You can choose the soft bed, but you have to take the big knives into the bargain, or you can choose the rough roads and take Jørgen Schwer into the bargain. Now brother-in-law Morten is standing on Hassler's terrace, saying to himself: No matter what happens to my crazy sister-in-law (who incidentally wears damned well and has the prettiest head and the nicest ass south of the Alps) I have here before my eyes *la citta eterna*, just down to the right the Spanish Steps, just down to the left Trevi, against the horizon the Castle of the Angels and Saint Peter's, off to the right Radio Rome and the Olympic Stadium in the middle and all the way around, the Tiber, and I won't keep myself from enjoying it, since I have only one life, too, and it needn't be worse than most people's. When he turns around he sees no memorials, but rather a lovely roof-restaurant where the tablecloths rise faintly and flutter in the spring breeze, and as sure as his name is Morten Terlow, he suddenly shifts his glance, tosses his head and follows a black, whirring dash in the air, a flashing comma, which proves to be the first swallow of the year. It's too much. Moved, he forgets Anna for a while, stands motionless, listening, but finishes, calls the waiter to him with a backward hand, Senta! and orders a grilled steak, salad, cheese, wild strawberries and a half, no a whole, Barolo.

I (Anna) feel hungry and trot up next to Jørgen Schwer. I ask him whether we shouldn't have something to eat at some point. Haven't had anything since the previous evening, but he shakes his head and I miss his long wig, which could have swung to and fro, convincingly. One, two, two--like a soldier he marches away, and after a while I place myself behind a tree like Joan Blondell in my childhood's Topper movies, I hitch up my dungarees (though it's difficult) and try to catch a lift. But there are no cars and no usable trees, and no Topper comes by with limousine and chauffeur, so I just trudge along after him.

At quarter past two we're still walking and haven't exchanged a word since Bracciano. I can't feel my feet anymore, only my stomach which opens and contracts in a series of offended cramps. Two cars have passed us, both with men's profiles and attentive eyes glued to the road and then when they'd successfully gone past, a glance in the rear-view mirror to see what kind of a pair of gypsies it was that they and their vehicles were glad to not pick up.

On the other side of the field the expressway from Rome to Florence comes into view. A row of high-tension poles toddle with their wires on each other's shoulders, visor-clad, from the field's southern side, turn eastward, cross the highway and show the way. The sound of traffic reaches us, a prolonged simmering, high-geared and occasionally thudded, disappearing when the wind, rising carries the sound away, increasing when it slackens.

I stand quietly next to Jørgen while we look at the highway sign two hundred meters ahead. I want to have at least some idea of what we should do, what we should watch for, what kind of a face we should wear if Karl Christensen were to suddenly come tearing up on a Vespa, shouting: There they are, there they are! I ask him:

--What should we do now?

--See about getting a ride.

--No matter with whom?

--No.

--How'll we know the difference?

--That's something I'll decide.

--And if the police come?

--Then we'll just keep standing there.

--And if they stop?

--Then we'll run.

Short, simple, and precise.

I forget that my feet are sore and almost that I'm about to die of hunger when we come onto the highway, which goes through *campagna*, shows up three hundred meters south between two hills and disappears three kilometers to the north at a curve. The traffic is heavy, and it seems as if everyone's travelling at the same speed. Eighty kilometers an hour, swi-ish, 90 km, 80 km, 90 km swish, swi-ish, swish, gone.

--Take your coat off, Jørgen shouts.

I take it off and lay it beside me at the edge of the ditch. Am just waiting for him to shout:

--Shove your breasts out.

I shove them out and lift my hair over my shoulders. Stand there with my scarf in my left hand, use the right hand for thumbing. Each thing has its time, I say, and here stands granny again, like in the old days, bending her arm over the asphalt, waiting to sing the happy songs of yore, but here there's no Tove and no Fris and no Leonard and no Dave, so I just do my job and watch the idiots drive by, the larger the cars, the bigger the idiots as always and the more speed. The pressure from the camions, who often stopped in the old days, hits us and sharpens the feeling of threatening isolation, evil fate, sudden death, violence. But then we catch sight of a procession of cars, which are different from the others both in their appearance and their slower speed. Without thinking about it, we both let our arms drop while the cortege approaches and it's only after the colored trucks, the dark blue limousines and the campers with red letters are really close that it occurs to us why we're actually standing here flailing madly. The first truck in the parade is very big, a kind of delivery truck with painted windows in back. It slowly drives up beside us, and when it stops, ten--eleven trucks behind it stop with a screeching creaking like an old-fashioned freight train. There's a flickering of stays and a scraping of cordage, two of the car radios are playing different stations, windows are rolled down, elbows laid out on them, faces thrust forth, butts thrown away, shouts shouted. The blue vehicle stops with its windshield at my height and I see myself reflected from the waist up in the bowed glass, but because of the reflection can't really see in. Jørgen stands with his hands at his sides, apparently unable to decide anything at all. The window on the right side is rolled down and a man with a red face, white hair and a big nose, which is thinnest at the root and then gets thicker, swells up, shines and dominates, shades his eyes with his hands and says in an odd mixture of German and Italian:

--Where are you going?

I (Anna) cannot answer and look imploringly at Jørgen. He smiles, for the second time in our acquaintance, and says:

--North.

With his right arm the man points to the tailgate, and without discussing it further, Jørgen and I run over to the body or cargo compartment and climb up. Inside the truck there is something, which perhaps, if it's assembled correctly can become a booth, a ticket booth or a little office and in the corner, close to the half divider between the cargo hold and the driver's seat, there is a rhesus monkey with a chain around its neck, watching us with its grey fingers running to and fro over the mouth of an electric microphone. The man with the white hair and the big nose has turned around toward us and points at a tarpaulin along one side of the vehicle. We sit down beside each other and for the first time I realize the driver of the truck is a woman. From the back she looks to be about my height, but her hair is black and she doesn't turn around to say hello--it almost seems as if she doesn't want to have anything to do with us. I remember all the feelings from back then, the instinctive feeling of whether it would turn out to be a good ride or a difficult ride, whether there was danger of advances one couldn't handle, whether there were particular obligations beyond a usual demand for entertainment and talk. I can't say what this ride involves. But on the whole I can't say anything at all about what is going to happen, where and how. Things have to come one by one, the problems be solved one by one--I'm not the one sitting at the wheel.

The woman's hair scraped up from behind and rolled into a wreath on her head. She leans forward and pulls the gear stick into first, the truck begins to move and the feeling that the whole snake in back will also be hauled along makes us thrust our feet against the floor and press our backs against the wall. Every passenger experiences the need to help with the driving, consciously or unconsciously, step on the empty floor in order to brake when they're nervous, reach out for the dashboard and straps for support, lean forward when the speed slows, but the hitchhiker is still more engaged--he puts his whole person at the disposal of the driver and vehicle, they've taken him along out of good will, and he must render something in return. Later a hitchhiker has the chance to become a good lookout since he watches the road uninterrupted, conveys his feelings of prospective danger, changing of lanes, curves, tractors approaching from side roads, low-flying planes and leaping deer to the driver through his body's tension, tiny outbursts, and zealous observant glances. It's a balancing out and demands tact; it's a question of making yourself useful without seeming forward, and one can see from Jørgen and Anna that they are preparing themselves now for their new task, though they don't have the chance to intervene directly with the steering. They sit on the tarp while the speed increases. They have their legs pulled up halfway under them, and they turn their heads in the direction of travel, where they can see the necks of their two hosts (the stout man's cheeks, too, from behind), the windshield and the road, which with even speed is sucked in under the truck. A few clouds in the sky indicate a possible change in the weather, but the cypresses and pines scattered in characteristic tiny groves and clusters deny every inconstancy. Now we're driving north.

The redbearded whitehaired man turns around and looks at Anna a moment. He fastens his gaze on her coat, her hair and the gold jewelry on her right wrist. He turns back again and says something in Italian which Anna can't understand. The woman doesn't answer, but opens the glove compartment and pulls out a pack of cigarettes and lights one with the dashboard lighter. The movement is unbroken and routine and concludes with her handing the package over her shoulder to offer the passengers some. I (Anna) accept the cigarettes and say thank you. I offer Jørgen Schwer a cigarette, and he accepts it, and it's he who lights both our cigarettes. Part of the opening ceremony has now been performed, but nothing's been said yet. We drive a while in silence; then the whitehaired man says without turning:

--Where are you going?

Jørgen stares at me and I answer, as we've already explained:

--North.

--Florence? the man asks.

I look at Jørgen and he nods.

--Farther.

I answer in French:

--Farther.

--Prato? the man asks.

I look at Jørgen. He nods.

--Si, I say.

I have no idea whether Prato is closer or farther, south or north of Florence, east or west, but the man seems to be satisfied. He sits back a while and the movements of the truck make a pad of fat on his neck quiver. Then he turns and says in English:

--You English?

Without looking at Jørgen, I have an idea of what I should say, but he steals the march on me:

--Yes, he says.

--Bene, the man says. You're lucky. We're going to Prato, too.

I open my eyes wide and translate quickly for Jørgen.

He says: we were lucky there--they're going to Prato, too.

Jørgen nods and looks surly. The woman concentrates on her driving, and the draft makes her cigarette smoke mix with ours in small gusts. The monkey has closed its eyes and appears to be sleeping. Perhaps the tobacco smoke bothers it. Monkeys are good subjects for conversation and I take the opportunity.

--What is the monkey's name?

The man turns and says:

--Chica.

He turns further around now, as if he wants to check whether I'm really interested. He looks at Jørgen Schwer, too, who doesn't look interested and then at me, who now looks very interested.

--It's one of the main acts in Circus Anastasia, he says. Chica is a trained monkey, unimpressive, perhaps, but one of the most intelligent of the rhesus species. He glances at the woman and continues.

--Chica has overcome her fear, controls herself completely, and is part of one of the most sensational acts in circus history. The act is called . . . can I say it in Italian? . . . "Colpa & Pena."

--Colpa and Pena?

--After the big *entr'acte* Chica runs out into the audience and

113

begins to steal. She dives down into pockets, unclasps necklaces, slips off wedding rings, unfastens watches, carries off small change, yes, maybe even goes so far as to sneak the shirt off of someone--and the audience, which is amused in the beginning, begins to get upset, can't tell whether the act is for real or a joke, some of them shout, others whine because they don't like the animal's nearness and aggressiveness, or its smell, perhaps. People appeal to the *Sprechstallmeister*, and at some point I give in to the audience's pleas, lift the whip, crack it, blow my silver whistle and a projector spotlights the gilded cage under the dome and at that moment two gerfalcons are released and fly out.

--Gerfalcons?

--Yes, two gerfalcons. Two trained gerfalcons, white, which in the blinding light now catch the audience's full attention while they circle faster and faster above the arena. Chica catches sight of them, too, throws down whatever she has in her hands, lets out a shriek, and leaps down into the circus track. She tries to escape, but the falcons are gaining on her. The music, which has been playing all the time, becomes more and more intense. The monkey keeps to the edge of the track where she draws the eyes of the audience to her, round and round and round, and each time the falcons lose height, flying with claws outstretched. I follow them, too, and when the two birds are right over Chica, I crack the whip again and everything seems to stop, to collapse--it's impossible to tell things apart--no one knows what they are seeing or really experiencing--everyone just *feels* a terror, an excitement, an enthusiasm, a loathing, *feels*. And the next second the falcons take off with Chica in their claws, fly across the arena toward the stage entrance where the curtains are drawn aside and the three animals disappear. And the curtain drops again, the spotlight keeps boring

114

against the silk a moment, then goes out, the music stops and the circus lies in total darkness.

The color of the man's face has become more intense, but the monkey still sits with its eyes closed. Jørgen Schwer has also closed his eyes. I think about the act, "Crime and Punishment." It's quiet in the truck. I don't know what I should say. As if to interrupt or to shift the conversation to something else, the woman turns on the radio with an abrupt movement. The news is on. The speaker's voice is animated yet neutral. The news isn't especially interesting but toward the end of it there's a missing person's announcement which I suddenly realize is about me. Anna slowly emerges from the radiophonic figure. But I have to strain to get her, to be completely sure it's me. Donna . . . danese . . . diplomatico . . . rossa . . . verde. Turn my head to Jørgen whose eyes are open again. He looks at the monkey, as if it too were sought, or could translate what he was hearing but didn't fully understand.

For the first time the woman at the wheel turns her head and looks at us. Actually the description on the radio could fit her too. Only the cut and color of the hair is different. I look at her and feel like I am between mirrors again. The woman's eyes catch mine. Then she turns and keeps on driving.

8

I've been graced with a high position, and I think it's time I looked at the world. It's true I can't see out my window, which hangs like a prison skylight three meters above my head, but still the location of the room is so good that I can think panoramically. I'm in Prato, a medium-sized Italian industrial city, west of Florence, south of Genoa, far from Denmark. It's a senseless place for me to be, but I'm here. Maybe if I had long hair like Rapunzel, I'd let it drop down the six stories and hope for a young mopedist to catch sight of it and begin to climb up, but I don't believe in fairy tales, and my hair is short. We--notice that I already say "we"--are to perform here this evening. All day since our arrival around six in the morning the people from the various trucks have worked to set up the tent. As a kind of payment for our ride, Jørgen helped with the rough work while I've been spared and for the most part organized the ticket sheets and tried to avoid conflicts with Chica, the gerfalcon's victim.

There's no doubt "they" know who we are, but for the moment neither Anastasia nor Roberto--as the man with the white hair and red face is called--has done or said a thing. In other words we find ourselves in a vacuum, but among friends. The location is oxygen-poor geographically, but as Roberto said when we asked him what Prato was and why we should go there: There are people! Travelling both from the coast and to the coast most people would have avoided this last city before Florence on the expressway with lightning speed except for someone on a particular errand. In Prato there are people. In Prato there's an audience that wants to see the circus. If I think about it more, I must admit I haven't had any particular relation to any of it--neither to the circus nor the audience nor--people? I don't know why I have a feeling of being locked in my tower room--in fact the door is open--I can open it whenever I want and leave. Perhaps it was our arrival, the appearance of the city, my situation, the weather, the ride here which gave me the feeling of having been escorted, deposited, and placed in custody. As far back as Florence the rain fell heavily through the darkness and on the way here it came in fits and starts against the windshield as if the speed of the squalls were greater than that of the truck. Even at low beam, the reflection of the headlights in the puddles seemed threatening when approaching traffic howled by. There weren't many cars at this point, and when we turned from the main highway hardly any. Maybe that's why I felt we had to be torpedoed, Roberto or the driver of the other truck go amuck and turn the steering wheels so we rammed each other radiator to radiator and disappeared in a tornado of bent metal and gashed chrome. But Roberto, who had taken the wheel after a very long siesta, drove carefully and I saw the city's empty streets and clocks with hands in vertical extension of each other, the naked, closed facades, barracks that nestled up to the last bit of unconsciousness before all hell and the next day broke loose in this ugly city. Roberto drove carefully, perhaps because he knew that he had valuable goods on board, perhaps because he was also interested in saving his own skin. I climbed the stairs slowly with my coat over my shoulder when we had gotten our keys, and while I slept in the morning I heard what went on around me through a gauze-like filter of nervousness. I don't know whether there were really people walking in my room, but the feeling was strong and was mixed with the sounds from outside: the traffic that increased steadily, the construction gangs working someplace in the city, hammers pounding, sawing, shouts. I awoke fully and lay a moment in the heavy immobility of aftersleep while the forgotten pieces of the puzzle arranged themselves. I knew that I had obligations. According to my upbringing, one good turn deserves another, so I couldn't just get up now and leave. The question was simply who owed whom what? In the matter of Jørgen Schwer there were problems enough. With Roberto and Anastasia (could that be their real names?) the case was easier. Yes, they surely wouldn't say a word if I trudged over to the rail station and booked a ticket to Denmark. I had myself gotten Jørgen into hot water, or out of it, whichever way you wanted to look at it, so hadn't I done enough? He really didn't have any claim on me, and what I was trying to understand was my own actions and reactions. But I should get the circus over with first, and when I walked through the city past the yellow, straddling church and the small cafes on the corner of the square with the yellow liqueur bottles and the bitters' cinnabar, my plan was conceived. I would offer them a day's work like a proper comrade and then I'd go home. I hadn't forgotten anything. In Prato everything was as clear as it ever was--my good marriage perhaps wasn't as good as everyone else's, even though it was splendid; my relationship to my children--particularly the youngest--was more than problematical, and my own relationship to myself? I couldn't say anything about that. So it was better to do something then, and I saw this thing before me like a grey abstraction hovering someplace or other in the room. I had often seen it before and talked with myself about it, and I think that someday I can have a good relation with my "thing." It comforted me at least while I walked through the streets of Prato out to a large square among demolished houses, where the tent was set up. I'm really very fond of my own common sense. It arrives just like foolishness without any warning. Hello, I say. Then let's take ten minute's common sense, relax our shoulders, remove the pressure around our navels and have a good time. I turned the corner and came out onto the circus grounds with the feeling still intact. Yes, the thing was really beginning to materialize: it was called travel, it was intrinsically called "back to common sense," and I discovered too late that it had something to do with the usual: to make decisions. But I still kept on, informed Anastasia that I would like something to do, and she put me in a tiny wagon, whose base and skeleton we had seen in the truck, more nearly a little house on wheels where I've sat for a few hours under the surveillance of a rhesus-monkey (which occasionally grinds its teeth) and stamped the date on sheets of tickets so that my fingers are still blue. I saw Jørgen and noticed that he was capable of handling heavy objects and at one point Roberto came and asked if I would like a cup of coffee. As I worked and when the monkey didn't look too threatening or hiss, I forgot where I was.

And now I (Anna) am here and I haven't bought the ticket and I haven't left and Christ knows why. I lie on my bed in the Rapunzel tower and know that the world's communication system is such that I could contact 1) my husband 2) my children 3) my family 4) my doctor (who?) just as I could in a few hours more or less be with all of them in person and be saved. I think that's what I'm up to. But now I'm lying here and am in limbo. I can't see my thing, but neither do I have the feeling that it's completely gone. I want to put my fingers up to my lips and say pluther pluther pluther, and I do it but tire of it quickly because it's a nuisance and finally boring when a thirty-five year old woman lies on her back in an empty room with a crucifix on the wall and says pluther pluther pluther. I begin to think about my clothes and get a little angry because my good, expensive clothes not only won't do anymore, but also have to be dragged through all kinds of dirt and mud and rain because of a crazy whim. One knows exactly what clothes are, and I love my encasements. I love to live in my prosperous regalia and leave and leave Nørrebro, through varying districts that become better and better, reach the center of town, leave it, too, friends, feel my whole organism become bouncy, straps tighten, snaps stretch, feel that things fit as they should, that I am invincible, can't be touched. I should have been one of the invulnerable, one of the charmed professionals who stare at me when I open Harpers Bazar and Vogue. I think I could have lived in these pictures. I understand their character, I feel within myself how meaningful and liberating their attitudes are. I say: they look at me but none of them see, none of them participate, none of them reflect anything except gesture, ritual conjurings, and an unshakable faith in the future, the world's continuity, well-being, and eternal salvation. They are invulnerable and beautiful, not only aesthetically perfect but invincible ethically, too, because they don't take part, but just are, because they aren't just are but also are not. They live like codes, unambiguous, incomprehensible signs which speak directly to us and encompass us completely. Their security is an abstraction, but their presence points directly at our chance of survival. They're professional actors and accept the conditions entirely graciously. Their possibilities are boundless. If I can get rid of my pathos, everything will be easier, but can I and will I? If I've been given anything, I'd better stick with it, get as much out of it as possible. On the other hand, these words choke me, and if I really think about it, it is they more than anything else that give me the feeling of sinking. My shoes are dirty, covered with mud right over the top, and when I lift my legs I can also see spattered, dirty water up the length of my Levis. Everything has its time, everything has its proper place. I would have sworn that dirty pants and me was a town in Russia. If it were only a matter of decorative dirt, of wished for and desired spots, mud that had to do with something other than mud. I think of Anastasia and see her before me in a different way, dressed in a strange fashion, her hair combed differently, her eyes looking at me as though she had a question I could answer. Maybe she's the only one who knows who I am, maybe she hasn't talked to Roberto about us at all. But I realize that my thoughts about the mirror, about someone who looks at you and scrutinizes you, aren't accidental, and today I will, if she asks me, do whatever she wants done, even if it's dangerous. What I've learned for now is that people don't always do what you expect, and this banality can be applied directly to my attitude toward myself. But I hadn't thought about it before, and it was only yesterday, no today, when I made decisions and didn't carry them out that I realized that there are more possibilities than I thought or had forgotten there were.

I lie on my bed. There's a knock on my door, and I've never felt the same way before when someone's knocked. The bed creaks softly when I breathe and answer in a military fasion: Come in.

It's Jørgen Schwer who enters, and it strikes me that the man has a tendency to look me up when I'm lying or have just been lying in my bed. He looks around briefly, perhaps contemplating his chances for retreat and so must recognize that they're not very optimal except for the door by which he came in. I keep lying there and have him half in frog's eye perspective. He opens his mouth and says:

--They'll be here three days. We'd better get going again.

I (Anna) am grateful in a way to be included now in his "we."

--You don't have to say "we." I'm not going with you any further.

He doesn't answer, but keeps standing there at the foot of the bed.

--I wanted to tell you in the afternoon, but I thought I should do something for them and didn't get to let you know.

--How are you going to get home?

--There must be a train--from Florence.

He turns and goes over to the wall, where the hotel has hung some oiled paper on a nail for cleaning your shoes. He raises a hand and touches it, then drops his hand again.

--What about the money? he asks.

--There must be enough for both of us, I say.

Two feelings surface when I've said that: Is it really so easy, and is this all there is? He looks as if he wants to protest, and I feel how the decimation or the halving of the we-feeling hurts me.

--Well, you can go back to Rome, he says.

--Why should I go there?

--You can get money . . . from that fellow Morten.

--Yes, but the police, what about the police?

He turns and walks over to the bed.

--They don't give a fart.

--What do you mean they don't give a fart? What's the point of the whole thing?

--Ah, you'll manage.

He touches the pimple's little sore on his neck.

--You have your passport, and besides, you're sick.

--I'm not sick.

--Aren't you sick? I thought you said you were sick.

--But there's nothing wrong with me.

--What do you have to go home for, then?

Again uncertainty, again the feeling that something that was just about to be true is true no longer.

--What are you going home for?

--I've told you why.

--Yes, you've said a whole bunch of ambiguous twaddle about going home to "connections" and getting money and I don't know what. But why are you really going home?

--I was on the way there, wasn't I?

--Yes, and so what?

--So I just want to go home.

He stands there hanging in such a way that I have to say:

--Sit down.

He sits down on the edge of the bed as if a hinge inside him gave.

--You were on your way home with a policeman to be sentenced and sent to prison and you want to "just go home" anyway, then? Perhaps you really think that it was me who kept you from getting home?

He doesn't say a word, just sits there.

Suddenly I realize that my prodigal son is every bit as conventional as school-tie John in Karachi. There's no reason to continue the discussion. I get up and go quickly over to the desk. Even though I divide the bundle of green bills into two, there are plenty for both him and me. With a stack in each hand, I feel such a strong irritation that I have to bawl him out. If people can't hear, you have to shout; if people can't see, you have to set fire to yourself. My irritation burns from the toes up and spreads out over my whole body. Red in the face, I stand over him, unable to say a word.

--It's important, he says.

The gall sinks again.

--You'll never make it to the border. They'll get you at the border with that passport. You may just as well turn yourself in here, and then they'll arrange the rest.

--And what about you, couldn't you do that, too, since you're so wild about getting home? Then it's just a matter of a few days' delay. Then maybe I could get by with an apology for having lead you astray?

--I don't want to go home that way, he says. Not now.

The ridiculousness of the situation is overwhelming. Diplomat's wife out on a lark has gotten herself into a hopeless jam. After following a schoolgirl impulse, she now sits in the ugliest city in central Italy with an ugly young man who doesn't know what he wants. The only thing that she knows herself is that she doesn't want this. If mediocrity is the principle here, too, the play very simply is played too poorly. It's a challenge and she intends to take it up. But can she, and are there sufficient grounds to do it? It's possible that dreams can be directed. It's a little harder with reality.

--Anyway, you don't have anything to apologize for, he says.

This answer to my irony is so touching that I feel tenderness for the young stranger. For a second there's an opportunity for action and I make use of it. I go over to him and lay my hand on his shoulder. We're a statue and could stand in Crome and Goldschmidt's hall, but we're not made of bronze yet and the statue would not have heard the knock on the door. I let my hand remain on Jørgen Schwer's shoulder and repeat my invitation in a different voice:

--Come in.

Anastasia has changed into a blue kimona and her hair is longer than mine, I see now that she's taken it down. She keeps standing at the door, looking at us. Then she comes in. Professionally she is more beautiful than I--her beauty is the kind that can be used for something. She glances quickly at the two piles of money and then speaks directly to me.

124

--I want to ask you to do us a favor. I don't know what your plans are, but a problem's come up with the show tonight. Signor Caduti has told me to ask you whether you might be so kind as to help us?

There's no ambiguity--ostensibly--in her words, and I don't know what to answer except to say yes. She comes closer as if she wants to take my measure and I listen to her strange accent with e's pasted on after most of the consonants. Her partner in the high trapeze act is sick, and of course the idea isn't that I should replace her--Anastasia will manage the acrobatics alone--but the act depends on a certain aesthetic symmetry, and since I was about the same height and with the help of make-up could be made to look like both Anastasia and her partner, she and Roberto felt it would be a good idea to ask me. Whether I'd follow her to her room for additional instructions?

Refreshed by this directness (and attached to this woman in the blue silk kimona and black hair over her shoulders), Anna circus princess feels on the track again. She exchanges a few meaningless words with Schwer, who remains sitting on the edge of the bed, and then she leaves the room and walks at Anastasia's heels down the hallway. They turn a corner and go up a little stairway to the floor above, where Anastasia's room is, which is almost identical to Anna's except that the windows with the French shutters are lower and have a view of the square and the slanting cathedral. Hanging on the wall is a tiny birdcage of braided wood with a goldfinch inside, and as soon as Anastasia has come in and closed the door after Anna, she goes over and sticks a long, ring-covered finger in between the slats. The bird pecks away carefully with his head shifting from one side to the other at the skin on Anastasia's finger, and the guest in the room doesn't feel any impatience. The sun turns round on the cathedral's spire, and a moment after the

125

two women have stepped into the room, a streak from the disc reaches along the edge of the wall and sends an opalescent shimmering against their retinas. The blackhaired woman lets out a little whistle which imitates the goldfinch's and then asks Anna:

--Have you ever performed before?

Anna shakes her head and smiles at the question. Of course she's played Trine in April Fools but it won't mean much to explain that here, and she doesn't feel like it, either. On the door of the wardrobe hangs a costume that consists of a white leotard with swan's feathers and rhinestones, a helmet such as pilots use but white and full of sequins, and on the bed are two pairs of white net stockings. Like a little girl, Anna asks:

--Is that what I'm going to wear?

And Anastasia smiles and goes over and takes the white shining costume and holds it up in front of me, talking all the while, and I think about my metamorphosis. Hand in hand we will go into the ring, the spotlight following us, and when the rope ladder descends from the dome, I'll hold it tight and Anastasia will disappear upwards, followed by still more light and the rising tension of the audience. The music is loud and strident, and there won't be more than two thoughts: the self-forgetting excitement and a feeling of beauty.

--Brava! she says, brava!

I sit down on the bed and put on one of the pairs of stockings, and she gets the pilot's helmet and buckles it under my chin. I myself think I'm speaking several languages at the same time, but we both start laughing when I suddenly say *sobresaliente* and am quite certain it's Italian until I remember what it means and explain to Anastasia that it's the matador's substitute, his *understudy*, that it's Spanish and I can't speak Spanish, either. We laugh and in the sun's fogshimmer the images tower up, do you remember, girls?--the sound of a bat hitting the asphalt, the sneakers' rapid take-off, the disappointed roar when you didn't get to your base or the ball really hit you and we ran among each other, changed sides, changed back, stretched our hands in the air and "died" when something was completely silly, left the court with arms dangling, quickly down to the lockers, and stood under the shower and thought about what our breasts would be like someday, what they were like now, how nice some of the others' were, how unfortunate some, whether we would get flabby stomachs and wrinkles, whether anything ever would be or had to be different. We dried ourselves and dressed. Then we went up the stairs, and a little later the next class began.

I feel the intoxication lessen, but Anastasia is indefatigable. She opens the door to the hall and shouts for Roberto, who appears shortly after, also in a kimona and with Chica walking beside him at the end of a thin leash. He looks at me and nods with a cigar between his lips. It's all set, I'm all right. And I ask myself whether I'm not. The two people talk with one another and I'm a little outside and can't really grasp their liberation. So far as I can tell, they know about me, know my story, yet still they treat me like an ordinary hitchhiker, dress me in swansdown and pearls, turn me around in front of their mirror and let me perform in their circus. They say I'm doing them a favor, but I myself feel it's an honor. I have no idea what I'm to do in the ring. Anastasia's explanation has been less complete than my own fantasies, and the thought occurs that maybe it's not for their sake at all but only for mine that they're doing all this. But what do they know, and where do I really stand?

The woman opens the door to the other half of the wardrobe, and there are new costumes hanging there. She bores in among them and pulls out more hangers, which she passes over to me. I

127

say--and indicate--that I'd like the white one, but she shakes her head and says that Signor Caduti would like to take a look at other possibilities. I look at them but have to accept their professional shamelessness. Probably people do things like that in their circle. Anastasia helps me again with the zipper and hooks, but even though I stand with my back turned and cover myself with my arms, the mirror gives the man a full view of my nakedness when the leotard drops. His eyes are half-closed, and cigar smoke runs in a trail on the right side of his nose up over his forehead. The monkey gazes with his face turned to the wall. It's sitting on its backside with arms hanging straight down. While she helps me with the pink taffeta costume, I think about Jørgen and fourteen hundred dollars in two piles with seven hundred in each and then I think about Morten, whose flight to Tanzania has long since left because he has to talk all the time to a depressed Tom, sitting at his rosewood desk in Karachi, sure that his wife definitely faces a longer stay at the St. Hans looneybin.

I ask myself what this combination holds but don't reach any conclusive answer. I'm left, if anything, standing there with the formulation: What's going on here? And I try to figure out what I'm doing myself (as I try to hide as much as possible of myself while Anastasia lets me change from silver to gold, from ochre to madda-green, from cherry to honey). I don't know what's going on, though I can register the feelings, and they alternate between fascination, anxiety, attraction, repulsion, desire and hunger. The monkey lets out a creaking little sound, a kind of unrecognizable cough with a tune to it. The rhythm is spirited and it stops suddenly. Roberto places himself behind me and puts both hands on my hips. They are warm through the dress, massive, lie heavily. Anastasia stands beside him, and they both look into the mirror at me. His cigar is close to my hair and I move my head a bit. The tiny hairs on the back of my neck rise.

--Bene, he says, bene, bene, bene.

But it's not the right costume. The first costume was the right costume. Their taste can't be so bad that they can't see it. It can't be accidental, either, that the first costume was laid out. I shake my head and the outer layer of my hair brushes the cigar, so I step back and walk away from the mirror. The other two remain standing there, but the atmosphere has changed for a moment. Signor Caduti says something to Anastasia which I don't understand, and then heads quickly out of the room with the monkey following him without his needing to pull the leash. As it passes me, it supports itself with the knuckles of its right hand and begins to walk haltingly because the man has taken its other hand. If I am to perform, it will be in the white costume--that I know for certain.

Oh, but the world isn't here anymore. Now I've succeeded in shutting it out completely. I'm seized by a feeling of tripleness, she who plagues me in Pakistan when the Danish newspapers arrive. Then I'm the woman who sits in a Danish foreign mission and reads about the problems of developing countries, reported to the Danish press by Danish reporters, directed to me, who sits in an underdeveloped country and doesn't know anything at all, either. I have to step back to the mirror to see if I'm still here, and in it I see Anna in a hideous costume and realize that nothing that is happening is true. Anastasia approaches me from behind, and although I again lift my hands to undo the hooks myself, she takes ahold of me like a nurse and works hard and unfeelingly with me. The pieces of clothing fall one by one, and when I'm completely naked, she stops.

--I have a proposal to make to you, she says.

My eyes, my breasts, my navel, my womb, my knees gaze back

at her.

--You're not going to perform, but we have use for you anyway.

I look at her and she knows I don't understand what she means. Her voice is low, but rings in my head. She steps up close to me and at the same time lays a hand over my mouth and one on my breast. I'm back on the plane, lifted but also afraid of falling. She presses hard into me and speaks:

--In a little while Roberto Caduti is coming back. He's spoken to someone you know. Yes, he's spoken with two. In the afternoon while you were working, we were called by the police here at the hotel. They had tracked you and your--friend here. And they've sent an additional friend off to Prato. You know him--he's a countryman of yours--I can't remember his name but he's from the police. They asked Roberto if he knew anything about you, but he said no. He admitted that there had been a couple of people riding with him who answered the description, but that they had gotten off in Florence. So no one knows that you're here, but it can be arranged easily. If you want that to happen, don't do what I say; if you don't want it to happen, do what I say.

I shake my head, try to shake my head, but Anastasia keeps on talking, and strangely enough she doesn't tighten her grip, but loosens it and simultaneously her hand slides slowly down to my stomach and caresses me. And I know that the buzzard would immediately emigrate to my neighbor if he saw this, but on the other hand I have no idea what to answer, for it's too complicated and complex, all of it. I thought it had been decided, it can be decided right now. It's so easy, a step back, a scream, done, but I don't do anything. I listen engrossed to the voice and feel the tiny speech-pearls collect on the rim of my right ear.

--The police are in the city, police from outside, probably your

130

friend, too. But we can use the costumes, we can hide you, we can dress you up and after the show tonight or perhaps better: during the show--during my act I can slip out and no one needs to see anything. You just have to do what I say.

She leads me from the mirror over to the bed. She holds me by the wrist with the trapeze fingers of her right hand, with the left she removes the blanket so the sheet is exposed. I try to pull my hand back and throw my body to the right at the same time, but she's all over me and strikes my upper arm hard with the back of her hand. The paralysis shoots like a leafnet all the way down to my fingers. I don't say a word but my larynx is thick. All this for the fresh air kid and--Minna. I see both of them before me, little tots.

--What do you want me to do? I ask.

--Lie down.

She's still holding me but lets go when I step over to the bed.

It stands before me, scaffold-like, cool. The sun has moved completely free of the tower, but has sunk a little. Its beams seem to come from below. Anastasia stands with her back to it, her figure in black, her face invisible. I get into the bed, kneeling. My face is turned toward the door, which opens at that moment. Roberto stands in it, and I feel a shivering over my left breast and my sex shrinks. In a warped mythological picture the man at the door stands with a white arrogant bird on each shoulder. He takes two steps forward and the birds, whose claws grip the leather epaullets on something that reminds me of a Roman gladiator's dress, sway back and forth while their eyes blink. I throw myself on the bed and tumble down onto the floor, want to run, run, run around, run. I want to get up and push something between me and this, want to run for my life, run around this room, run. But before I can get to my feet to face my first obstacle, I see Roberto

131

spin around in a desperate turn, against which the birds can't stabilize themselves. They release their grip and take off in a screeching flap toward the ceiling while their feathers fly from them and Jørgen appears in the door with the revolver in his hand.

9

Problems are made to be solved, as my old mathematics teacher, Miss Hellbrun, always said, and if I've learned nothing else, I've learned this, that in certain situations you do very simple things which turn out to provide solutions, if not definitive, then provisional. When Jørgen Schwer stood in the door with his revolver and the two birds took off and tried to get near enough to attack their prey or just flee, I did the following: grabbed as many clothes as I could from where I lay, held the blanket up in front of me like a flag, went past the two men in the doorway and ran down the hall. I thought about my heart, which I hadn't heard before, didn't know whether it just began beating now, but felt it beat a fast syncopated rhythm between each slap of my feet on the marble floor. Near the bottom of the stairs, one of my feet got twisted in the blanket, and I strode airily domineeringly forward like Winged Victory at the top of the stairs in the Louvre, standing, while I fell. But even in the fall the blanket acted like an immense wrapping paper--I became a protected ball whose rolling speed didn't stop until the door to my own room. My purse was gone, but I could see my coat in the open wardrobe, had just barely thrown it over me when Jørgen Schwer stood in the doorway swinging the black weapon like the policeman on St. Hans Square back home. After that I remember mostly my feet, my feet and heart, feet over a coer runner, right foot that struck something wet and sticky, which I couldn't remove because we ran and had to run, my feet against a warmer floor, wood, the warmth of the kitchen range, my heart rumbling in huge pots and spaghetti vats, beating against tile walls, wheezing in the doorspring's vacuum and finally breath like a knife in the throat. Faces turned after us, mouths opened, but we never heard anything--there was no sound but this rhythm and the feeling of a liberating, absurd singleness of purpose. I jumped into a car without knowing where it had come from, saw by the ammeter's quivering needle that the motor was already going, bent backwards according to the laws of motion when Jørgen released the clutch and the automobile accelerated in first gear with the gas floored, only then felt the weight in my lap and saw the gun between my coat-tails, softly creeping with the barrel between my legs. We drove through a gate and the light was red in the dust from the vanished sun, first felt the car's broadside around three corners with burning tires as a kind of rash *tour de triomphe*, but realized, as the narrow heights of hotels stooped in over us with the uppermost windows glowing that the man at the wheel was looking for a specific way of escape, which we found. Drove straight ahead, straight ahead, and when I picked up the revolver and laid it on the shelf under the dashboard, I saw that my purse was there too, and that the car bore Alpha Romeo's heraldry on a tiny enamelled circle. Exhaust opened from the little pipe, was expanded in the car's cooling system, rumbled against the facades and remained hanging like exploded giant bubbles behind us. As always, when you expect to drive in a definite direction, think you're driving in it, but are, in fact, on your way to a different place, you feel a certain nausea. I was sure that we would drive down the Autostrada del Sola, but discovered that I didn't know the names on the roadsigns, didn't realize either that the distance from Prato to the main highway could be so long, read the name of the city Pievepelago and began to ask questions. Listen to what you ask about when you're in flight:

    --What road are we driving on?

    --North.

134

--Yes, yes, but why don't you take the Autostrada?

--It's a toll road.

--You want to save money?

--No.

Silence. He, too, has to overcome a kind of nausea to answer anything he obviously considers a less than gifted comment or question. He says laboriously:

--You can't get off toll roads. They're guarded. You can't just turn off--they want their money, and you pay according to how far you've driven.

--Where are we going, then?

--North.

The landscape is fresh and green. I wonder whether the swallows have come up this far. I feel cold under my coat, discover that I'm sitting with a pair of pants and a jumper and my brassiere in my hand.

--I'm freezing.

--Put your clothes on then.

--Here?

He shakes his head as if I were his wanton daughter who simply will not listen to reason. I put the clothes on the shelf, but keep the trousers and lift one of my legs to try to get them on; the coat slips aside and he stares straight ahead like a madman. I've taken my underpants off and put them on again in a car before, but never in an Alpha.

--Where did you get the car?

--Rented it.

--And then you think they can't find us because you're not driving on the expressway?

Now I sound like the wild and wooly schoolgirl during the noon break.

135

--I didn't have to steal a car. There was a car rental on the square. We can swipe one in Reggio.

It's that easy then. But who can guarantee that the next car will be one of the same breed? How different it was when I was young. I can remember. I can remember it absolutely clearly. Yes, how I remember. When I was young we thought things over, we really did. When you had a problem, you sat down and thought: if you do such and such, maybe this and this will be the outcome and conversely if you don't do such and such, maybe nothing will happen at all or maybe something completely different. That's the way it was when I married Tom. I said to myself, there's no doubt that you'll marry Tom, but what will the consequences be? You'll have to give up your study of human physiology and biology. You'll have to adapt your life according to his; he has a career, yours hasn't even started yet so it can be shelved without too many tears. But isn't that, in a way, to give up your independence? Yes, that's true, but can't one preserve independence in a marriage *in another way*? That's what I said to myself. And I spoke further: If you marry Tom, you'll be given something, too. It will be an exciting life. You'll be able to travel, get to see new and exotic places. You'll have a responsibility, and with your knowledge of yourself, your engagément in matters human and political, there will be more than enough to fill up your life. All these truisms I thought over intensely, or maybe it wasn't that way at all. Maybe it was more a matter of feeling, and yet there was no way getting around conscientiousness. If you want to have a real life, you have to work for it and probably without too much nonsense. Not because we were puritanical, we really were not, and I've said before that both his and my appetite were big and that we (I) had known how to satisfy it (with him?), that we'd created and acquired the things we

136

wanted, including two children who could win first prize at any dog show. But I thought a lot back then, and I think I also thought, even if it was never completely clear on my intimate electric scoreboard: if you marry Tom it means quite simply social advancement. And perhaps in the final analysis that's what brought me to the place where I am now. To La Spezia. Where I still marvel over (but soon will stop doing it) what a flea-trick it is to be a criminal. I haven't defined the concept for myself before or connected it with my own person, but there's probably no way around it, Donald Duck--I'm going downhill and at full speed. Tell me, why does it feel like a privilege? Is it the same process that's set in motion when one arrives in the East? Anyway it's just as delicious. Yes, the condition may be characterized as a liberation. You emerge from the fogs of the Niebelungen, dismount from your Serimner, pack up Grundtvig and the united European democratic and cultural pretensions lovingly in mothballs and relax because things are finally put into place. The master-slave relationship is a matter-of-course. You learn in less than a week to put an extraordinary value on the swift run of bare feet in the corridor, the little cup of tea which is always at hand when you need it--yes, one goes completely crazy over the good Victorian custom of the servants' being called by their first names while they stick Sir in front and Master in back, Memsahib in the middle and for a long time called Tom "Massa," until with the last bit of my guilt feeling I got that abolished, a fine double-moral maneuver which gave me a still greater possibility of enjoying the servility/devotion, which is *natural,* yes, simply a side of the culture in the Orient. Isn't it so?

My glass of Martini/soda doesn't answer. The Mediterranean Sea behind my shoulder, Pernod-colored against my red hair, doesn't answer either. Jørgen Schwer not at all because he lies with

137

his head against the garden table and the checkered table cloth and sleeps. He's worked hard and been man for a series of happenings which would have gone well with his long hair, now lying in a trash can in Rome or already being worn as a wig by a happy sixty-year-old society whore while she promenades her dachshund in the gardens at Fregene. Anyway, it's a fact that my clothes fit miraculously well when you take into account that they were acquired during a break-in at Signor Meyers' clothing store in Parma about four o'clock in the morning. Perhaps there is guilt in my excitement, or maybe you just feel happy when something succeeds very well, no matter what it is.

As Jørgen Schwer promised, we changed cars for the first time in Reggio. It happened this way. We drove into one of the smaller streets without anyone as much as casting a glance in our direction. He parked the car, and I got out with my coat buttoned and the evening chill (remember it's still March and we're heading north) like a cold thermal around my buttocks. We walked from one street to the next, and Jørgen let his hand bump against all the car doorhandles along the sidewalk like a boy who walks along the fence with a stick in the summer. When one of the doorhandles gave and the car proved to be open, he seated himself behind the wheel and I got in from the other side. He asked me if I had a hairpin and I wanted to say idiot! because he should know that my hair style didn't call for pins, but then I happened to think that in fact once in a while I have a clip on my right side to keep my hair away from my eyes when it's newly washed, and just shook my head. He sat there for a moment as if the message had knocked him out, but that was probably just to see if the coast was clear. Then he opened the door again, came back and pulled the little handle to the left of the wheel and the hood sprang open. He lifted it all the way up and disappeared behind it. The streetlight over

138

the car smouldered in the reflection of the finish, and I wanted to ask: What does one do, What does one do, but as soon as the motor started, the streetlight slipped into place, extinguished its indirect light, Jørgen sat beside me and swung the Fiat out from the curb. We were on our way again.

All the while I try to figure out my travelling companion, I really do, but it isn't easy. If you treat him as an equal, he gets sulky; if you give him the coolie-treatment, he buttons up; if you keep your mouth shut, he gets nervous, drives poorly and makes tiny noises with his teeth; if you question him, he automatically lies. But at the most surprising moments and when you least expect it, he's nice, yes, downright thoughtful, and I sit there with my lady-heart and say: It was right, I chose rightly, I found my messiah, my little flowerman, my Carthusian monk--for there we were in Parma, and in the middle of the godbedazzled dark he said suddenly:

--What was that you said when we left?

--When we left?

--Yes, weren't you cold, for Christ's sake?

--Yes.

I had almost forgotten it or gotten used to it or considered it a part of the game that I should be cold.

Without saying much more, he pulled in to the right, turned off the car lights, and beside us there was enthroned a display window full of wax mannikins and the name MEYER in capital letters and in cursive lettering underneath: *haute couture*. We sat a little in the dark and let the sound of the asphalt run out of our ears. Then he's in motion again, opens the door, steps out. He looks around and goes over to the glass window, puts his face close to it, shields his face with his hands and stares in. Then he turns and nods to me. I don't know what he means, but suddenly he strides over to the car and swings my door open, as if he were a bellhop or doorman at Cardin in Rue Faubourt Saint Honoré. And your ladyship gets out, goes three steps in front of him over to the window, takes a look at the selection from Louise of Rome, Yves Saint Laurent, Courreges, Nina Ricci, nods but is still suspicious, for the last time we got outfitted together, the request went in a somewhat different direction. I don't grasp the change, but accept his subtlety and interpret it as a compliment or a gift. I nod again and he takes me by the hand while we follow along the facade and slide in along a portal and around into a courtyard, where dimmed windows look at us drably and introvertedly, while a door with a skylight above it seems to offer a possibility, from the look of Jørgen Schwer. When he's being professional, a good deal of his infantilism is brushed aside. He preserves his childlikeness, but I discover more and more that it is energy, enthusiasm, or outright optimism that characterizes him when he's "at work on something." It looks as if he's saying to himself: "This is damned good, this here, man." His sulkiness and awkwardness step into the background, yes, I want to say it right out that his unconscious depression is replaced by something which shines, radiates with something, perhaps it is charm?

Ready for business, he instructs me mutely. He shows me the window and then points to his shoulders, moves closer to the door and stands a moment while I can't decide or figure out what he wants me to do. But it isn't so difficult--he flips his shoulders, invitingly, imperatively, and in order to accomodate him, live up to him, I unbutton my coat and take it off. Panties and bra in Parma at four o'clock in the morning--that's equal to Mad Magazine, girls, but are there any of you who have tried it? I crawl up on his back and a moment later stand tottering and scratch with my nails into the wood to get to the height of a small

transom window, but my gratitude and amazement at his strange
generosity give me strength, and my luck holds and a moment
later I've gotten the unclasped window ajar and can hang firmly
by my upper torso while the sill scrapes against my breasts and I
swear softly and want to scream, but get even more furious because
the drop window presses down on me from above and cuts into my
spine, get more energy and go up through with my hips and the
rest and fall like a sack of kindling wood on the floor with a crash
that should be enough to awaken all the Parmasaners in the
neighborhood. But I'm in and open the door for the former hippie
and apparently there are no alarms ringing and no sirens howling.
The stillness after the crash is enormous and we walk on
mousetoes through the back room and into the store itself, where
the glow from the streetlights makes the shadows around the faces
of the wax figures tremble. It's warm, relatively warm in the store--
a faint scent of roses seems to stream in from the painted screens,
perfume wafts from the tiny cabinets where Parma's ladies in the
clear daylight let their hands run across silk and brocade, tweed
and nylon, saying their "Che' bella!" And I say the same, let my
hands run over shelves with underclothes, blouses, feel the skirts,
hurry over to the racks with dresses, take them out, hold them up
against my body, lift, choose, replace. Am at last a girl in a toy
shop, I think, whirl inwardly, remember the scent of my bed when
I woke after such a dream and it continued with its vibrations in
the dark and happiness was uncomplicated, the feeling whole. I
can't see Jørgen Schwer's face in the dark, but he's absolutely
quiet, probably following me. He doesn't rush me, whispers no
orders--he's quiet and watchful. I understand that this respite, too,
is a kind of gift, the patience an extravagance he can allow himself
in the dark and on secure, forbidden roads. Again I want to live up
to him and restrain my intoxication, come down to earth, choose

141

sensibly and not too much. I kneel beside a rack of drawers, lean on the pile of necessary items I've scraped together and will finish with hose, preferably pantyhose.

As I pull the drawer out, I come across something which amazes me by having a temperature different than the other things I've touched. It's remarkable that it feels warmer, or can seem warmer when you touch other people although we share about the same 98 degrees. But skin temperature has to change or else people would have fevers. I'm not touching the skin directly, but a trouserleg, and the registering thoughts are like a tightly loaded marron shot. Everything happens instantly, the man's reaction, too,--he stands up suddenly and his black overcoat falls off and unmasks him as a mechanical skeleton, an ancient watchman who's been sleeping or been so stiff with fright that he couldn't react until my hand brought him to life. He opens his mouth and simultaneously lifts a hand with a knout or a totenschläger in it and everything shines black and white at the same time, the stick's glint in the streetlight and the grey deep in his open mouth, from which comes a howl that starts the picture in furious animation. Before he gets to hit me, I'm rolled a meter away with the emperor's new clothes in my embrace, and his blow creates the prelude to a still greater crash than that I made when I went in through the transom. The cudgel travels obliquely backwards and shatters a showcase of corsets--the sound of the last fragments of glass on their way to the floor give, with their celeste-like contrast, possibility for counter-action, any action at all, and I don't become dumbfounded or feel anything before with my pile of clothes pressed to my face I've followed Jørgen Schwer through the four by eight window in a tumbling confusion of overturning clothing dummies and the supersonic whistling of bursting glass.

Yes, ladies and gentlemen, we kept Fiat 1500 until the city

with the amusing name Poppemoll, where my guide and companion thought it reasonable to change it for a Simca, the more precise specifications of which I will not mention because I know nothing about them. Socially regarded, our automobile swap was a decided setback. We were simply petty-driving, but considering that Jørgen, via a cut artery in his knee and on his left wrist, lost about three liters of blood on the floor and seat of the Fiat, the Simca denoted a step forward in spite of everything. We no longer got wet feet. While he drove, I dressed his wounds with two scarves from Schiaparelli and abstained from gloating because he suddenly had to see himself saved by something which he's previously held in contempt. A proper bandaging was out of the question--it was more like a binding to prevent the blood from immediately gushing out. The loss of blood had weakened him, and that's why he's sleeping now. Just before daybreak we reached the coast, and he stopped the car. The following conversation took place:

--Why are you stopping here?

--I have to piss.

There was nothing to say to that and I looked straight ahead. He opened the door and stepped out, forgot himself and hobbled more than he would have if he'd thought about the cut on his knee. I followed him out of the corner of my eye and felt, strangely enough, a little ambassadress-shocked over his choice of words. Respect for the Danish representatives abroad! In my circle we don't piss, we pee. I belong to the generation that found it risqué to use locker-room language when there were women present. We have our modesty and it can't be rooted out. Can it, Anna? For ten years we have fought our way to a somewhat free social convention, but the privet hedge can grow anywhere, even in the Pakastani salt earth, and it's cosy because the staunch leaves give

143

off a scent that reminds me of the days back then. He has hung it up nicely before he shows up again, and when he opens the door I see that the cymbalquivering frostmoment just before sunrise isn't far away. A high layer of sheet clouds holds in a certain form of warmth, but I'm not crazy about getting out when he asks me. I think, too, in my sceptical cartoon-balloon the repeated motto: what is he up to?

--What do you want? I say.

--We'd better get rid of it.

I look incomprehensibly at him. But he kicks the car's right front tire.

--They're on the lookout for stolen cars today, all stolen cars, and the reports on them will be sent out faster than yesterday.

--What is it you want us to do?

--Push it over the edge.

Somewhere within me I feel once again something that resists mischief, something that hurts. What was that I said before about our puritanism--that we were not puritans? Yes, but here I stand, kiddies, and inside me ticks an indelible message: Remember to clean up your plate, remember to clean up your plate, be frugal, not so much mustard. Whatever's left on your plate is how the manufacturer makes his profit, and be careful of your clothes, and have you forgotten to put your bicycle down in the cellar again?

--You want to push the car over the edge?

--Yes.

--Yes, but . . .

--There where I pissed it was at least two hundred meters down. It will drop straight into the water if we're lucky.

Again the challenge. I will live up to his vocabulary, but I won't give in right away. I will live up to his choice of words and his . . . his prodigality, his generosity, but he must give me a chance to breathe first.

--How will we go on, then?

--Walk.

--Walk!?

--Yes, hitchhike just as at first, part of the way, anyhow. I think we've shaken them off for now, so if we can get rid of the car and go north along the coast and wait until later to turn inland, there should be a chance.

--Yes, but the descriptions, they're certainly out?

--Haven't you gotten new clothes?

The sentence is so packed with meaning I can't answer and have to settle for nodding. His pride, close-fisted matter-of-factness, uncertainty, revolutionary aggressiveness, his bourgeois obstinacy.

--In La Spezia you'll go to the hairdresser's and buy a wig. He takes his hair off, I get new.

--What about yourself?

--I'll buy new clothes.

And, oh, it's a pretty situation. The light crawls forward faster and faster across the fields as if it came from the edge of the layer of clouds on the horizon and now chases us, pushes us, hurries us. What kind of coincident nervousness and calm is this, and the strange talk about what he'll buy and what I'll buy. With *my* money, friend. You'll buy clothes and I'll buy a wig, and if you want to trace the farthings, you'll have to go through the Danish treasury and a hodge-podge of industrial operations, coffee mills, packaging plants, iron foundries and the Terlow Mansion to find out where they came from. My money in my purse, a lot of money in my purse. I could buy you, Tom Thumb, and your Simca and your Schiaparelli scarves which now so wonderfully decorate your wrist and your knee as if you were an infant they were afraid

145

would vanish from the ward. And what is it that you want me (Anna) to do? Help you push some poor Spaghetti-Frederick's car over a high cliff so he'll never find it again and will have to dash from office to office, where they'll stare at him with the greatest suspicion, investigate his handwriting and his dossier, his family relations, eating-and-sexual habits, before half a year later they agree to declare the car lost and pay him a fraction of the money he has asked for and a minimum of the money that the car is actually worth.

Jørgen Schwer goes over and starts the car's engine again. A single car has passed the road three hundred meters behind us with its lights still on, the cones swinging, hopping on the lowest branches of the eucalyptus trees, the sound of the motor approaching, passing, fading away. But daylight is upon us, and I swallow my idiosyncrasy. For an entire twenty-four hours I haven't given Minna a thought.

The Simca is parked twenty meters from the cliff with its wheels turned wrong. He gets in and turns the car and drives slowly in first up beside me. I'm nearly twice as tall as the car. His face is opposite my breasts in the open door. He speaks calmly:

--I'll drive it down to the edge; then we can push it over together.

I nod.

--But if we can't get up enough speed, I may drive it up and jump out.

I shake my head. He looks at me. What does he want me to say? That he mustn't? But that would be crazy. Here's your chance, your chance! I say it to myself again, step forward on the little stage and speak to Anna, who sits leaning back in her tawdry rococco chair and has already heard the prompter long ago: Take your chance now, woman, it's the only chance to get the fellow off your hands. For the rest of your days you can swear that everything you did with him you were forced to do. It's true and can't be contradicted. Didn't he threaten you, gun in hand? Hasn't he pursued you from place to place through the most horrible challenges? Hasn't he dirtied you, scandalized you, wounded you? Hasn't he taken you from the good road you chose and led you into a plane where all values are broken down, all lines of direction collapse? Then let the bum drive himself straight to hell and blend himself with the other carp at the bottom of the Roman sea. Let him believe it's Mare Nostrum, but find out that down there he's all alone.

The car is on its way toward the edge, and when it stops he turns off the engine, waves me closer. I go over with my head bowed and the scent of the wool from my new clothes blends with the salt from the sea and the sound of a car passing on the road behind us. He leans against the car, holding onto the drip moulding tightly, but when I stand by the back window he comes over to me, puts his hands against the metal and arches his back to increase his pressure. I take the same position, and I remember Jerusalem and feel the comic wailing wall on rubber wheels roll forward, but slowly, slowly, much too slowly. The last stretch before the edge of the cliff slants up and if the car is to go far enough out and we, simultaneously, are to be concealed by a pine grove between us and the road, then the car can't be pushed into the sea but must be driven.

The performers on my stage are silent. She is walking in the wings, doesn't want to enter, but knows she's there because the theatre has no front, no back, no walls, no ceiling. The sun works its way forward between the cracks in the cloud layer, a little way out the water is struck with flashes, is illuminated broadly from the line where the nightcliff's shadows stop. A choice has been

147

made, or will be now. Everything is quiet. A gull passes in a long, gliding dive, rises on an updraft of air and is also struck by the sun. Jørgen Schwer says:

--It won't work.

I (Anna) know very well what he means, but give the statement a broader interpretation. Learned from my mother, who always said: I know you don't like me. And hoped and believed and didn't believe, suffered and trembled with delight when the answer came: Oh, but I do.

He gets into the car and again the procedure itself is nothing. The Simca jogs around itself, drives backwards slightly like an airplane getting a head-start for a take-off--he gives it the gas and accelerates, the right front door rattling, toward the edge. When I was little and was to go on a summer vacation and didn't want to be sick or have it rain, I prayed with lightning quickness to God as many times as possible.

I prayed the same way this morning, a dry, reeling, meaningless string of words. Ourfatherwhoartinheavenhallowed-bethynamethywillbedoneonearthasitisinheaven and again and again, until a grey whirling let itself lurch out over the grassclumps and the car with the same rocking as a little plane gathering momentum, went into the air and disappeared with the back wheels idiotically spinning in the unaccustomed element. The breakers drowned out whatever sound there must have been when the car struck the water. Gone was Simca when we looked.

I get up and go over to the terrace railing. It's just as far down here as it was at the other spot, but there are bathing huts on the beach and in two months the sand will be covered and no one will expect to get anything dropped on his head except sunshine and gullshit. I put the key to the hotel room next to Jørgen and go into the hotel. I'm politely shown the way to the hairdresser. It's not difficult and there are numerous possibilities. In an intensely internationalized city, there's no sign of surprise, either over the time of our arrival, our appearance, or the difference in our age. Oh, Jesus, that was it. He's twenty-one. The city's sophistication is probably so pervasive that people don't listen to the radio, either, don't look at newspapers, don't listen to the wanted reports, don't take part in the rest of the country's nerve-wracking pursuit of two dilettantes who are on their way, know the general direction, but don't know how they'll reach their goal and have no idea what they'll do once they get there.

Am received kindly in the salon because it's expensive. If you go into an expensive place, people automatically think that you can afford it and the service is good. It's off season, and I'm the only customer. The French-speaking hairdresser brings out a selection of wigs, comes with them on his clenched fists and looks like a puppeteer in a Punch and Judy show and smiles at me in the same way in the mirror. Just look now, my little girl! He combs my hair up and presses it together on my head; then he tries the blonde wig, but my skin is too delicate. I become too transparent with the blonde hair, ask for the black, le noir, and when it's pressed down over me, it's the same as seeing bird and nest at the same time, securitive and protective strokes of wings on both sides of my face. Along my cheeks the flightfeathers puff out, but as I'm about to take off, chuckling with satisfaction, there passes in the street, seen through a looking glass and plate glass, a person whom I know.

10

The truth, they said, remember the truth, Anna. I stood in the
kitchen on Vibe Road and father was leaning with his hips against
the gas burners and mother stood with her back turned, cutting
onions, but looked over her shoulder at me, for it was one of those
serious moments when important matters of life are discussed. And
thus it is that the desire for truth is bound forever in my
consciousness with the smell of onions and gas. I hadn't lied--it's
never been one of my habits to lie, but it often happens that when
I tell the truth people think I'm lying. Maybe that's because what I
say doesn't sound particularly trustworthy and maybe, if anything,
it's because I myself can't tell the difference between what's right
and what's wrong. Or perhaps I always lie because the mixture of
onion and gas is disgusting to me. As, e.g., now, when Morten is
sitting opposite me, and his head had changed into a huge shallot,
and the gas lies heavy in the room as if all the lines were leaking at
once. The place: La Spezia. The time: three in the afternoon. The
scene: my room with a view of the sea and the horizon. My
brother-in-law has just taken his hand from his head, which he's
been supporting because his burdens or my attitude seemed
unbearable. Now he turns his profile to me, and it is he, in fact,
who looks out at the Ligurian Sea. Yes, he's not only not in
Tanzania--he isn't in Rome, either. He's come here after he and
Karl Christensen fanned out in all directions with the police in
order to intercept us as quickly as possible, or as Morten says:
before we do any more mischief. He's aware of most of the
"mischief." I've made no secret of anything, but every time I admit
to something, he shakes his head and either thinks I've told him

150

too much or too little. All the while he says: let's begin from the beginning, and laboriously I begin from the beginning, but if I begin from the very beginning, I'll have to go over to the other side of Vibe Road all the way back to Gemmas Allé, where I was born next to a tilting stove while my slovenly old father walked around stuffing papers in the cracks so the wind wouldn't blow in on my straddling mother and the doctor, who (it's said) tipped over the ether bottle and wouldn't send for the midwife because he "could do it himself." But then Morten says, no, no, no, that's not what I want to know, and I realize that I should move on to a later point, all the way up to the point where he himself and Tom enter the picture, but apparently that doesn't help either. I tell him about my mornings, very seriously. I say to him: Morten, in Karachi for a long time I woke up early every morning with the irresistible urge to cut up my youngest child. I don't know whether I would really do it, but the feeling of uncertainty, the inability to use my reason to control my desires and eventual actions left me in the dank and the dark, where unnameable creatures move about and dead fish decay slowly while their white bellies look at us.

For him this is clearly gobbledygook. He listens sympathetically, but as soon as I stop short, he shakes his head again and wants to know something more concrete: How I came in contact with Schwer, what my motives were in seeking him out, why I performed the stupid maneuver in the Rome airport, why I didn't call 1) himself 2) after that, Christensen 3) both of them 4) the Roman police 5) the Danish Embassy. I say to him as matter-of-factly as I can that the impulse to "do something about Schwer" was spontaneous, but at the same time considered, too, that it had something to do with thought, but also--to a large extent--with feeling. He looks terribly distraught, as if this explanation was not at all what he wanted to hear, and while I myself am feeling a bit proud and excited that I can really account for (although confusedly) a good deal of what has happened to me in the last few days, he steamrollers along with his questions, which could confuse anyone. When he says: we have to begin from the beginning, he really means: We have to go on, and when I go on, he wants to go back to something I've already said but which he doesn't understand or refuses to understand. It's a very long conversation and at one point I'm about ready to say that he can just lift up the receiver but then it occurs to me that he's protecting me in a way, is so thoughtful that he wants to let me make the decision. It's thus they are taught in the old companies, and the East Asiatic Company hasn't lived in vain. At the same time it gives Jørgen a chance to finish his good night's sleep. Strange Morten has considerately called for a local medicine man, who has bandaged Schwer's wounds properly and without any further ceremony accepted an explanation that he had been hurt on a polo field in Salerno, our last whereabouts before we headed north. I think they play about as much polo in Salerno as ice-hockey in Mozambique. The thing about the stolen car was the worst. He kept on harping about that. If he knew that I'd also helped dump nearly a ton of tin into the Mediterranean, he would have left the room some time ago. "You're aware that you're guilty of theft?" he says. And I nod. "You're aware that you're guilty of criminal mischief of the lowest kind?" he says. And I nod. He shakes his head, says nothing for a moment, then he sighs and gets down to it. When on my own initiative I try to tell him about the circus in the city and a monkey that is attacked by gerfalcons, he raises his hands dismissingly and shakes his head even more fiercely. It's too much. He won't have anything at all to do with it, and besides he thinks it's irrelevant in this context. But what about the cars? And what about the burglary of Mr. Meyers' store, what about that?

152

What will come of that? And was it necessary to break so *much* glass? And calm and quiet I say to him: I was freezing. Completely frustrated he gets up and begins to walk back and forth across the floor. Now he speaks without asking any questions. He has reached a conclusion. He can see it all before him. He won't hide the fact that he's worried, but at the same time he's satisfied that now a decision can be reached. In Rome he sensed that there was something wrong with me, but now he knows that I am . . . (he chokes a little on the word) sick. There's no doubt. A person who does such desperate things must be sick. A person who has up to now lived not only a socially well-ordered, but a thoroughly *engaged* life can't be transformed overnight into a criminal and anti-social person without its being a question of mental disturbance. His method of prnouncing the word *engaged* made it charmingly clear how much he despises this *engagément* in something that everyone feels a prick of bad conscience over when they quickly leaf past certain pages in the Sunday paper. But, he emphasizes, it's still not a question of any catastrophe. With my background there's still a possibility of getting out of the affair with a minimum of damage. It's definitely an advantage that I am "sick." It's an advantage so far, and then there's, thank God, Jørgen Schwer who with his dossier is as good as convicted. There has been talk of coercion, hasn't there? He has threatened you with a gun, hasn't he? Against your will he has led you through a series of incidents that no judge in his right mind would ever suspect you of being mixed up in. You with your past, your marriage, your family. I ask whether he is thinking of his or mine, but he leaps over the digression and makes his demand. Total surrender now, unconditional capitulation--we call the authorities in La Spezia, and I can be released on bail on the spot. In addition, you have your passport, haven't you? Don't forget your immunity.

153

Perhaps it's the immunity, perhaps it was what he said (or didn't say) about the family that makes me go amuck. Perhaps it was his halfjabbering insinuations about my "sickness" that make me furious. Anyway, my actions are so desperate and feverish that it's only later that I realize that from this mundane place, on this mundane headland, over this mundane railing, I've thrown my red passport out among the gulls, which, startled, follow hearts and leaping lions on their journey down toward the waves. It can quite simply become a habit, this throwing things into the Mediterranean. I turn, and he makes the classic remark:

--You shouldn't have done that.

And now I wish I could say a kind of truth to him, but he has prevented it. So it has to be a kind of question, instead.

--What is it you want me to do? Should I give myself up? But there is nothing to "give up." I haven't really done anything. And even if I had done something, you say it doesn't mean anything at all. I'll go free, anyway. What is it you expect of me? Anger? Or reason? Or both? Yes, but Morten, I've just been out to play!

--It's no longer playing, says the schoolteacher. You're sick, Anna, but you don't know it yourself.

--Sick, I say. *Mensch,* from the moment I got into the plane I was well. But, of course, I didn't know it then.

--That is to say, you'll give up everything . . . everything out there . . . everything?

--If you mean Tom and the children, I haven't given up anything at all. I think that it's more that I've given up giving them up. I left, among other things, so I wouldn't kill my daughter, but maybe I would have started on the others if I had stayed. Or maybe I was already about to.

Morten is so nice to look at and so disconsolate. He looks like a schoolboy who's gotten bad grades and simply can't understand it. He's tried so hard, sweated and strained, and written a formal hand and done everything he was told, but a pixie in some mystic manner has changed the grade from honors to average. I discover that even my use of the grading scale is what Jørgen calls "flipped out"--it makes me weak for a moment, but then zealous again, decisive. I say:

--It's not just a question of me alone . . .

--Yes, he shouts, that's exactly it, it isn't . . .

And I continue through the approaching fog.

--It's also a question of Jørgen Schwer.

Apparently Morten has been waiting for this observation because his face resumes its normal lines again. The blubbering edge along his chin falls into place, the contours of his lower face sharpen. His nose jovially cuts the air. He's on the negotiation level again. Compromises can be made, solutions found.

--I knew you would have to say that sooner or later, and even if I can't understand what sympathy you can have for the fellow, I'm willing to make some concessions.

--Concessions?

--Yes. If you'll come with me now and give up any more digressions, I'll agree to give him a head start.

--A head start on whom?

--The authorities, who are so close to your heels now that it's only by chance that I got here first.

--How did you do it, really?

--I knew you and Tom had taken a trip from Monte Carlo to Rome by car, that you had been in La Spezia before, that you like to *return,* and then when I imagined Mr. Schwer's "cunning," an intricate trip rather than one straight north had to be considered a possibility.

--I've never said anything about La Spezia.

--No, but you give off vapors, sister-in-law. Didn't you know that?

--Give off vapors?

--You give off vapors of wishes and you stink of resolution.

--What kind of talk is that, Morten?

--Haven't you heard of mediumistic abilities?

--I had no idea you were acquainted with things like that.

--No, but maybe it's something that runs in the family. Both families, I mean.

He smiles for the first time and I weaken. My bedroom out there is so beautiful. It gets lighter slowly and the paintings and the curtains can be seen more and more clearly, the sounds come nearer, the ravens walk on the lawn, and on the corrugated iron roof my guardian sits, watching lighthouselike the day's first garbage cans.

--I can't leave him here, I say.

--Why not?

--He's wounded.

--Where does he plan to go from here?

--I don't know.

--If you knew that he was sure to get away, would you give up following him and go with me instead?

I don't know what to answer. The question mark circles about the room, and I feel my wig itch. Should you scratch it from above or should the wig come off before you begin? To be honest, I had forgotten that I had it on. A good deal had happened since I left the beauty salon, went the other way and literally trampled right into Morten at the first corner. He was prepared with apologies in his best Italian, and if he hadn't been so worried, maybe he would have begun a flirtation with this Modesty Blaise, who stepped first to one side and then to the other in order to get by, but finally had to look up and thereby let herself be recognized. I don't know how we'll go on from here, haven't thought about it, haven't had time to think because I suddenly have to account for all these things I haven't had time to think about, either. Of course, it isn't the wig that itches but my own hair underneath. The telephone rings.

I recognize Tom's instantaneous anxiety in Morten's face. The telephone is synonomous with disturbances, making up one's mind, business with the unknown. But the nervousness is always brief and superseded by decisiveness of will--every complex is conquered by the ability to act. I've no need at all to discuss with myself what I should do: whether I should pick up the receiver or not, what I should say if it's not who I think it is, what apologies I will make if the person calling accuses me of something I either haven't done or have done. I see the change in Morten's face between the first ring and the second ring; then he's standing next to it and a series of Si, si's and No, no's streams out of him. Then he shifts into Danish, and Anna hears him say the following:

Yes. Yes, it is. Yes. No, no I haven't. Got here two hours ago. I don't understand it. Absolutely not. But how could you track me down here? Yes. No. No. Yes, but why should I do that? That would be absurd. That they've registered here? That's impossible. I'm staying here myself. I came here right from the station, I mean . . . I drove right here. I delivered the car to the porter--it's back with Hertz--and I've reserved a seat on the train to Rome. Yes, it's absolutely necessary. I can't put my trip off any longer. No, I'm absolutely certain. I just came to . . . yes, exactly. And you? Nothing . . . ? No, no, of course. Yes, but . . . but then perhaps you're wasting your time? I understand. Understand completely. Yes, I promise you. Yes. Goodbye.

He puts down the receiver slowly and looks at me as if a

doctor had informed him he had an incurable disease. No, it's more like he looks at me as if I had told him I'd gone to bed with his father.

--I lied, he says.

--You lied?

--It was Christensen, and he knew you were here.

--Where is he?

--In Milan.

--Why didn't you tell him we were here?

--I don't know.

--Yes, but then you're in on it, Morten!

--What do you mean?

--Then you're an accomplice, then you're in on it . . . you're with us out playing!

He looks at me and draws back as from a leper when I embrace him and lay my strange hair against his cheek.

--I'm not in on it! I kept the police off because you haven't said yes to my plan. I have to have more time.

He gets up from the chair by the telephone and pounds the same piece of the rug as before, to and fro in front of the open window.

--I'll have nothing to do with your crazy . . . affair, nothing. Do you hear? I don't want to get mixed up in any part of it. It's not only immoral, it's simply too childish. Do you know that it *costs the taxpayers money* for you to run around with a former *criminal* and play fandango? Have you thought about that?

--Yes, but why didn't you say to him: Come, Christensen, the birds are here!

--I've just told you, because I don't want you to give me the slip now.

--And so you begin talking about money instead. It's typical.

158

--Shut up.

--What?

--I said: Shut up, Anna.

My stomach sinks, and regret rains in me like a cloudburst. What kind of a person am I? How am I treating my men? Anna, Anna, Anna. I lean back and close my eyes. My wig is made of iron, and I hold both sides of my head in my hands, lift it up, take it off, sit penitent with my scraped nunnery hair and listen.

--What do you want me to do? I ask.

His astonishment over my transformed head or the humiliation in my carriage changes his attitude. He apologizes for his outburst, but it's strengthened his self-esteem. Morten speaks calmly:

--Even though I don't have the slightest sympathy for Jørgen Schwer, I'm still willing to take him with us for a way in the car. As you heard, I told the Chief Detective--wrongfully--that I had returned the car and was ready to go back to Rome. There's no doubt that he's on his way here now, probably by plane, and there's hardly any doubt, either, that the Italian police are as good as at the door. But I'll only do it if you'll promise me to give up travelling any farther in his company.

--Will you force me to do it?

--Anna, is it really a question of forcing you?

I stand with the wig on my fingers, trying to spin it around, but the ends of the side-hair run into my wrists. What is it that he wants me to say? I feel a kind of narcosis set in. "Now that you've told us the truth, you'll have to admit that we're right, too." Gas and onions.

--We'd better get going.

I go over in front of the mirror and stand with stretched legs bent forward to get the wig to sit straight. Morten's voice is distant and not so threatening.

--I'll drive north toward Genoa. It's not certain Christensen can get through so quickly to the carabinieri as to me. What's your friend's room number? Perhaps they haven't blocked the road yet.

I sit in front with Morten, who's had time and taste enough to rent a Ferrari for his little chase. No matter where you travel, you should travel in style, as his mother always said, or she didn't, by God, for she wasn't that dumb, and secondly it's obvious. I watch the road from the coast into the city. I look at the afternoon traffic in La Spezia. I feel completely relaxed. I'm still balancing between the realities of the big car's leather-upholstered, rosewood instrument panel and the wretchedness of the Schwer outlook. He's sitting in the back seat biting his nails--the tiny clicking sound comes at intervals when he has gotten ahold of a chip with his front teeth, and I'm thinking that there's just a pair of steel plates, a little enamel, and a snap spring between me and the traffic cop on the corner, who would give half a month's pay for the chance to bring me in, but at the same time wouldn't understand a thing or think I was crazy if I went up to him now and began to yell that I was Anna guilt-Anna, colpa & pena. It's pretty here, so friendly and inviting. In the past I'd only travelled from the north, a summer evening in hot August, when the moon rode on the rails beside us at the same tempo and we had ice-chilled melon for dessert, and the strange thing is that my mood now is nearly the same, yes, perhaps there's extra spice on the melon, helping me feel better. Perhaps one should have suggested that Morten rent the Ferrari right from the start so we could have avoided all the detours. But no. No. It's as it should be. A little toward evening, the weather clear, two men in the car, the coast out there to the left, the numerous curves, houses that cling, speed limits, the murmuring excess under the hood, vacation. My

160

cavaliers are strange gentlemen. I don't know them, but they interest me. Outside, there are a lot of people who are interested in me. It seems to me like we should have a picnic. I'm like an actor we know. He always celebrates premieres well in advance. He never goes to premiere parties--oh, unless he's had a big and sure success--but when he knows that he has to go to one of his everlasting examinations and isn't sure of the result, he celebrates by himself. It's a healthy practice. And we haven't told Jørgen about the plans yet. It can be a kind of farewell party. Now I say it; now I say it to the other two. It can be in Rapallo. It would be lovely in Rapallo. I could buy Minna a rubber duck, a flat one that could be blown up sometime. Maybe we could try it on the beach. But won't say goodbye this way, hoo, hey. One shouldn't get sentimental, naturally, but on the other hand one shouldn't rush it, either. And we have time. Maybe Jørgen doesn't have so much time, but then he doesn't appear to be very busy, either. Isn't his point of transfer unimportant and I wonder if Morten has thought about dropping him off somewhere nearby, anyway? We drive slowly and no one speaks, Morten because he won't talk to Schwer, I because I'm thinking about our picnic and can't say anything without saying something wrong. I'm a little bit intoxicated, as I always get when I ride in big, beautiful cars and their motor vibrations spread up through the seat. For a moment I'm in an interspace, the space between one thing and another. Someone has decided for me what will happen now, but I'm not sure I've promised him completely. Haven't myself decided anything, but have a feeling, anyhow, that I've chosen sides. John, Tom, Minna are far away in a fog under a lopsided and reversed moon with a star on a leash. When we turn around a corner, there's a man swinging a red, shiny stop sign up and down. It's directed at us. The sound of the hippie's nailbiting ceases, and the car makes no sound when it stops. The policeman lowers the stop sign and two plainclothesmen step forward and come into the windshield's field of vision. It's a two-door car and Jørgen Schwer can't get out unless he goes over me or past Morten. I imagine how loud the sound might be if a revolver of his caliber were fired so close to my ear. I remember how afraid I was New Year's Eve and feel the burn scar on the inner side of my arm blink, tiny scab hole from a Chinese sparkler from back when things like that were allowed. I pray that no one will shoot now and that no steam whistles blow. I would like to sleep, dive down under my quilt and sleep. Each of the two men lifts a finger to his hat, as if they were used to wearing caps and forget that now they have fedoras on. Morten pushes a button and the window slides down. Faces come closer and the word *carta* is heard, *identificazione del automobile* too. There's no sound and no shot, not a fingernail falls to earth. Morten bends forward and picks up the yellow folder with the Hertz papers. He sits with them in his right hand, while with his left he finds his wallet in his pocket. He puts down the Hertz folder again, open his wallet and finds his driver's license. It's pink and is kept in a cellophane protector. It's touching. He hands the two men the license and the folder with the car's documents. I've watched eels through water-binoculars when the spear goes down over them and they thrash about at both ends, swim, swim, but can't go anywhere. The men look at the driver's license and at Morten; they open the folder with the papers, read down through them, compare them with something written on a pad. Then they look at Morten again and ask him (first in Italian and then, just to be sure, in a kind of English) to get out. They open the door for him, and Morten moves his legs from the floor mat of the Ferrari to the asphalt, unfolds himself, stands up. The men say something which I can't hear. Jørgen's way out now goes just over a seat which can be pushed down. Then one of the men sits in the seat and the way is blocked. The man takes the wheel and turns it hard to both sides. First hard to one side and then hard to the other. He really tugs at the wheel. The other man leaves Morten and walks over in front of the windshield again. The man at the wheel doesn't pull at it anymore, but puts his foot on the brake pedal and stamps hard. The man outside shakes his head. The man at the wheel lifts a hand and waves dismissingly. Then he bends forward and turns on the ignition, reaches forward with his right arm and flips down a switch. The man outside nods. The man at the wheel flips the switch to a different position. The man outside nods. The man at the wheel steps on the floor switch to the left of the steering column. The man in the front of the car nods and throws his arms out to both sides. Then he walks to the right along the sidewalk to the rear of the car. The man at the wheel looks in the rear view mirror. Then he releases the wheel and the brakes and gets out.

We celebrate our picnic, not in Rapallo but in Nervi. I hadn't expected that they would say yes, my two men, but the sudden nearness of the forces of law and order, and the thought that something is *decided,* softens them or makes them haughty. The nervousness has left them but now it's after me. Only not so hard that I can't fight it. I find it amazing that Morten speaks with Schwer. The all-Danish players after the game--no one can remember who won and who lost. We sit on the edge of the square, and I read the gas pump's flame-yellow sign: *Supercorte-maggiore.* Why is Jørgen less aggressive towards Morten than he is towards me? Is he really a coolie? Or is it because I'm a woman? Listen to what they say:

--Geneva's best.

--Yes, I think you're right. The throughway goes north. And Christensen's in La Spezia.

He drinks his spumante.

Morten lifts his glass simultaneously.

Jørgen sets his glass down.

--Why are you helping me?

--I'm not helping you. It's a deal.

--A deal?

The swallows have indeed come to Nervi. One tries to build a nest up under the roof of the gas station. Strange swallow, strange intoxicated swallow in the middle of the octane's methyl high. Doesn't it care for its children at all?

--I've arranged with my sister-in-law for her to come with me when you've said goodbye. That was the condition on which I warned you and took you along.

He nods and looks as if it were obvious.

Lift my glass and feel as if I'm put out of the game. Soccer widow.

--But still I can't help asking you to turn yourself in now . . . as quickly as possible. It will pay off.

Jørgen Schwer looks at Anna. He looks at me.

--What about her? he says then. She'll be in a lot of damned hot water, too.

--That will be taken care of, Morten says and makes the usual gesture with his left hand for his wallet. Senta!

The rest of the way to Genoa is simple transportation. I've taken off my idiotic wig and sit with it in my lap. There's no particular reason to comb out my hair. The rubber bands are allowed to remain. Anna (I) thinks about the Carmen Curlers that she after the damnedest trouble had sent out to Karachi by diplomatic pouch. They weren't right, either. The trip is short and the approach to the harbor city not much, as usual. If you're not in the particular mood that makes chemical factories, gasworks, and loading cranes something sensational. Yellow fog, dust, stench, transit.

We--still we--continue to Piazzale Autostrada and drive into the gas station by the approach road from Ventimiglia. The sun is on the rim again, balancing between two houses, intersected by power lines, veiled by the exhaust from passing cars. We get out, Morten on his side, I on mine, Jørgen hesitating a moment, then following his fellow masculine friend. I turn my back and prepare a suitable ritual: Goodbye and thanks for everything. Goodbye and have a good trip. Goodbye and take care of yourself. Goodbye and thanks. It was very nice. Goodbye, say hello to everyone for me. Bye, bye, and good luck. Au revoir. Bon voyage! Ciao! I involuntarily bend my loins a little to follow the ceremony, an outstretched hand will do, a little bow, a nod of the head--and see two black cars drive into the traffic circle from the same side we did a few minutes ago. The most marked thing about them is that they are identical, identical and very black. They obey the lights and signs, stop once for crossing traffic, start again, apparently move the hood searchingly, sniffingly, but it's impossible, leave the common circulation and steer right for the gas station. Two cars.

Before they get all the way onto the asphalt under the enormous overhanging roof, the back door of the first car springs open and a shape in a light coat and brown hat leaps out and begins to run alongside the car while he (it is a he) searches for something with his right hand under the lapel of his coat. Before he gets to reveal what it is, the echo-hall's space resounds with two booms, drowning out all the motors, all the horns, all the wrenches pounding, and the man falls, first lifted in a backwards ballet-leap, then thrown to the ground. I turn and before my eyes there shines in the flash of the double explosion an undulating dragon, black with a fire-red tongue sticking from its mouth and the word: Supercortemaggiore.

11

Anyone who's ever had geography in school knows how difficult it is to see what it's really all about. A map is flat, even though it says on it that brown means higher areas, dark brown mountains and particular numbers particular heights on particular mountains. You see borders as red lines and agricultural products as colored symbols. Everything becomes jumbled and one-dimensional: wheat, wine, olive, wheat wine olive, yes, the funny thing is that even your own country, strictly geographically, doesn't seem to represent anything concrete. Are the cities on Fyn anything more than a lesson until you yourself have noticed how slanting the streets are certain places in Svendborg, how the square in Bogense gazes at you with its bowed windows, how cold it is in Odense in the winter when you walk out of the railroad station and the wind comes whipping across the park?

I've never given the timber-line a thought before today. Naturally I heard about it back then many years ago, heard about it the same way I heard about everything else you had to learn: it was noted, tucked in and forgotten, stacked up, stowed out of the way and repressed. Well, that's not completely true, for if you had asked me what the timber-line was, I would have been able to answer: The timber-line is where the trees stops when you go up a mountain that's high enough. That would have been a piece of homework, a good, intelligent student report on something that she's learned. There would have been no actuality behind it, no feeling or experience, no revelation like today, where a long forgotten theoretical knowledge suddenly found its poetic confirmation in reality. They hadn't lied to me! And I felt a great tenderness that put me in direct rapport with my past, my childhood and school, not the one I feel I'm still attending, the one

167

with the girls, no, the very first one where we sat at stationary desks and the pointer against the map made a tiny bobbing sound that came again and again, every time we shouted the name of a city in chorus and the teacher moved the pointer farther: Mons, Liege, Namur, Bruxelles, Gent, Brügge, Antwerp.

Today we passed the timber-line, and it was a borderline. Without any particular transition, the woods stopped, and you could see that it wasn't just a local phenomenon by looking at the mountains around you. They all had woods but at a definite line they stopped. I've crossed borders before, in the last few days as well, and it's easier to perceive the artificial dividing lines as accidental than the definitive of the timber-line: up to here and no farther. Maybe it's because we haven't crossed the political borders in the normal manner that they don't seem like they used to; maybe I'm so exhausted that the thin air makes me hallucinate. It's as if we had come out above the world, and I'm afraid. Jørgen has decided to go against all the rules and for the moment it's paid off. I just don't know whether I can explain myself why "paid off" in this context is a vulgarity. I'm too tired. We've done the opposite of what they expected of us, i.e. sought the most thickly populated, most heavily travelled, best guarded areas, and no one has paid us any attention at all. Of course, we're in the wilderness now, but on the way to a junction, too. He plans for us to go over the Little St. Bernard's Tunnel, not through it, but follow it a way on top until it disappears into the mountain, and then climb the rest of the way into Switzerland. I still don't understand his love for the most closely guarded borders and the heaviest concentrations of traffic, but it was as if the big car cut through like a butterknife, ploughed down the expressway until we turned west at Serravalle, hammered through Ovada on the narrow road, went a little north again to Acqui until we found the road through Spigno west toward France. The draft in the car was fatiguing, and the sound a distorted whistling from the holes where a shower of submachine gun bullets had gone through. We drove until there was no more gas, and discovered, when we ditched the car in a thicket twenty kilometers from Briancon, that the howling sound had not only come from the bullet holes, but also from the capless gas tank. That explained why the tone had become deeper, shifted, rose and fell with the speed, and ended like a roar just before the tank was empty and the motor began to buck just before it quit.

Since then we've walked, and I don't know how long we've walked. Most of the time we've followed rivers and streams, some up, some down. It isn't clear how much of the time we've been in France, but I really would have rather stayed there, but he shakes his head and says Switzerland, Switzerland, as if there were no such thing as a big prison with orpine and edelweiss on its roof. We ran into the road northeast of Bourg and were still in Italy. Got a lift to the mountain north of Aosta, where two hours ago we crossed the timberline and have been able to see the approach to the tunnel all the while like Midgaard's serpent which is determined to embrace and devour this massif, but a little way up chooses a secret path and bores its head into the mountain to reach the vital nerve. It's impossible to cross the Matterhorn at the end of March, but we can manage its neighbor, which is easily a few meters lower. I have no idea how it will go, but it doesn't interest me very much, either. At this point I'm not the one who's taking the lead or giving directions--not even my old compulsion toward the north is still active. After a certain point, I've allowed myself to be led--you have to do something. From the moment I saw the left front wheel of the Ferrari pass Christensen, who lay on the cement as if concentrating on looking for something he definitely couldn't find, I've been passive. My powers of reasoning have become thinner and thinner. I have difficulty activating Anna, speak to her in a low voice, say:

--Anna, this isn't too good. Simultaneously overrule the choice of words and try again: Anna, things aren't like they used to be. Do you remember? Once upon a time knives were something that hung behind a door in the high-ceilinged kitchen where Mirres and Ahcmat and the others rule. Anna, knives were something that gleamed in the morning's earliest waking dreams. And they were deaf and dull and blunt even if you were afraid of them. You wandered in your morning walk from your bed through hallways on the cool tiles. You took the knife and shivered when you touched the edge, you opened the door and walked slowly into Minna's shadowroom, where you leaned forward and jabbed again, again, again, but you never did. You never did. You lay in your bed and the dark was thick with possibilities, but you never made use of them.

--Anna, what do your clothes look like? What kind of a spot do you have down at the bottom of your skirt? How will you wash it away? What is it? Who put it there? Whose clothes are you wearing? Where's your family, your husband, your children, your brother-in-law, your brother, your father and your mother? And I get cocky at this inquisitorial murmuring and answer:

--I'm here. Here I am. I only have a stocking on one leg. I'm carrying a purse that belongs in Le Grand Vefour, but crosses the timber-line now. I'm in possession of about 1000 dollars. With them I can buy a mountain goat to ride on. I'm in the company of one Jørgen Schwer, soon again long-haired, probably a murderer. I'm his accomplice, although still a relatively innocent accomplice. Or am I? Why didn't I remain standing by the Gilbarco-automat where the glass will always be full and you can pay with tourist coupons? Why did I automatically move forward as soon as my pupils widened after the flashes and my ears heard the roar? Why did I open the door to the car, get into the seat and watch Jørgen Schwer as he flayed away at the ignition key and drove off between the two black cars, where six men in coats tried to get out of the way, while at the same time they cocked their submachine guns, pointed them at our car, pulled the triggers and fired? I can't say, but maybe I followed him because I want to have the answer. Anyway, that's what I tell myself.

I also tell myself: What is your relation to Jørgen Schwer--is it the same as before, or have you ever had any relationship at all with him? He walks up there in front, an indefatigable mountain goat. I know that boys who are sent into the country early in May to the large camps to gain their strength and cast off their slum greyness as a rule aren't sent away because they are weak but because their teachers can't stand their unruliness in class any more. And so they come to the fresh air camps where they have vitaminized porridge enriched with all sorts of minerals, calcium and phosphorous, radium and LSD. The boys go on looking just as pale and grimy even though they eat and eat and eat and finish up with snacks and half a kilo of jam. They maintain their color even though the sun shines and they walk around in its rays from morning to night. But someplace or other they build up a strength, a toughness, which I know of from home, too, but haven't thought about for many years. I want to shout, brother, lend me a little, give me a little of your proletarian, sullen, asocial energy, but I can't do it because I don't know him. We haven't talked about anything, haven't exchanged a sensible word, *ever*. When I begin in the East, he snaps at me--not only in the West, but over on the other side of the world. Our relationship is just as meaningless as his shooting down one Chief and travelling Detective Karl Christensen, who lay on all fours and tried to see if he could find himself in his own blood. And brother-in-law Morten's mouth open, saying without a sound: no, no, no, just as it always said no when something came crushing in, demanding its reality, explicable or inexplicable, good or bad.

But the worst thing is my own callousness or passivity, my mental jargon when I ask for peace and calm on the premises. What if it were Tom who had come out of the black car and suddenly had lain there? Would I have kept standing there? It could have been him. No one in the flurry could see who came out of the car. The shooting was a spontaneous reaction, the act of a person who knows he's caught but doesn't have imagination enough to understand what the consequences of his actions will be. The one who was shot was a man whose clothes and manner of speaking appealed to my sense of humor and perhaps to my tenderness, too. He was nice, as I've said, and at home there's probably a girl who's stood on the corner of Hambro Street and Niels Brock Street, waiting for him, thinking he was *handsome* or who had sat at home, keeping the coffee warm, and the children had been sent to bed, but had been allowed not to go to sleep before they had said hello and kissed papa, who was coming home late because he was a hard worker and the police often let him work overtime.

The thing that interests me is the same, really, as interests Morten. How did this process begin? Who's responsible for it? And when will it end? I (Anna) am here as a Northern European middle-aged person with certain experiences from a life that has given me quite a few possibilities. I've travelled, I've studied, I've been both rich and poor, I'm committed (or closer perhaps: have been) politically committed--the actual reality with its ups and downs is unknown to me. I know, for example, that this March there's a state of emergency in Spain (vexes me), crisis in the Middle East (can't evaluate it, detest equally Israel's militant aggressiveness and the Arabic infiltration of guerrillas) that

Nixon's in Rome, and came too late for me to wipe his raisin loaf of a face with a rotten tomato, that the bourgeois regime back home (my husband's high superiors and my coming judges) drop with stress during the performance of their duties and the implementation of the law, who at best are characterized by mediocrity and have hardly ever appealed whole-heartedly to anyone at all. How what I am and what happens to me falls together in any manner, I can't see--certain images just seem to keep hanging in the air: the knife in the dark, the buzzard, Mirres' hands, Tom's shape against the lighter window, the water from the river wandering over the lawn toward me, I myself kneeling naked across from Roberto, the monkey's teeth and the leash from the neck to the hand, the revolver, the kneeling man who looked for his own mirror image in a sticky liquid on the cement. Three partridges bluster up next to us, and their noise opens my ears again. A new factor makes itself felt, and when the shock has subsided and Jørgen has thrust the revolver back between his shirt and his body, we hear the sound of the traffic in the tunnel approach reach us. It's impossible to judge how good the view is through its grillwork construction, but it's obvious that we have to watch out and probably will have to wait until nightfall to attempt to force the cement snake. We stand there crouching next to each other, and when I stop in the middle of a movement to rise up next to him, I stagger a moment and have to support myself and notice how tightly his ribs lie against his skin under the shirt. We talk, and the talk is typical. He says:

--They can see us from the tunnel.

--Yes.

I move my hand from his body when I've regained my balance. The tires sing against the reinforced concrete of the highway bridge.

173

--Why do you want to go this way?

--They don't expect us here.

--What if they see us?

He shakes his head.

--What if they've seen us?

--They haven't.

He crouches down even farther and makes a movement with his hand which indicates that I too should crouch farther down. I do.

--Run behind the ledge.

I look to the left where a rock sticks up like a lost gigantic cap with its shadow pointing at us. Crouching, I run into the shelter behind it. During a break in the traffic he follows me. We sit with our backs to the stone and look at the way we've come. Four-five kilometers down to the right there are houses opposite our angle of incidence from the road. Smoke rises from one of them. It's a long time since I've been in a house.

--We'll never make it, I say.

--Do you have a better suggesion?

I shake my head.

It's not hard to remember what I've seen before me most of the day: a broad mountainside with a tunnel entrance of concrete, pillars, blasted rocks, the sky full of clouds submerged between the mountaintops, the approach which for a way is quarried through the rock instead of running around it. That's what we have to go over and up, from ledge to ledge. You can't climb on vertical cement, even though that's what I thought we were going to do. And why not?

--What happens when we get up?

--We go on.

--Up into the mountain?

174

--Yes.

That, too, I remember, the mountain in back. It disappears into the clouds, and I think about the reason the tunnel has been made to avoid the rise into the pass. If there is a pass.

--It gets cold at night in the mountains, I say, cleverly.

He nods.

--And we have hardly any clothes on. You have hardly any clothes on.

It occurs to me that this *is* the way conversations with Jøgen Schwer in the Swiss-Italian alps are, have to be. But I don't let myself get cowed.

--What do you think will happen? I ask.

--What? he says.

--What do you think will happen when we get across and up the mountain and down the other side--alive--and into Switzerland. What will happen then?

--We'll go on.

I warm again at his "we" and continue.

--Why are you doing this? Why don't you shoot me, too, and be done with it?

Schoolgirl's voice.

--Shoot?

He laughs.

--Yes, maybe I will. But there are only four left.

--Four what?

--Four bullets.

--But you were big enough to sacrifice two of them on Christensen?

--That was because of the confusion.

--Did you know it was Christensen?

He shakes his head. He turns, crawls forward, and looks up

175

toward the mountain road. He gazes up there for a while. I can see his soles and they are thin. One of his socks has crept down around his heel. I look at my missing stocking. He comes back and sits down.

--We'll have to try it in daylight.

He's torn off a straw while he's crawled. He sticks it in his mouth now, and I think of the fungus that grows on it right out to the tip and which in a little while will spread to his gums and his palate, change into a monstrous mycelium which will fill his whole mouth, choke him, drown him, fill his nostrils with mildew.

--Aren't you sorry you shot him . . . killed him?

--Who, Christensen? The cop?

--Yes.

--No.

I sit there getting agitated and recognize the agitation from other situations. Dad in his rocking chair with the paper to Mother: It says here that a railroad worker in Tørring kept his daughter locked up for fourteen months and only gave her potatoes and flour gravy while she sat chained to an iron bed. Mom: What did you say? Dad: I say that it says here that a railroad worker in Tørring has kept his little daughter locked up . . . Mom: That's just awful! (comes closer) Dad: And that he only gave her potatoes and flour gravy to eat for fourteen months . . . Mom: (clasping her hands) For fourteen months. That's just awful! Oh, how can people do things like that! Dad: And it says, too, that she was chained to an iron bed when she was found . . . Mom: (crying hysterically) No, stop, stop, I just can't bear to hear such things. I don't understand it. I don't understand how people *can!* Dad: (shaking his head, looking further in the paper) No. Mom: (stands a while with her hands at her side, then goes back to the ironing board, begins to iron) Do you want coffee now or later? Dad: Later.

It's well over a mile to the tunnel road, the rise about forty-five degrees. The wind has shifted and a faint smell of diesel wafts down to us and mixes with the dampness and the smell of grass. There are bluebells next to one of my shoes. They haven't blossomed yet. I don't pick them.

--It's not certain he's dead, either, Jørgen Schwer says.

--He was bleeding, I say. He was bleeding a lot.

--Only if it was the thigh arteries. I aimed at his legs.

--You aimed?

--Yes, I aimed. Didn't you see the way he jumped?

--Yes?

--That's what happens when you're hit in the legs.

--How do you know that?

--I've been in the army.

He says it with pride and contempt. Almost with an extra stress on the first syllable, as if he were a waiter and spoke about bearnaise.

--Maybe you thought I hadn't been?

I don't know what to say. I hadn't thought about him in that role. He's very young.

--You can get off here if you like, he says, and I feel a dizziness like that which comes when you've taken too many empirin. A road, a car, a mountain, innumerable choices--it's so easy, left right, left right, up on your feet, march straight ahead, down the mountain, over to the house, up to the fireplace, over to the telephone, off with the receiver, hello, hello, good day, good day.

--Why have you dragged me up here if you don't want me along any more? Anna asks.

--I haven't dragged you, by Jesus, he says, pouting.

There's a burr in my hair. I take it out and bend the tiny

177

curved hairs softly between my thumb and forefinger. I think about my children. Perhaps it would be one of them who'd pick up the phone. That would be lovely. I would hurry home to them as quickly as possible. It's wonderful to be reunited with your children, and I can notice now, too, how badly I miss them. The first forty-five minutes you have with your children again after a long separation are blissful. Then the blissfulness stops. But can you ask for more? Isn't the rest romanticism, this exaltation? I go my way, and their existence ceases except maybe just at the moment when missing them is physical and tangible. It would be lovely to talk with them, touch them, sit with them. And then? Yes, then nothing, it would just be lovely. My sentimental moment makes me conscious of my body, and I feel the warm murmuring from someplace under navel spread out over my hips and on the inside of my thighs. I do, Jørgen Schwer. And now you and I jointly have disturbed my whole life.

He gets down on his knees again and gazes up toward the road. Then he looks at his watch and nods to me. It must be close to four o'clock. There are at least three hours to twilight. He seems nervous, but energetic, too. I myself am continually afraid deep down because I can't foresee the consequences of what lies ahead. You are literally tiny when you stand on a mountain slope, have a mountain (maybe more) in front of you, have to go over the top, down the other side and are dressed in shoes from Reuben Torres, one stocking from Dior, and Rabanne's skirt. But you are perhaps even smaller because for reasons that can't be made rational you're cut off from turning back. Strange to travel away and home at the same time. That's something I've tried before, but never heading toward Denmark! That ridiculous country with the residential streets and the most comical social morality in the world: We're doing damned well, but our taxes are too high! I wish I were sitting by Degne Marsh, feeding the ducks.

We haven't slept much for three days, but the sleepiness, and the warmth that comes with it, disappears when he signals in a way I've seen in war films. Avancér, forward, crawl, now, act as if you were a man. Avanti, Garibaldi, sempre avanti.

There's about fifty meters from the boulders to the ledge on the way up to the tunnel, but because of the rise it will take time to go across the plateau. I'm exhausted by the time I throw myself behind the first boulder. Three minutes later Jørgen comes and, breathing heavily, lies beside me. He explains that we can only run when there are gaps in the traffic, and we accustom ourselves to this rhythm, figure out how long ahead of time you can hear the approaching cars, when they will pass, and their possible view of us, learn to distinguish between when there's one or more coming, use the bigger intervals for longer runs, forget that there's any danger in the effort to avoid it. At quarter after six we are so close to the approach that we can't be seen from it. The last part of the way to the rock wall above the tunnel we walk, and I realize the challenge consists of a perpendicular climbing trip of over two hundred and fifty meters. Twenty-five times the staging in a monkey-cage of the same character. I don't care since I can't feel anything. My knees are in shreds and my legs numb. I listen half-conscious and half-unconscious to the general, who says:

--It's a matter of getting up there and going on before it gets dark. Otherwise we'll lose a day. And if we're spotted, it's even more important. The higher up we get, the better our chances.

--Yes, I say, without saying it, that's all right for you to say, you subnormal cretin. I've *never* said I was a mountain climber, but if I had to give a lecture now, it would be to the effect that you should have used your wonderful strategy and your terrain-walking abilities for something else than a life of crime. But

179

perhaps it's only in the military and in the criminal world that you can use that kind of thing?

He looks appraisingly at me and smiles. The revolver must cut into him the way it's sitting. But to hell with that, he doesn't notice that, either. Porridge and LSD.

The sound of the cars fifty meters above us is loud and nearly constant. Maybe there's a particular border-migration just before mealtimes. The thought reminds me of my own bowels and Mirres' grey nails and whatever is lying under the silver dish when he holds it forward and lets Memsahib be served first. I'm lonely and mute and feel like crying. I can't invoke my girls now, who are sitting so far away in their offices or in commuter trains or are standing in their kitchens, swearing at themselves because they can't decide what to cook today, even though they've bought meatballs. Suddenly the desire for meatballs is gone, hidden by a kind of thick wall of nausea and loneliness--think, if there were a mountain in your pan, with eternal snow on top and a lump of margarine--that would be something to serve, wouldn't it!

We decide (or rather he decides) that I should go up first because he can support me if I should slip or faint along the way; that last point I suggested myself without saying it. We decide to take a break every twenty-five meters. When I put my foot on the ledge and lift myself upwards, my calf muscles quiver and protrude like oarblades. Thickest on top and painfully tightened below. But still it's easier than I thought. The ledges are fairly well placed in relation to one another, and it's he, in fact, who stops me by whistling when I've reached the first fifty meters or more. I find a wide shelf and sit down with my legs tucked up and my face turned toward the hillside and the valley. I'm so high up now that I can see the roof, a ribbed reinforced-concrete roof between supporting arches on the approach road, which is covered, I suppose, to protect it from snow and snowslides. We are completely protected by the wind which blows the other way. Maybe that's why I don't pay much attention to the noise which blends in with the sound of the traffic and don't really see, either, at first what it is that's coming. But when I look down and see Jørgen pressing himself hard against the rock, I realize that the dot increasingly bearing down on us and the mountain and producing a high, clipping hum, is a helicopter.

This is worse than anything else. Helicopters aren't ordinary or simple like airplanes. There's never been any civil habituation to helicopters. They're not the kind of thing you can meet sitting on a ledge on a vertical stone wall without being terrified. I can feel the chill and the vibrations rise up from Schwer. Helicopters haven't been seriously introduced into democracies. They belong to the forces of law and order, are at home in Vietnam or are used to spray poison. Against the helicopter you're exposed and defenceless. At the sight of them you get sick with terror, are naked, and helplessly full of hate. They themselves are time's chitinlike nightmare, things that fly in all directions at once, at all heights, but slowly, searching and ultimately purposeful. But there's a disadvantage even with helicopters in that they can only come so near a mountainside, and at the point that I am just about to lose my grip and drop helplessly, the helicopter changes its course and begins to fly along the tunnel approach to the right. Before it can turn and come back, we have to find ourselves another spot. I don't know where. But Jørgen begins to crawl up to me, and I remember to breathe for the first time in a long while. Then the helicopter disappears around the rocks while its sound is drowned out in the moving traffic. For some reason or other he lowers his voice as if he were afraid that the men in the copter or the people in the cars would hear us. I can't hear his words and shout: What did you say? What did you say? hysterically like a drunk, and he turns and points and shouts: The roof! The roof! and then I understand with heart-stopping certainty that he wants us to move out on the highway roof's ribbed construction in order to get in under the rock projection itself, from where we can't be seen. Since the width of the individual cement ribs is under fifty centimeters and the drop to the highway fifteen meters, it's a hazard, a sheer hazard. And with the image of the green cloth in Monte Carlo before my eyes, the words Pair/Impair ringing in my ears, I follow him and have gotten to the first girder when the helicopter in a steep bank appears five hundred meters away and bears directly down on us. Jørgen Schwer turns his head from it to me and back again and back again; then he runs with his feet in front of him like a huge hare, grabs ahold of my hand and roars: Now! And before my stiffness has turned into indissoluble cramps, I follow him with closed eyes and feel the flapping gigantic tug of the helicopter's rotor blades as it passes and before I myself am whirled in under the rock and scrape my knee once more and drop down by the side of the boy from the fresh air camp in the dark.

We lie in this black V with our faces toward each other. His nose touches the hair on my shoulder and I can feel his breathing and think again of the rodents, white rabbits, frightened, hares out of their wits caught in a car's headlights or leaping between a shotgun's evil hail of pellets. We lie quietly, but the noise is all around us: the cars from below, the diesel moiling and toiling upwards of a camion, the wheezing, singing of speeding cars, more intense, intense, falling, the helicopter which disappears, rolls out over the valley, banks in order to turn around and comes back, vibrations everywhere, as if the highway itself were alive and conspiratorial, tremors transmitted to the mountain, moving it in an enormous seismography, which seems to be connected to the very powers and threatening uproar of the earth's interior.

We lie completely quiet in the mouth of the mountain and he moves his nose so that it touches my neck, and I turn and hold his neck with my right hand. Shortly after we're a part of the shaking, want to bore into the warm center, want to go through and out, want to explode the mountain and preserve it. The pain in my legs disappears and for a moment the hovering helicopter speaks through its megaphone to us without our listening or hearing. Then they force themselves in with three languages, primarily the last, the repetitions and their echoes out over the plateau, the threat, the judgment: Bedingungslose Kapitulation . . . Kapitulation . . . ion . . . ion . . .

But the darkness falls, and the helicopter has to leave. I embrace the thin body, but he twists free and looks at me a moment. I (Anna) can feel my own paleness. He creeps out of the crack and watches the helicopter's navigation light as it disappears. Then he takes my hand and helps me to my feet. I straighten my skirt, and shortly after we're on our way upwards in the dark. We get around the tunnel when the darkness is nearly total. Jørgen takes my hand and leads me upward, on. I notice something stick against my face, prickle, melt and disappear. It's snow.

12

I think about recuperation, fugitives, and explorers. The connection isn't immediately apparent, but I'll try to take up each point separately. Anyone who's been sick and gotten well again knows the joyful feeling of being reborn, of *returning*. You're stronger than you thought possible, even though you're still weak. You have the feeling of unlimited possibility. All the evil is behind you, all the good things ahead. Something's been given you by somebody, and at first you won't acknowledge that it's your own body, you yourself, in other words, and no metaphysical being outside you, which is able to offer you so clear a pleasure, so matter-of-fact a resurrection. But in that moment you understand it's the body that's won its own battle, happiness flows so strongly that it takes your breath away. You haven't been given anything; it's your own resources which have stopped the disintegration, have said: Halt and withdraw! And in the middle of the weakness, after the weakness, the feeling of strength is intoxicating. A victory has been won, and thousands can be. The air around you is thin, every step a dizzying, bold expedition which is crowned with luck when you walk from the bed to the easy chair and you make it without your legs buckling or losing your breath. I think the feeling can be compared to the bulbous plants when they begin to stir anew after winter. A compactness, a pressing in the sleeping cambium expands, dreams locked tightly by stonehard earth and cold, choked, feel a directional longing upwards, after rising and liberating themselves, after blossoming in the light.

But whoever flees from death is a fugitive, and even if he escapes, the encounter will have left its traces. In a way all fugitives are running from death or its synonyms, but in her euphoric clarity, Anna (I) may ask whether it's not a matter of legal flight and illegal flight. A Jew who flees from liquidation in a concentration camp is a legal fugitive from nearly every point of view but that of the SS. But a soldier who flees from the front because he's afraid of being killed by the enemy has suddenly a more limited legality. He can be called a deserter, even though a pacifist would maintain the fleeing soldier is acting ethically. His flight is a deserting--he betrays ideas, even though they're not necessarily his own. This fugitive's situation is ambiguous. Whereas a fleeing criminal's flight is unambiguously illegal. He has committed a murder, perpetrated an offense, so to speak, against universal laws--although naturally there may be a question of mitigating circumstances. But everyone must be interested in seeing such a criminal imprisoned and rendered harmless. Maybe the flight fills him momentarily with a hitherto unknown feeling of freedom, recuperation, of possibilities and energy, but the moment the trap snaps around him and he has to face the bill, he will realize with awful certainty that the feeling of freedom was a fiction which already carried the dream of perdition and judgement within it. But what can you do with a person who has slipped from the jaws of death and is a fugitive, but will not compromise with his rashness? and how should you characterize a fugitive who can't give more than one and a half reasonable explanations for his flight? Is Anna a fugitive--isn't she more like an oblique traveller, a meteor, who more or less voluntarily has left her course and simply wobbles? Her flight has no definite direction and on that ground alone must be regarded as illegal. No one has threatened her with death, although she herself has toyed with the thought of depriving others of life. But the flight from a

185

dream or rather: the flight from the nearest possibility, namely, *to awaken*, is perhaps the greatest crime of them all.

Fugitives flee outwards, flee away from something; explorers flee inward. From the outset nearly every fugitive will consider his flight legal. The explorer has a goal even though he doesn't know it. Columbus absolutely wanted to find India, but he found America. It can be called an accident, but it's a simple geographic consequence. Columbus is a great man. Byrd, Scott, Amundsen travelled savagely toward the South Pole--one of them had to eat his shoes before he could lie down to die under the canvas of his tent. Scott became a tragic hero, but he was a great man. Stanley went into the jungle after Livingstone and found him--he had to presume--but he wasn't disappointed, and did Livingstone live up to his expectations? *Had* he any expectations in mind before he set out, and did he know what he was really looking for? Stanley was a great man. But Cook was a swindler, and André a criminal, although no one can really fathom the secret of them all. At a point, their actions resembled triumphs, but each of them in his own manner ran inwards and away. Their fates have become symbols, even their tragedies and mistakes are made legal and realized--their myths are truth.

It's a question of confusion: the dimensionless, accidental, unnuanced, neurotic are fused enough to give an expedition mystical and ethical cogency. I (Anna) haven't felt so well for a long time, and even if my situation and my person don't justify it, for a while I'll observe everything as facts and tell all about them. I'll try to sharpen my reasoning powers, but without rocking a jot or tittle my, yes, I shrink from saying the word: idyl, which now surrounds me and which I'm a part of.

From where I sit I can see out a window with tiny panes. A strong indirect light from the snow strikes the ceiling. The sun has

186

passed this side of the house, but it still drips from the eaves. The room is warm; a black, cylindrical oven, it's lowest door open, burns evenly and steadily. Over my bed hangs a three-cornered shelf with dried wildflowers in little jars. At the foot, a crucifix has been placed half a meter up. The house, an Alpine farm, is owned by the Stürmer family, whose home is really in another part of Switzerland. During the war they were more or less driven from their place by the military because it was too near the German border and was to be used for surveillance. Maybe that's why their conduct toward fugitives is so open or maybe in Switzerland a good part of the population has an historic hospitality determined by the climate, the snow, St. Bernards, and the four different borders facing four different countries. You would think they would have had enough of this gadding about. The Stürmers are probably not at all characteristic; a pessimist would say that their old grudge is the likely explanation, but today I'm willing to make concessions to everyone, and I can say that without having to, the family has done more to protect us, much more, than a simple human demand could have asked.

The story of how we got up here is one of Peter Stürmer's favorites. I know it inside out, but it can't do any harm to tell it again because it gives me a little identity. After dinner we sit at the table under the oil lamp like a family in a Danish summer cottage, and when the first two glasses of Glühwein had vanished behind his beard, Peter pushes the straw hat he usually wears when he comes into the house back from his forehead and looks expectantly at us, as if it were us and not he who could tell a good story. Yes, he says, yes, there you sit. In the beginning we scraped our feet a little because there was no refuting the fact, but it demanded anyhow a kind of recognition or applause. Now we just sit quietly and wait, smiling, for him to begin. He tells it well, warms up gradually as, in his opinion, the drama and the spice in it increase. Renate Stürmer walks to and fro--there's always something on the fire and she doesn't have any of that middle-class-produced terror that anyone, and certainly not her husband, should get too much to eat. When the pot was empty, it was filled up, and when we went to bed, it was put away. There is a little clearing of the throat in the beginning:

--Ahem. Yes, it wasn't all that easy.

And: Yes, eh, ahem, hm, bad weather. Really bad weather.

Until the wheels take hold and he describes the preliminaries, each time painstakingly with an elucidation of the situation surrounding the evening milking, what he had heard on the radio, what--ahem--they had had for dinner, and it was precisely that day the boy (who's surely over thirty) was sent to town, yes, precisely, to town and not half an hour later the roads were closed, and they've been closed ever since. The roads and the fields and the forest farther down, all closed. And then he had gotten this *feeling* or this *impulse* or if anything this *warning* that there was something up, something about to happen. Naturally, at first he pushed it out of his mind--it was just the weather, the thought of the boy, who wasn't home anymore, that made him uneasy. But then he noticed from both the animals and the dog that something unusual was on the way. He told his wife, who naturally shook--hm--her head and told him to come in and get his dinner and stop thinking about such things (after the remark about his wife, he always glances at her or looks for her to be sure she's listening, that she's sufficiently appreciative she's included in the story.)

At last the unease and the presentiments became so strong that he puts his clothes on, straps on his skis, calls the dog and begins to ski down through the dark and the storm. His wife entreats him to stay home, but of course knows there's no stopping him--ahem-- and when he has skied a few kilometers and can still see the stile and knows that he can find his way home, the dog begins running like hell and disappears baying and howling and he has to call it like crazy to get it to come back. With his pole in one hand, the leash in the other, he struggles forward. The dog hauls and tugs; its tongue hangs like a sausage (here he looks around again) out of its jaws. At last they come to the goat shed and when he gets the door yanked open--the wind is bearing right down one and pressing against it--at first he can't see anything at all, just hears the groaning of the animals and feels the warmth from them, but when he gets out the flashlight and clicks it on with his numbed fingers, he sees something that is so fantastic that he has to break off the story, lift his glass, take a long drink, stretch out the moment of the release of the central point to its utmost, dries his beard, gazes at us, his wife, looks around for the dog, breathes deeply--and then it comes:

--Wes ik denn dort gesehen heb'!

In the gleam from the light there lay two people, he and she, jammed so tightly up against each other one wouldn't think they had a chance in heaven of breathing. There they lay--in his goathouse, on the straw, among his animals--and the dog barked and they didn't even so much as stir. (He tells the story each time like all real story tellers, without paying any attention to the fact that his main characters are present. The story *an sich* is the most important thing--reality is too abstract or uncertain to really take into consideration, and then he is right: we were not present at the time he first saw us in the goathouse.)

Two things make up the narrative's high point: the way we clung to each other and my clothes. Both things appeared (or appear to him now) risqué or in any case spicy. As a rule, the wife turns her back or stands by the stove when Stürmer comes to this point.

--Deese Kleider, he says. Shakes his head, and repeats the outburst--Deese Kleider! And then he speaks exhaustively about my naked legs and my shoes, and the torn skirt, and I've heard it so many times that smiling I have to think of Ruben and Paco and Nina and Yves who sat in their gilded sewing rooms and their mirror-bedecked salons and don't give a thought to the fact that a change from their genial subtleties to a cotton sweater three sizes too large, two sweaters and a pair of ski boots can once in a while feel like a promotion, or a blessing, anyway.

The story ebbs out, for the rest is heroic, very simple and therefore uninteresting. But the truth is that Peter Stürmer, seventy-two, went up to the house first for blankets, came back, wrapped me up and covered Jørgen, hauled me over his shoulder up to the house, delivered me, went back and, tottering, half-dragged, half-carried him home to safety, while the dog barked. Renate injects her observation that he should have joined the Olympics when it was in the neighborhood a few years ago, and then a satisfied, redeemed silence falls over us. We nod like women around a sewing table, and I look at my hands, which are still swollen and have a black edge down along the forefinger from something which could be called frostbite, but which was probably more like gangrene. Out of politeness, Stürmer invites us once in a while to narrate something, but when Jørgen tried once, it was without success. His German quickly went to pieces, and I discovered that the request was not meant seriously. Our presence, for which no one has demanded an explanation, is entertaining enough in itself. In a house where there probably isn't very much spoken daily, it's the duty of the guest to shut up when the host and hostess finally get their chance to talk.

190

The first few days we *couldn't* talk. The storm whirled outside like a bulldozer, which every once in a while pulls back a little, lifts its bucket, shakes it, revs its motor, makes a new run and comes dashing ahead with new strength. It was hard to tell day from night, but the first time I showed up from the place where I fumbled around in a directionless, silent darkness, I thought that it was night and I lay in Vibe Road in the beginning of the forties and a poster with a tender, protective mother and a little child, warning against diptheria and urging vaccination against the same, was hovering before my eyes. I had finally gotten this horrible sickness, and now there was a person bending over me with a knife to cut her way past the pus, through my neck under the larynx, so maybe I could breathe again. But I would rather be choked than cut, so I try to scream and toss my head wildly when a hand takes hold of my neck to position the steel better, but the nightmare fades and the smell of bouillon makes me understand that it wasn't a murderer but a rescuing angel who stood over me and I had a long forgotten feeling of returning, a flinging myself headlong into a boundless, unqualified tenderness.

Day by day the light became more distinct; the ability to distinguish the hours returned. It stopped snowing and the wind subsided. The icicles outside and the high-stacked snowpillows on the roofs made soft and transparent shadows, and when the water dropped from the ice in the strong March sunshine, there came a singing sound that reminded me of the pulsebeat's increasing strength and peace. As the days passed I tried gradually to think back, but the coincidence of my weakness and my reluctance to take up far too complicated problems yet, makes me just repeat obscurely our wandering from the fall of the first snowflake until we drowned in the storm's cutting, rushing tumult. I stopped at the point where I lost my shoe. I wouldn't walk any farther. I laughed in the dark and wanted to take up my hand and plather plather plather with my lips and send a greeting to my free girl friends, my hovering free girl friends in Danfoss Ventilators' central heated paradise. I wanted to sing my last aria and stick a cork into the hole where the rain and the snow came in and then I wanted to sleep, but the boy from the Knudsminde fresh air camp turned around and came back or forward or up or down, or whatever it was and shouted for me to shut up, and that made me so furious that so shortly after, that he so shortly . . . after what?-- could speak to me in that tone of voice, that crying I walked on, crawled scraped, slid, sobbed without thinking anything but that it was too much, everything was too much.

But here it's everyday and everyday is quiet as if we had lived here in Sleeping Beauty's time. It's no ordinary everyday, either for the Stürmer family or for us, of course, but because this life in isolation among strangers makes special demands and contains special possibilities, everyone tries to respect the silence, strives to make the everyday so everyday that occasionally it seems to me monumental. We're cut off from the surrounding world, and the border that is drawn around us is so soft and massive and subduing, so *definitive,* the change leaves its mark on us. Jørgen Schwer goes to and fro as if he were the prodigal son's substitute; the family Stürmer must be at least his grandparents' age, and the generation-aggressiveness that perhaps might have been expressed against people of a younger age and which he still shows toward me, is laid on the shelf with the Stürmers. Jørgen gets up at the same time as Peter, they go out to the stable together, and when it gets really light and I get up, the two men are sitting at the table, drinking coffee. After a week goes by, their sitting position at the table is the same: both of them have their elbows planted in front of them, hold their huge cups raised between their hands, blow on

192

the coffee with pointed lips, and drink in tiny swallows so as not to burn themselves.

I try to make myself useful, but Renate Stürmer senses, per instinct, something about me which I think she conceives of as "great lady." It's not a question of a master-slave relationship as in the East, here it's more an old bourgeois manifestation of snobbery or maybe an urge to protect the delicate that asserts itself. So far as I know, Heinz is their only son--no one's mentioned daughters, and there are no photographs of girls who could pass for Peter and Renate's children. Maybe I'm playing the role of the dreamed-of daughter and am such a new and wonderful gift that I must be spoiled at any cost. Most of the time I'm with her in the kitchen, where the stove doesn't seem to be able to glow enough to compensate for all the heat the family thinks I've lost and must now have back. But in the afternoon I go into my own room and try to read the family-weekly magazines that got through before the storm closed the approach roads. The stories often remind me of my own, but I get distracted anyway because nowhere can I find the grating *longing* in them and the sudden ambushing blackness I know from myself.

When the helicopter came the first time I didn't know what it was. Approaching airplanes aren't non-existent one moment and there the next. They announce themselves like oscillations, at first unconsciously, then consciously, without really waking recognition. They become a kind of echo chamber where at first there isn't anything with which to create echoes, but then the sound gets louder and the echo disappears, becomes a constant oscillation which is thickened to humming and as far as the helicopter is concerned, ends in a slobbering roar.

I sat up in bed when I heard the sound and fully realized we were being visited by a machine like the one that followed us

193

along the mountain. I went through the possibilities and saw a series of stupidities before me: Jørgen with gesticulating revolver in the courtyard, four shots to choose from, one for the helicopter, one for the pilot, one for the farm's cat and one for himself. I was tired of childish activity with fatal consequences, but on the other hand would rather not leave now, not be hauled away under a sheet in the blue cockchafer or sit up straight in a plastic dome and let myself be indicted politely but firmly. I wanted peace and ducked down under the blankets as I saw the shadow of the copter slide across the wall and a moment later the helicopter itself, a different smaller type than its predecessor on the Italian side of the border. There it was, out on the other side of the window, and I felt so protected by my new environment that I spoke aloud into the room: If you want something from me you can come and get me. During the ensuing slience my nervousness increased and I remembered my childhood appendicitis, They came and got me late in the evening and drove me to the hospital. Strange men and women undressed me and felt me. They asked questions and one of the doctors stuck his finger up my rear end. They talked with each other so I couldn't hear what was being said, and since I had no idea of what was to happen but surely knew what usually happened to appendicitis patients, I said--and I meant it to the bottom of the soul I had never heard about: Can't I get up and sleep? I'm so tired! Anna was operated on the same night.

Everything got quiet and no strange men came tramping into my rustic room. The sound of the helicopter's rotor began again and light snow whipped against my window, while the shadow glided in the opposite direction and disappeared. Not immediately, but half an hour later Fru Stürmer came in to me, and when I asked her who it was who'd visited us and what they wanted, she said:

--Nichts, Kind, der Peter hat's gut jemacht.

Two days later the helicopter came again, dissatisfied with the negative result, but the lookout functioned this time because Stürmer took us through the connecting shed into the barn, buried us in the hay and made it out the front door of the house before the copter got near enough to prepare to set down. That Renate also managed to get our bedclothes out of the way and the rest of my "habengut" in the stove before the men stepped into the room I knew only later when the old people fetched us and the bed in my room was flat and unsuspicious under a cross-striped fustian.

Before I begin to tell about my lover, I have to clear my throat a little and find a suitable vocal pitch even though I don't have any idea why it's necessary. There was the temptation to put on a dashing tone and shout a triumphant: Hi, girls, I've taken a new man to bed! But that would be odd, not because I feel anything particularly pathetic in that connection--it's just more intricate, complex, perhaps. The pathetic is easy enough to deal with, but for the most part it deals with *imagined* feelings. Pathos can be true enough, but the comic element that appears when it's described too unambiguously and too simply is nearly always unintentional and unmanageable. I can't act pathetic toward the little Mohammedan, who now promenades a big sore where the gun has chafed against his hipbone, which sticks out like an antique potsherd. But I can't laugh at him either. So I hang between the expressions, unable to choose.

He comes into the room evenings when the two grandparents have gone to bed. He steps in and stands a moment inside the door as if he were my valet who's just waiting for the madame's yes before he dares to come closer. But that isn't his attitude and that's not why he stands there like that. It's more a matter of he himself wanting to decide when he will show up instead of giving others the advantage of calling him. If ever anyone is going to feel impatience, it won't be him. He comes, anyway; he goes as far as the door, in it, but then no farther. When I had accustomed myself to the procedure, I no longer paid any attention to it, but one of the first evenings I turned around and looked questioningly at him, whereupon I discovered that he was sticking his tongue out at me.

You've come a long way, Anna, I say to myself in the morning, when everything is going as usual in the ice-castle, and I have to maintain this tone, not only to deaden the guilt feelings that lie behind the fence all along Vibe Road, eavesdropping on me, but also in order not to succumb to the ethical and emotional barrage which is on its way toward me in one incessant wave. I talk sense to Anna. I say, little Anna, you went home to be cured, but why spend money on an expensive doctor-man when you can solve your problems yourself? The argument isn't good enough. I didn't go home to be cured even though the words used were something to that effect. I wasn't sick. I've never been sick. But it was so wonderful to hear Tom talk. It was a fine morning under the banyan tree when he gave his lecture and understood all my problems at once and more, too; yes, he let himself simply get inspired with them; he waxed poetic, not confused like one speaking in tongues, but calmer and calmer, more and more experienced, tolerant, and intelligent. But I say this about him in a tone of voice that is like an accusation! I myself believe in my sickness, and I was thankful that it was so easy to talk to my husband about it. Probably I would have been disappointed and hurt if he hadn't understood me, but why circumstances brought me here and other places, I haven't understood. I wanted to be completely irresponsible and eat my own actions like earned candy, but I can't do that, either. Someplace or other the mature Anna speaks, but her voice is cracked, and the *responsibility* she speaks of is unreal. I listen like the horrid Meta to the good Meta. It takes a person's whole life and fills a person's whole life to give birth to, love, and bring up children. It's a responsibility that mustn't be taken lightly. If you were a dolt and a dummy you could excuse yourself by saying that you had allied yourself with a man and added two children to the world for fortuitous reasons. But you aren't a dummy, you're gifted, sensitive, brought up by a loving mother and a strict but fair father. You've attended a good school. You've taken an interest in many things of both a theoretical and practical nature. You've gone far down the road of knowledge to study the human body and life functions in general. There's nothing wrong with your social consciousness. It's possible that once in a while you go a little out of the way to utilize the advantages of your place and position, but that's forgivable for basically you feel and act morally in most situations. You're not interested in excesses, you have an excellent sense of humor and a good disposition. You want to kill your little daughter . . . Anna kicks the loudspeaker, but nothing more comes out of the apparatus. She hits the dial with her elbow, but that only results in making the light flicker. The sound of an idle electric humming fills the room.

He comes into the room and walks over to me now that he has let himself slip free with a matter-of-factness that makes me defenseless. None of my men has ever been like that. I don't think one of them came without reservation. It's either been gate crashers who slogged away in order to camouflage their insecurity or they have shown so much consideration that their consideration became oppressive and had more to do with themselves than with me. It's not like that with Tom, but the most noble confidence, the most perceptive Winnie-the-Pooh argot, the most obvious old boy's devotion can have its problems, too. Oh, Tom you are still there, you are still there, my friend, and when I think of you, it's not without pure pathos, and genuine tears of salt and water run down my cheeks. But when the obvious, insecure, bony, criminally innocent young man comes over to me, I feel something I never thought I would experience. And the first prize in the laundry soap contest goes to whoever can describe in a few words whatever it is.

I (Anna) hear this word *innocent* fired off and see it stick up like a cow parsnip in an oatfield. I hear the shouts from the great amphitheater, innocent? innocent? who innocent? This unwashed bandit, this has-been longhaired *hippy,* this tough, this dope shark and dealer, this coldblooded *murderer?* He who in cold blood shoots down a policeman, kills a potential father and lover, seduces another man's wife, lies, sneers and sticks out his tongue, he *innocent?*

Don't know what I should say, but try to describe *me,* what's happening, what I feel. He comes in and suddenly demands are made on me. It isn't just me who furnished the expected goods. Here comes a hungry carnivorous cat in the door, wanting food. But he doesn't just want to devour and gorge, he also pelts me with the most grudging enthusiasm and awkward ecstasy in the world. He makes love to me and sticks out his tongue at the same time. He looks at my breasts and wants to eat them and kiss them and drink from them and spit them out all at once. Come on, then, with this talk of ethics, and I say that he is a furious, giving, loving, hating, adoring and disdaining cannonball who burns these impoverished ideas away in the space around me, in me, everywhere.

We talk together in a different, perhaps a little different way than before. But there aren't many subjects. We can hardly talk about what has happened, and we can't talk at all about what will happen. Anyway, I don't dare say that there was anything amusing

198

or bizzare in the way . . . yes, I don't know myself . . . how should I say it: we met each other. He wants to know what Anastasia and Roberto were up to with me, but what should I say to that? I hardly know myself. Counter-thrust by asking him how he could know something wrong was in the wind, but then he becomes sulky, and I begin to wonder whether he hadn't been nearby all the time, whether he had peeked through the keyhole and followed us and had sprung aside at the last second when Roberto came and went.

We lie in bed together in my room. He always comes to me-- I've never seen his room. I can't say whether he's protecting me again or feels more seductive when he visits me. I think the first. We've turned off the light, and he breathes as if he were already asleep. I think about considerate and technically perfect lovers; I think about grown men and my clothes, which long ago have blazed up and disappeared through Renate's chimney, or in the case of the Roman ones are worn by Anastasia Caduti while she trims her husband's gerfalcons or curls his monkey. I think about the frequency of orgasm and vaginal stimuli and begin to laugh so much that probably it is the shaking of my body that wakes the glowing fresh air kid. He says in the dark:

--I read a poem.

The laughter disappears and I listen. Why is it strange that he says it?

--Yes?

--I couldn't understand what it was all about. It was something about someone or other who went to visit his father at the hospital.

There is a silence between us.

--Do you know it?

I shake my head, answering simultaneously:

--No.

--I thought maybe you might know it.

--Tell me a little more about it.

--Well, I don't know. It was something about a father who was sick and his eyes or one eye lay down at the foot of the bed and there was something in his brain that shouldn't be there. And he had a big foot, too.

--A foot?

--Yes. It was the foot, I think, that had the eye in it.

He turns and lies with his face toward the ceiling.

--I didn't understand it. I don't know why I read it, either. It was just by chance. It was pretty good. It was about his father.

He says nothing more. I don't know what to say, either. I haven't read poetry for many years. There is something about the silence that is different. I think about what it is that has changed until it occus to me that the sound I hear outside is the rain streaming down over the roof and the window.

13

There's no doubt that we look a little more proper now. The uniform is more suitable for our form of travel. Jørgen's hair has grown, if not to its former hippie-splendor, then to a length that makes him suitably road-slovenly. My hair has gotten long in three weeks, too. I feel younger; I'm a kind of mermaid in my much too large clothes-basin. I've become longhaired, and the tips that used to sit on my cheeks are gone and instead my hair falls freely down over my back and turns every time I move my head to see where we are now, where he is now.

When the snow disappeared, we had to go too. Even though we easily could have spent the rest of our days there. And no one said anything, either--it was just natural, like a change in the weather that had to come. We strode down the lea hand in hand through the mud at the side of the road, and when I stopped and turned to wave, he gripped my hand tightly and wouldn't let me do it, as if he felt that if he let me I would either go back or turn to salt. And I didn't need to turn around because I knew how they would look, Peter and Renate Stürmer, two peaceful old birds who followed us with half-closed eyes until we became blurred in their sight. When we had half disappeared, they would go back, he to his work, she to hers, and when some time had passed, maybe a week, maybe a month, Peter Stürmer would begin to talk about us, and at last we would become just as alive, near and distant as the dancing peasants and musicians hanging on the wall over Peter's place at the table in the kitchen.

We could have stayed. Practically, we couldn't, of course, but that strangeness which wasn't very apparent among us from the beginning gradually disappeared entirely. At the last, Renate no longer treated me as if she were Putzfrau and I Frau. Her motherliness became more democratic, she began to make use of me, and I went around like the good daughter and did the jobs I was given. We could have stayed there as the young couple on the farm, but would Heinz have put up with it when he came home after the snow? Or would Jørgen be forced to use yet another of his heavy bullets on the man who was the rightful heir to the place? Perhaps we could have found a way. Perhaps we could have stood next to the old couple when the son arrived and have greeted him and said that we were distant relatives who had come to help make the farm better, to expand it. We could have said a lot of things and maybe Heinz is an enterprising young man who could see the advantage of having us there, too. But we didn't get that far.

When the thaw set in, we had to prepare ourselves for the fact that it was over. As soon as the road was passable, *someone* would come--no doubt about it--even though the helicopter had been there twice in vain. With the melting snow the conditions for our presence and the half unreal foundation that had made it a fairy tale flowed down the mountain. We hadn't talked about anything with our hosts, i.e., we had talked a lot, but never about who we were and where we came from. All the terrible circumstances surrounding our appearance could be used for re-telling, for embroidery and fantastification, but all the while there was a so-far and no-further. The two Stürmers didn't need to tell anything about themselves--everything was crystal clear on the walls, in their food, in their way of walking and talking or not talking to each other, but they would never have dreamed of talking about themselves, either. They would have considered it a violation of common modesty. Perhaps that's the difference between civilized and uncivilized people, that a machine product, an urban jellyfish

202

like me can uninhibitedly blabber away about me and mine whereas neither Jørgen Schwer nor Peter nor Renate are capable of saying as much as a word, giving so much as a hint--verbally--of where they come from and how. The question is, then, which of us is civilized.

It's the kind of situation one would call untenable. But that doesn't keep me from thinking that the stay at Stürmer's farm is one of the most tenable things I've experienced. I could easily have stayed there. I could have kept getting up--after my long curved sleep, where I felt not like a stone but like something living inside a warm stone--and gone down into the kitchen every day to see the circling shadows of rings on the wall above the stove where Renate snatched them off with her hook and stoked the logs so that the sparks leaped and forced her head back, forced her to blow in self-defense and lift her hands to protect her hair from the embers. I could have continued all the peaceful morning following her from point to point in the year's rituals, baking, washing, preparing meals, milking. I could have slept again the two hours in the afternoon when everything became calm and only the sound of the animals and the weather and the fire penetrated softly into my room. I could have sat evening after evening and have noticed the story of myself and my friend get larger and larger, more and more unreal, farther and farther from ourselves until perhaps I could tell it myself and forget completely that it was about me. But most of all I could have stayed in my room at night and heard the wild person's snarling shift to peaceful breathing in his sleep. But I'm not certain that the lynx would have stayed there for my provisional time and forever. When the rain set in that night, he woke later and got up. He crept over me, and when he heard the weather--maybe that's what it was that woke him--he stood by the window and bent forward to look out. I was a little cold under the blankets, but the cold didn't seem to touch him even though he was naked. He could scarcely be distinguished in the dark, but the light that was in his skin made the outline of his body smoulder. He went down on his knees a little--a sprinter's movement before he crouches forward and gets into the starting holes. A little later he got up and went over into the corner where his clothes lay on a chair. I heard the sound of his matches in his pants pocket when he picked them up and shortly after a snap and an elastic click of metal against metal. He was cold when he lay down beside me, and I said to myself like when I was a child: Dear Lord, let the rain turn to snow, let the rain turn to snow again, let everything be white and smooth in the morning, dear Lord, let everything be wise and good and white and smooth so that we won't do anything except what we have done to now, so that we won't be forced to stupidities, so that we won't be forced to make decisions and changes, dear Lord, let it still be skating weather tomorrow, don't let my snowman melt, don't let the rains come, let it always be winter and clean and cold.

Have tried to ponder beyond all reason my relationship to the boy, but don't understand much. Maybe one's own mechanism, when you've forced it over a certain point, forces you not only to accept the one you've chosen, but also to lose yourself in him and under him. I called him lynx, but he's not a lynx--he's a rabbit, perhaps a wild rabbit or a hare, but no carnivore. I call him carnivore and really speak more about myself. For I've gotten my freedom for the first time in Sleeping Beauty's castle, and I don't understand anything but this: his charged person, his lack of proportion in his relationship with me and our chance confinement makes me free of guilt. In the goat pen, behind the snow wall I've experienced a freedom I didn't know existed. The primitivism, which I know can never be mine, was on loan--that is simply all too clear--but one has heard of vacationing children

204

who were happy on their farms and got a keepsake that--as the saying goes--was for life. I have, with contempt for my confinement on a different level and with adult delight and satisfaction, stuck my hand under the damask and found Tom at the table, but when *this* blind masculine being boiling with contempt and gasping with longing thrusts his branch against me, there opens a feeling that has to do with lost land, unlived life, painfully repressed dreams. And the flight, the heavenward flight I couldn't do alone or better: the dream I couldn't dream, we dream together, running, rising, spreading, enlarging, and gathering, light-tracks across a black arch, darkness and sleep.

The perseverance of the police probably declines with the newsworthiness of the case. As long as one is *hot potatoes* in the press, the police are also on their toes. It's a matter of prestige, and is also felt as a kind of compliment by the pursued. As long as one is alive and moving, he's worth pursuing--disappeared, the pursuer quickly loses interest just like the cat that's bored with a dead mouse. But at the same time the monstrousness of the judicial system is shown. There's no time for the intermediate phases--no one interests himself in the period from when the tracks disappear until the fugitive's bones stick out of the melting snow. There's no glamour for the police in natural tragedies. A murder is good because it contains drama, possibility of detection, disclosure, imprisonment and judgement; there's also something attractive about demonstrations where the ordinary policeman, in the same way as the soldier, can get the opportunity to do something with his education: hit, kick, grapple, and subdue. But with fugitives who won't let themselves be caught--that's not much. They don't give any prestige, more the opposite, and if results fail to materialize, it's best to forget the prey as soon as possible. Perishing in frost and cold is indeed only just, and at home, certainly, waits neither father nor mother, but conviction and punishment.

We have travelled through Switzerland as if we were honeymooners, penniless tourists who have been south in the early spring and now have to go home to the university or to the office or day-care center to scrape a few pennies together for the summer vacation. The first few days we travelled mostly by night, but after passing Lausanne in bright day without so much as a fly blinking one of his three million eyelids, we've used the days, too. Yes, in fact, just one day, because we got a lift all the way from Bern to Basel on E4 and then went eastward along the Rhine. We stayed some distance from the river and the border so as not to run into the arms of too many guards, but at some point we had to choose, and I don't know whether it was so beautiful that we chose just this place, but suddenly it occurred to me that spring was in wild gallop, early April, there was gorse up and down the slopes like yellow sparklers. We had wintered on the mountain, but the weather had gone around us from the Italian, and that morning when we chose to take a left turn, it occurred to me. We lay in the grass behind a blackthorn hedge and waited for the day to pass, and I teased him because he still wouldn't really tell me anything about himself. Now that I feel that he belongs to me, I have to have the intellectual (neurotic?) need satisfied too. He has bought four Pepsi-colas for us, and I'm surprised again at his childlikeness. Tom would have bought beer, but there we lay with our sweet colas, and I thought about his age and about my age and about the machine at home which produces youth on an assembly belt, youth, who have enough in themselves, youth, who don't have time or talent to ask what it really means to be young now, but are satisfied with the noisy propaganda for this excellence: to be young. I would like to say to Jørgen Schwer: Now listen here

206

old (young) boy, I'm the kind of person who wants to know something. I've driven my husband up the wall by plaguing him with questions about what he felt, why he felt that way and how it felt to feel that way. I have difficulty seeing how things tick, how I myself tick, if I don't see how others do--perhaps it's just that faculty or characteristic that forms the basis for my illness. Everything has to be clear to me, and then when it is--black or white--it seems I can't control it or that it grows unclear anyway. I haven't told you about Minna--yes, maybe I've said a little--but the catastrophe in that situation is simple enough. Certain values in my existence are devalued, but Minna I have decided (or something in me decided) shall be valued highly. Therefore she's the most endangered, too, and my *understanding* doesn't help a bit. I can't live with her for then she must die; I can't live without her for then I must die.

All this I didn't say. But I turned in the grass and pulled off my sweater and unbuttoned my shirt. My brassiere, if it had been sold by Mr. Meyer himself, would have brought in a good many lire. It's--aside from my panties--the most expensive clothing I own now. Perhaps it can entice the slum-snail to talk. A bra from Real has been known to loosen a proletarian tongue before. I turned in the sunlight, let my legs shift, rested on my elbow, pushed the hair away from my forehead and said to him:

--Where were you born?

He sticks his finger down in the cola bottle and lets it pop out.

--In Copenhagen.

--Yes, I know, but where in Copenhagen?

--In Hvidovre.

I think: Hvidovre, Hvidovre, Hvidovre--one can't be born there. That district has only become inhabitable--if it's inhabitable at all--in the last five years.

207

--And then what?

--What do you mean "and then what"?

Well, then what afterwards? Where did you go to school? When did you graduate? What did you want to be?

--Be?

--Yes, be. What did you want to be?

--Christ, I don't know.

--Well, but at some point or other you must have wanted to be something, something or other. When you were a boy, didn't you want to be something when you were a boy?

--Yes.

--But what was it, and why didn't you become it?

His glance moves from my legs up over my navel to the brassiere. It stays there.

--I didn't want to go to school.

--You're not answering my question! Tell me what it was you wanted to be when you were a boy. Tell me.

--Why do you want to know?

--Because I want to know something or other.

--What's the difference, anyway?

He looks at the stretch between my breasts and navel. I sit up and face him.

--Then I can tell you, too, what I wanted to be. I wanted to be something, too! I did!

--You are, too, he says.

--I'm from Vibe Road, Anna says.

He looks at me. He can hear from my tone of voice that it's information which in some way or other should make us equal or intimate, but he can't differentiate among the values, can't decide if I'm being condescending or straight.

Where's that, he asks.

And I straddle him and hammer with clenched fists down at his chest which sounds and feels like an empty orange crate.

--Nørrebro, I shout, Nørrebro, Nørrebro. Tell me now what you wanted to be! Tell me! Tell me!

He catches my arms and holds me tightly. My hair is so long that it touches his face. I sit across his crotch and my thighs are on both sides of his body. The revolver scrapes against his hip and cuts into my leg.

--Put that away, I say.

He lets go of my left arm and reaches down for the weapon. He lays the gun next to him in the grass. It's like a much too big blackblue beetle that can't get down any hole and so has tipped itself on its side, helpless. His hand comes back between my hip and thigh. He releases my other hand and I bend farther forward, and while his rod pitches forward up into me he says:

--I didn't want to be anything, I didn't want to be anything, I didn't want to be anything, I wanted to have someone like you.

We slept in the grass and when the sun began to leave the sky I got dressed and unrolled the extra sweater for night. We were on the other side of Schaffhausen, probably halfway to Konstanz and figured that if we headed straight down we would have to hit the lakes, one of the smaller ones leading up to Bodensee. We held hands, but when I realized that I was walking slower than Jørgen, I let go and followed him in the dark. His steps could be heard all the while, and when a car came, we automatically stepped to the side and stood among the trees. I remembered a trip with the girls a hundred years ago where with sudden recklessness we decided we wanted to go to the beach in the middle of the night and walked and walked through hedges and woods with a bicycle lamp about as big as a pilot light. There was the same mixed feeling of great security and an unease which stemmed from the dark and the faint light, but also from the thought of everything that lay in the future, the possibilities, the victories, the catastrophes, the defeats, the tragedy. The hike itself was something complete, already concluded when it was decided, but inspired, anyway. It belonged in advance to the established memories, yes, was already memorable as it unfolded. It became spacious with the feelings it washed up. Each person in the dark had a chance to think and dream his own dream, but the unease, the nervousness, the time, the shared excitement, security, age made the joint omen great and awe-inspiring. Mr. Pan was present, but there was the cycle-light, too--all nature rumbled at the shoreline and the sea rose white, but Ursala had to pee, and that was also arranged. We wandered home hand in hand, not saying very much, but when we found the summer cottage, I went out into the kitchen to the schnapps bottle and took a slug before I crept down into the sleeping bag next to the others. They breathed in different rhythms but all calmly. Before my own breathing blended with theirs, I heard a bird scream outside in a tree. I thought: it's good to go for a walk in the woods at night, but it's good to come home and lie down and sleep, too.

In the darkness above Bodensee I felt the same mixture of indefinability and fate, giggles and solemnity. But I was both secure and uneasy, and I thought about the future.

When the Jews and the resistance fighters fled across the sound during the war, the crossing seemed to be unbelievably hazardous. That was before we moved from Gemmas Allé to Vibe Road, and when we walked along the beach in Amager I often thought about "the other side" and those who sneaked on board boats in the dark and sailed across. I got goose pimples at the thought of the dark nights, the cold, the terror, the strange shapes, the sounds, all those Germans who were everywhere. It was inconceivable that it should happen when you thought about everything that was done to prevent it. And it wasn't only a matter of two or three people, my father said, there were hundreds, yes, thousands, some every day, perhaps right now, where we could see two speedboats with the black-white swallowtailed flag and swastika patrol between Røsen and Middlegrunden. I knew I would never dare, if it were me, and I knew it would never go well. But now here I am with two countries behind me, two borders, more, and everything has gone well. It's been close a few times, but usually when we've been most cautious. Is there a lesson in that-- that you should just plod off with all your might and main through life, reckless in regard to yourself and others so the borders are rubbed out, the guards disappear, the police rush to forget, the soldiers bury their bayonets in the earth and turn their weapons around?

We reached the lake where it narrows and becomes the Rhine, and since there were no people in sight at the boat pier that was closest, we went out on it and untied a pair of lines and pushed free. The lights were distinct on the other side of the water, and since the other side of the water could be nothing but Germany, it was just a matter of steering. If we had come out on the river a little farther west, we would probably have landed in Switzerland again and have yet another border to cross, or at least have had the false sense of having crossed, but now we just let ourselves drift with the current and Jørgen used the boat's rudder to keep us partly at a slant and going in the right direction. Six - eight kilometers down the river we crossed the middle, and about the same distance farther down we had to give up coming closer to land. The crossing was more hazardous than I can imagine any flight across the sound 1944 to be--without oars, without poles, without sails--and when we were only a hundred meters from the bank and the current very weak, we gave up coming closer. I was

211

glad that my purse lay somewhere on the slopes of the Matterhorn so that I didn't have to have it in my mouth on the swim in. Twice I went under with the same feeling as when the snow overtook us, twice I came up again in the hands of the fresh air kid and his forearm's sinews of piano wire. When at last we had firm bottom under our feet--or whatever you call Rhinesludge--I was still glad that my purse was gone with my driver's license, my contraceptives, and the rest. I kept falling and put out my hands and hawked and spit and could only concentrate on one thing-- getting out of this hateful, ice-cold element, and getting a chance to lie down no matter where, whether it was a hard cell cot or in a doghouse.

We slept like the foetus back home on the shelf, which at certain angles and in a particular light with all its wrinkles can look like two people pasted together. Against all reason we crawled on board a barge on the outer side of two others, and when we got below, and in the dark staggered forward to something that seemed like sackcloth or bagging, shaking we helped each other off with our clothes and rubbed and rubbed with the rough cloth until I moaned because the warmth came and my bad fingers bled and I had a feeling that the dark and the smell and the faint sound of the river against the ship's sides were all made of blood and iron. I had the kind of pain all through my body that you have in your throat after an unreasonably long and strenuous race and I coughed and didn't know whether I had lost my sex, whether I was man or woman--there was only the feeling of pain and abandonment and defeat. But with the warmth came drowsiness, too. We buried ourselves in the damp sacks and I only woke when I heard his laughter and opened my eyes and saw him sitting beside me with his hands on his thighs while he laughed and laughed in a way I'd never heard him laugh before. I covered myself as well as I could because I felt that it was me and my nakedness he was laughing at or thought that it was a last, definitive, gruesome joke which now proved we were both crazy. But then I got a look at him and realized what it was that made him laugh. The sacks we had rubbed each other with in the night and later slept under and on, were coal sacks. He looked like the stupid Black in an American comedy from the thirties--his eyeballs shone, his teeth flashed, and I couldn't keep from laughing because he laughed and I had the feeling that I myself must look like a cross between Aunt Jemima and Dorothy Lamour on the road to Morocco. The laughter rang in the empty barge, but stopped suddenly because somebody stuck his head down the hatch we had crawled through the night before, and as if our laughter hadn't been proof enough of our crazy appearance, the head let out a scream and disappeared. I don't know whether German river people are especially afraid of blacks or Albino-Blacks--which we perhaps resembled more--anyway, it was our chance since they stood paralyzed with their hands up to their mouths when we came out of the hole with our clothes in our arms and ran naked and coal-black (in spots, anyway) across the two boats, into land, crossed the road and disappeared among the trees.

Since then the trip has been nearly luxurious, and at the present point it's reached heights we hadn't dreamed of when we stood in the river mud. We've become members of a club. We've made new friends. We aren't travelling a definite route, but we've been guaranteed that we'll get to the north. At some point. Sometime. At some point we'll reach Frankfort, that's for sure. For that's where most of the club members are from. But it's necessary to begin in Stuttgart, for that's where the initiation ceremony took place. At this moment the vice-president sits--or more correctly-- the vice-president lies in my lap. He is heavy and dignified and fairly dead drunk. And he's an American like the other three gentlemen, members Jake, Hank, and Flip. Member Gus is the gentlemen in my lap. We passed Meersburg, Ravensburg, Biberach, Ulm and came out on the Autobahn Winthertur-Stuttgart around Tübingen. In Ulm we bought new clothes in an Army Surplus store and maybe it was all this khaki and grasshopper-green fatigues that has inspired our friends. The trip came to a halt when darkness fell and we wandered down a narrow sideroad until we came to a lopsided little gas station at a big crossroads. It shone in the dark and was so anonymous and distant that Jørgen insisted on having his cola there. I stood looking at the map on the wall when the club came in. Through the window between the flyspecked centerpiece of oil cans I could see a Mercedes convertible of elder vintage, enormous, with the top down, in front of the gas tank. The three men, G.I.'s, crewcut but not in uniform, sat down by the gas attendant's desk, moving their heads back and forth. As if they'd gotten too much air in the open car or couldn't catch their breath. One of them belched. Jørgen watched them but looked away when all three of them began to stare at me. They kept on staring a while, then shook their heads again and tried to catch their breath. They talked to each other.

--Where's Gus?

--Backseat.

--In the backseat?

--Yeah.

--He's stewed.

--Oh, Christ I need a drink.

--Take a coke.

--Fuck.

The last word brought their attention back to me, as if it were a command and not an exclamation. Their faces looked guilty.

214

One of them got up. I took the chance, the sudden advantage. I stepped over to them and asked if they were going farther and where. Yes, they were going on, but they didn't know exactly where. Whether they were going north? Yeah. Whether maybe they were going to Frankfort? Yes, they were. At some point. But now it was the weekend, Ma'am, and they were out on pass, and ohdohohdohoh . . .

I'm not sure what Jørgen thinks about my initiative. He hasn't said anything, just sits there jammed between the two men in the front seat while I have buddy Gus lying across me and Hank pressing in from the other side. I'd forgotten how cold it is to ride in the back seat of an open car in April, but now I've learned it again, as well as that the human warmth from another body can feel protecting even if it comes from a very drunk and heavy person I don't know.

Up to now we've been in three places, and I've uninhibitedly utilized the clubmembers' offer of Schinkenbrot and ein grosses Helles and Doorkaat Schnapps while Jørgen has held back even though we haven't had a decent meal since Switzerland, and have only a few wet banknotes left of those that fell out of my purse when it plopped down toward Grossglockner, or wherever it was. I'm a little bit tipsy because I've had a cognac, too, and I'll probably get more because the soldiers have figured out how much English I can understand, and can't do enough to compensate for their *faux pas*. They are very young and very drunk and very American.

Admission to what they call RFS (Reverse First Society) occurs at every stop along the way. The big Mercedes, you see, can be started in only two ways: with a crank and then by driving a way in reverse. I've helped them push and am therefore accepted as a member. It's a little more uncertain in Jørgen's case. He's worked

215

with the crank all right but he hasn't yet succeeded in starting the motor. I really don't know. The thing that's charmed me most about the group up to now is the soldiers' completely awkward and exaggerated *politeness*. They have changed their tone of voice --they belch, to be sure, once in a while and Gus breathes against my thigh, but it's not anything, certainly, that I'd want to tell the girls about. When Anna was on a trip through the woods with four Yankees in an open car in the middle of the night. The time Anna invited herself on a trip through the woods in a big Mercedes Benz from before the war and sat in Raststätte in the quicksilver light and played the juke-box and drank Weinbrand. But at the next spot I'll have coffee.

I've been afraid a .number of times because the brakes on the car are mechanical and pull unevenly and because there's no doubt that no matter who drives, the driver is drunk. The cold and the countless beers make the club members' bladders sensitive, and we frequently drive onto the shoulder so they can relieve themselves. We're on the Autobahn now, and I figure that they're driving north and will keep on doing so. Maybe that's why they want to relieve themselves, prepare for a long hike in the cold without a heater, without a top--although it isn't down; it simply isn't there. We turn off to the right and drive down a narrow road in among the trees. Flip says to Jake that he shouldn't turn the motor off. Remember, he says. It's impossible to get it started. Not backwards. In the dark.

The car stops and Flip gets out while Jake sits there. Hank pushes himself free of Gus and steps out. Flip goes over to my door and opens it. I look at him but he doesn't say anything. I smile at him because I don't need to pee. I'm a woman. I have a larger bladder. And I'm warm because I have Gus for a quilt. I see Jørgen's neck at the same time Jake turns off the lights. It's quiet after the wind pressure from the road has disappeared. Gus is very heavy. His head and shoulder fall heavily against the leather seat when I'm pulled out the side door. I don't scream for one of them already has his hand over my mouth. The car's motor is still running in the dark. My clothes aren't easy to get off because I'm wearing long pants. The clothes are new and sturdy, but the men tear at them and at last rip the slacks in the fly and I feel how my limbs come out of my pants legs as out of a case. I bend my legs, pull them together, roll away and bite, but it's difficult to get ahold of anything but the hand which tastes of lighter fluid and disappears at every bite and comes again and closes my mouth and a new hand comes and grips me around the neck so that the light grows violet and radiant behind my eyelids and then I lie down and one of them tries to sit on my breast while he leans his full weight against my face.

It's only when you're dressed over your upper body that you're really naked. I feel my terrible vulnerability and finally manage to scream something or other, some name or other, some word or other: Tom, Minna, Jørgen! The scream is repeated, or anyway a new noise breaks out another place to the side, farther out in the dark, and when a strange flesh presses against mine and my legs are forced to each side, I perceive that the cataclysm is above me too, has come closer, come here. I twist onto my side and am struck brutally in the face by something that can't be hand but must be made of iron. With the free hand I get ahold of the revolver and lift it against him lying over me, creeping into me. The muzzle must be against the body for when I fire and sense the cordite and the explosion's pressure against my face there is immediately a smell of burnt flesh.

14

In Germany nothing ever changes. I thought the same thing when I came to Lübeck with the girls right after the war. Maybe it was a question of economics, but it couldn't have been that alone. As soon as we saw the customs officials in their green uniforms and caps with the tipped-back high crowns, as soon as we saw the boots, black, and the lesser officials with their thick, ugly military ski hats, we said: Yes, it's the same all right, nothing has changed, everything goes on as before. Naturally it was unthinkable that a broken nation would be able to supply its uniformed public servants with clothes which differed entirely from those of the Third Reich--where would the money and material come from--yet there was something more to it, a kind of ineradicable symbolism that was probably produced by our own idiosyncrasies and victorious sentimentality but was also tied to an ineradicable revengeful symbolism among the conquered. We were quick to cram the feelings into our pockets, and I have done it since, each time I've come to Germany. I've done it faced with the appearance of Germans and their language, I've done it every time other places in the world have demonstrated their incorrigibility, and I remember how many knocks a journalist took when he gave a derogatory opinion about the German's vulgar ability to *occupy* southern Europe; with their quick and massive money in complete democratic legality to straddle memorials and restaurants and metamorphose every alegria to Knödelsuppe. For the whole century it's been considered good manners to consider Americans and later Swedes as intrusive, rich, and swaggering, spoiled, demanding, and childish. That's not the case with the Germans.

They're protected in a special way. The crimes of the past have put them in a class by themselves where atrocities can scarcely be noted and in any case not criticized. So it's a question of simplification and discrimination. The German's are no different than other people. They are no different than, for example, the Danes. Negroes are no different than Norwegians, either. Maybe they have another color skin, but their different background, conditions, environment, historical fate, etc., don't make them different. We live in a grand epoch of equalization, and that isn't peculiar when you know what has happened to people and races during the last decades because some determined *by law* that they should be different and inferior. The Germans are in a strong position there. Their atrocities were so great that you think they themselves must have lived through a kind of purification. Their lesson has been so hard that we, to camouflage guilt feelings in connection with the crimes we have in our righteous revenge committed against them, create a kind of immunity around them--every time we want to protest some dangerous tendency like, for example, the New Naziism, we're quick to say: No, that can't be right. It's a dream-- it's like a nightmare, maybe, but it certainly doesn't have anything to do with the *Germans*. The nation has gotten smarter, the boys have learned their lesson, and the extremists are, as with us, *extremists,* people on the lunatic right whom you can't consider and let us finally clean up our own back yard before we begin on others. It's possible that the Germans have suffered from guilt feelings over the bygone time, but these feelings are nothing compared with those which the more or less active killers of Naziism have about the Germans.

What is it I (Anna) want to say with all this? Does she want us to stick out our tongue every time we come to Germany from now on? Does she want us to nail down with seven carpenter's nails that the Germans are vulgar, swaggering, trigger happy, incorrigible, and insufferable, every last one of them? No, but she remembers. At this moment she remembers so much and so simultaneously she wants to say something that is true, not about others, but about herself. She can't and won't judge, but feels a right to talk about her own feelings, tell about something that's happened, has taken place, is concrete, even if it's history. Her situation is double like most people's. She has her head and her feelings, though she's not always able to tell which is deciding what and when. But back then, she says, let's try to hold tightly to *back then*, now that everything is shifting even more than before.

It was the same time of year we came to Germany. Late in April. We crossed the border at Krusaa; we had gray passports, which had lain in the British military mission for a long time, but were now supplied with visas, large blue stamps, oblong columns with the signature and sanction of officers. We travelled from the North, and we were victors. I don't think we conceived of ourselves as victors. Rysensteeners didn't move in that kind of circle, but still we were different. For five years Europe and Germany had lain down under us on the map like an odd, inconceivable lump. We were too little--and my family was too poor--to have travelled before the war. Now the border opened, even if it had to be coaxed a little, and we were on our way to Lübeck to bow down before the city's great democratic son, a freedom fighter related to our cotton-coat-clad cousins and uncles. We were uncertain, to put it mildly-- our legality and superiority were encumbered with so many but's and hm's and stamps and ornaments that we almost felt illegal. It was less than two years previous that we had seen the columns of defeated, hungry, louse-ridden, ass-dragging soldiers marching south, and now we were going--already!--down to them. Maybe they stood there waiting for us, maybe they stretched steel wire

220

across the road at the height of our heads, which would fly off in a gurgling twitch when the bus passed. We stopped in Flensborg after having driven through the razed woods north of the city, and when I was given a soda bought in a ZOB bus station, I didn't dare drink it. How could a punished, cowed, beaten, downtrodden, guilty nation produce soda that wasn't poisonous? Mustn't their simplest products for many years have been made of pressed rats, rotten kohlrabi and vulcanized ersatz coffee? I went around behind a shed and dumped the sugared water down through a grating.

There was no one who took revenge, no grinning werewolf with a knife between his teeth and old stick grenades tied to the pull- and release- chains on the public toilets--everywhere there was first and foremost a natural blend of servility and insulting matter-of-factness. The Grössel family pumped coffee into me and the customs officials looked like standartenführer; the Grössel family felt their way in bristling Danish, but everyone else spoke that language which for so many years now has seemed gall-like and puke-producing. When on the way home, we stood at Sankelmärk in the high sun and blue air and intoned "The Easter bells were gently chiming," while the larks tried to drown us out, it was with a numbing feeling of uncertainty. Everything seemed provisional and at the same time determined. History itself sloshed like a bubbling sea of true and untrue around us, fixed and flowing. We yelled away with trembling hearts and an unredeemed knowledge of all the ideas, all the values we now paid homage to as established for time and eternity were annulled in even our absurd presence. I don't know which miracles or crimes we awaited, but when we drove home across the border, the uncertainty hadn't vanished, on the contrary. It was good, of course, to come where they said "a" for "I" and the post boxes were red, but the meeting with the open Europe and the first country after our own border had not provided any redemption. The bus stopped under the sighing elm trees after the border station (do you remember, girls?) and the last ones customed and visaed came running, laughed, and found their seats. The bus started off, we were home, had crossed a border. I think it's true when I say that I can remember what I thought: What are you fleeing? Where are you fleeing to? What are you fleeing from?

Everything was not so clearly defined and stated, naturally. I just had a feeling. I had crossed a border and expected that the action, the movement itself, would give me clarity or certainty. No, I didn't expect that--just that I would be different, *changed*. Was the same, was the same in my freezing uncertainty and historical indeterminism, yes, God knows, in my immaturity, and I knew that my whole life I would travel back and forth across borders.

All this comes streaming now through the crack between the lid of an empty potato pit and the half-rotted casing around it. It comes running on the sunbeams and down the larksong through my eyes and ears, and in my nose it's all there, too, for the smell is the same as back then. I bear the lid to the pit on my head while I very carefully peek out into the morning and feel an excitement in my heart which would be recognized by those who have stood facing a goal or are so close to getting their wishes fulfilled that it's almost already happened. I don't know where I get my surplus from now, a bizarre Anna-surplus which makes me want to boast, to sing, to twitch my rear end, to dance, to buy a drink, to be rich, to toss off literary allusions. I don't want to close the lid now, but to open it up even more to my wizened flat, fruitful Nolde-landscape of sprouting sunflowers and women in yellow, but that won't do because the world is full of fierce dogs with long sniffing noses and behind me among the potatoes sleeps Mr. Jørgen Schwer, who's told me that we have to wait for nightfall as usual before going on and even if neither of us knows where we're going and why exactly there where we have to, we just keep on going, going, going, and I begin to understand him. People without a country can't live, people with a country have a duty to return home. Fifty kilometers to the north is my country--it's there I have to go.

My mood isn't in harmony with the situation, and it hasn't been all the while. I don't know how prisoners on death row feel, but I can imagine that under the impact of their sentence, the definitive, they must feel something similar once in a while. We neurotics fumble between two views when we are farthest out: total blackness, or a liberating excitement about letting things go. If you want to manage the days, you should just imagine you're doing the thing that helps. It's a balancing act on the edge of a knife, but that's the way we'd rather have it, wouldn't we, girls?

I shut the lid, and it's black in our pit except for a few streaks of light coming through the cracks and holes. We've both lost weight. I don't know whether it's that or just the fatigue which once in a while makes me nauseous (I've thrown up three times in three days) but it's fun to lose weight without a weight chart, something triumphant in getting thin without counting calories. We have no problem with mayonnaisse and cream éclairs, even the cokes are a thing of the past--socially we are reduced to a sub-sistence level. Maybe that's how things should rightfully be when you run away from your responsibilities.

I know I'm back into my half-jargon and go round in circles. So then speak breast and legs:

Twice I pulled the trigger in the dark according to the primal prescription for thoroughness and double assurance, and twice I thought my wrist snapped. Twice I pumped my terror and contempt into a swaying, hard and soft shape in the dark, and when the cordite and the smell of sweaty roast pork hit my face, I cried and threw up through the corner of my mouth. The violent movements around me ebbed out and I felt the cold again, the draft around my legs and my nakedness. Got my foot free and found the torn trousers while someone ran away and the leaves rustled in the low trees and bushes. Jørgen's knee hit me on the shoulder when he came over looking for me and I said Here! Here! and stretched up my arms. He helped me to my feet and turned his face away in the dark because some of the vomit was still lying on my shoulder. I bent down and pulled off a tuft of grass and cleaned myself. Then he asked where the revolver was and I handed it to him. We went over to the car, its motor still running in the dark. My underclothes and one side of my khaki shirt were drenched, but there wasn't time to do anything about it, and I bent completely into the lee of the windshield when he put the car into gear and drove out onto the road. The headlights seemed shameless and revealing, but we couldn't drive without them, not fast, anyway. We entered the Autobahn before the triangle where Nürnberg Road swings off, but it wasn't until thirty kilometers before Darmstadt that the intoxicated man in the back seat began to wake up. I had forgotten him and screamed when his hand prodded me from behind. Jørgen turned halfway around and looked at the American, but continued driving. It was only when he came to a natural Abfart with parking for trucks that he turned off, and we came into the woods again, which closed around us on both sides and pressed us into a tunnel of light ahead and blackness behind. When he stopped the car and turned off the lights, he must have turned the key instead of hitting the light switch. The motor died with the lights. I sat still and could hear that the man behind me said something, mumbled something or other or swore. It was faint and incomprehensible. He only began to shout aloud--as if he were surprised and a little annoyed--when Jørgen began to hit him and I heard myself shout, too, when I realized that the dull sound, regular and mechanical after the man's protest had to come from the revolver butt which chopped down on his cranium. My sickness returned and I leaned out over the car door and threw up to get myself out, to get away. I only regained consciousness when I heard the sound of a crank and realized that we hadn't gone farther because we hadn't fulfilled RFS's conditions. As ghosts the club members were still with us or rather: eccentric cars that won't start don't start because two of the other owners or passengers are dead and the other two vanished. I wiped my mouth with my arm and crawled from my seat across into the driver's seat, but my hands shook so much that I couldn't hold the wheel or get my foot to release the clutch properly. After the fourth try the crank lugged the pistons into the correct position, the ignition caught, and the motor started. But in order to make contact, the car first had to be put in reverse, and I flayed away at the gear shift until the gears meshed, and while Jørgen pushed I got the car swung into the brush and the motor raced so much that the shift from reverse to first gear was possible. I don't know whether the procedure is correct, but it worked, anyway, and we were driving again.

At first I didn't understand how Jørgen would dare to drive on the main road, but then it occurred to me that locally, anyway, the balance between our crime and the one committed against us was more or less even. It isn't likely the fleeing Americans would be very interested in reporting anything at all to any authorities whatsoever. On the other hand, there was the question of time-- when the next alarm would be given. Felt that I occupied myself with considerations that lay in a different plane than those I used to have: the habitual criminal's gradual hardening, postcoital or the accomplished rape's possibility of flight from depression, or the confirmation of a cynical process which had long been in motion without my having suspected it?

We passed Frankfort and drove hard toward Giessen by way of Butzbach. Dawn had the same color as the man in the back seat. I was so cold that my teeth chattered and I had to hold onto the car tightly in order to sit still or to get the shaking to stop. Didn't know what Jørgen Schwer's plan was, just looked at him every now and then while he sat bent over the wheel with the metal circle and the threecornered star in the middle. He didn't say anything, probably because he couldn't either. He sat in the daybreak and drove the car and I remembered the gaunt, seedy Henry Fonda in Ford's film and the text that was shown before the film: "This is a film which takes place in the USA. It shows that not all social relationships are as they should be and that not all people live as they would like to, but the circumstances of the orange pickers arc different now, and the people who were driven from their homes have got other and better ones." Or something to that effect.

We ate it up at the movies, but it was wiped out after the film and only came back in the daybreak when I looked at Jørgen and thought about what had brought us so far. I thought about the propaganda phrases, the Roosevelt period's mixture of optimism and half-heartedness, and I thought about the international story of the tourist family, whose grandmother dies along the way, who stow her in the trunk until one day the car is stolen in front of a restaurant while the family is eating dinner, but at the same time I knew that that wouldn't be our way of getting rid of the corpse. While I froze in the merciless morning wind and saw the sun halfway up--a yellowish glazed eye between ponds and fields on the horizon, I thought of my changed relationship to crime and punishment and was astonished that it really was different than

226

before. The hard thing wasn't to act in action, the difficulty was to act when the distance between good and evil, right and wrong, crime and punishment was so small you couldn't tell when you went from one to the other. A large distance between character and plot, ethically considered, gives violent effects and strong winds, action; little or unconscious distance, doldrums and stagnation. It was an unethical argument, but after all it is in the pyschological calm that the greatest, most savage and protracted crimes are committed.

As I said: it was easy. We drove the car down a slope to a bog. Halfway to the water's edge Jørgen braked the Mercedes, and we were again hidden by trees. Together we carried Gus, who stank of half-digested whiskey, around to the front seat. It was difficult to get him behind the wheel, maybe because the morning chill had hastened the process of rigor mortis. One of his arms kept lying on the windshield when we tried to bend him double and get him into place, and for a moment the image combination was there: a mad Göring driving for the last time with upraised arm in greeting through the yelling crowds on Unter den Linden. Jørgen shoved the arm back from the windshield and it fell down along the dead man's side like an old-fashioned directional signal.

Back in the car my travelling companion found a jerry-can with gasoline, and we didn't need to use the radiator hose he had disconnected from the motor for a siphon. He asked me to get back and when I reached the trees a little way up the slope he doused the car with gasoline. He himself stepped back from the car, pulled out a box of matches, empited some of the matches into his pocket, set fire to the rest and the box, swore loudly and laid the box on the ground where it burned peacefully and slowly, ran over to the car, opened the front door and released the handbrake, rushed back and picked up the burning matchbox, swore again, hurled the box toward the rolling vehicle, turned toward me with his hands over his ears. In the second before the vehicle caught fire, I heard the sound of a soaring jet plane, then the explosion's deep cough came, a hot exaggerated breathing as with someone who's trying to save his bursting heart. Together we ran across the field away from Gus and his burning chariot and it was only by my back and ears that I knew the car had reached the water.

Now we are here in the potato pit, and I understand why children love holes and rabbits that live in them, why they like to think of things down under the earth in the dark and be protected themselves on all sides, overhead by a ceiling, underneath by a floor. I think we could become potatoes ourselves if we could get through the summer, could shake ourselves down into the earth, and when the new spring came we would begin to sprout and grow and put forth tubers, and there would be health in the root and white poison in our flowers. We could have left here before but something is holding us back--I don't know whether it's anxiety about the decisive step or the desire to stretch out the suspense. At night I open the lid to the pit all the way up and stand like a gopher with my nostrils sniffing in all directions. I feel I'm shining like a flower, deadly nightshade, nature-bred, free and dangerous. But I can't get my roots into the ground and something gathers in the dark and begins to talk to me when I close the lid and lie down along the wall to keep the moles and woodlice out. Singly and in chorus they speak, come every evening and night and pronounce my booming name, Anna. I know all of them. My father speaks first. He's not severe and stands there with his cap in his hand that he can't wear because of mother, twists it back and forth. He says:

Anna, when you were born everyone said that you couldn't live. No one said it, but I could see from the doctor's face that he thought it. He looked at me as if he wanted to tell me that it was my fault we lived that way. But what should I do, and haven't I done everything since that could be expected? I stuffed papers in the cracks and burned a pair of my old shoes so you and your mother wouldn't freeze. I stole Kjeld's wooden toys and stuffed them in the stove, and as I did it I thought that God would surely punish me because I stole from one child to save the other one's life. But I was sure that he would forgive me, too. He did, too, for you lived, and you became the sweetest child in the world. You were so beautiful, Anna, and everything you did was right. You brought light into my life, and every time I've seen you and thought of you, I've seen this light and said--it must never be put out. With you and Kjeld things got better, you didn't die, everything changed and we no longer lived in the back shed but could move because I got a job and the war came and I got even more to do. I was proud of my children, and I'm proud of you, Anna. You always did the right thing, and even though I know that a marriage and career are nothing, I still can't help feeling proud when I see your name in the paper or a picture of you in a magazine. They said you couldn't live, but that's just what you did, and we all lived better because of you. I was the one who hadn't lived before or couldn't live, but when you were born, I said to myself: For Anna's sake, for Anna's sake you will live and make things better for yourself and your family. But now what? What is it that's happened now? What have you done and what does it mean? Where are you? I can't see you, can't see you in the dark, underground. Anna, where are you? Anna!

I listen to his silly pathos and sit up in the cold sour stink, saying, here I am. I'm here in a hole in the ground, and I'm on the way home. There's nothing to worry about. Everything will be all right. Everything will be good and hard and smooth as flint. Anna is resting safely in Schlesvig's earth. But there are other voices, and they don't harden her as much because she can argue and not just buckle under, longing. Tom speaks in the dark. He says:

--I think I know more about us than you think. I'm not that distant. I don't lie sleeping in my sarcophagus against a lighter window. I have my eyes open under the closed lid. I know that you're awake in the dark. I want to talk to you, touch you, lie with you, remind you of things which you've forgotten, but I can't. When I get up and sit down next to you, you push me away. Not literally, but by your shutting me out. You don't have the ability to let the dreams and memories of others occur in you. They don't exist in your consciousness. You give and give, but can't accept. Your problems are superhuman and can't be solved by people, only by yourself, or God. When my dependence on you on one level ceased or grew less, you wrote me off on all the others. One has to be a bird on a corrugated iron roof before your care can be alleviated. One has to be a slave squatting in a hospital corridor before you will give birth to one's child. But I love you even though you don't know what it means.

Ha, Anna says in the dark, listen to Noureddin, listen to the spirit of the lamp, listen to the clever one's speech. But her voice is uncertain, and she turns in the dark, scraping against the potato wall, unable to find an answer. Then she gets halfway up and says in a different voice:

--Why didn't you come? Why did you make me believe that metaphysical chit chat about willpower and subconscious desires was enough? Don't you know that it's precisely the concrete, the tangible, the ametaphysical, the banal that we have together? You say that I can't give, that my care is stifling, that I need something that needs me. I thought that was the principle, the engine to it all, Tom. One also wants to know one is a thing, object, person,

230

need, desire, weakness, strength. Suppositions and speculations, considerations and *interpretations*, analyses of motives is love's antipode, its negation. Maybe I can't hold the memories of others, who came, but I can remember *us*. And no matter where I end up, I'll have the bedpiece from Vibe Road framed and hung on the wall. No, that isn't necessary. It's here now, wide, oblong and sharp in my breast. And God how we laughed when it cracked.

Then Morten comes, and it's almost touching. He's so easy to get around, his voice so boyish and moral. He says:

--On closer inspection the dossier is not inspiring. I've never had anything against my sister-in-law--quite the contrary. There are no family principles that say one shouldn't accept a person from a different class (I'm not fond of the word) as an equal member. Anna has always met with openness and warmth in the Terlow family, yes, I'm not afraid to use the word "love." We all thought she would make an excellent partner for my slightly weaker, older brother, and it may be that this sounds a little bizarre, but since evaluation is a part of reality, there's no need to skip it. In most respects Anna has failed, and her last actions mark her as both irresponsible and erratic. She's often used her time lecturing me on humanness and every form of social philosophy--I just don't know how she will get an invalided policeman, countless larcenies, two murdered Americans, vagabondage, and flight from prosecution to fit into the picture. We've bent over as far as we can for her. Anna is written off.

For a moment she is about to say "Ah, yes" and smile a little, but two images can't be effaced from the potato sky: a man falling under the flameyellow Supercortemaggiore! and the revolver butt's muffled arc through the blackness. Where is the margin of exoticism, where is the border of the picaresque?

But Karl Christensen doesn't say anything, and the others are dead. He was in service and the others intoxicated. But the choir increases, the voices blend, increase, get louder. They gather, they gather, the transfigured ancient ones, and farther out in the wings chirp a choir of girls with strange hairstyles and medium dresses from the end of the forties, hound's-tooth wool and permanents laid in cement. Anna, they call, Anna, it's you who must give up! Anna, you're it. Anna, you're out, you're out.

Finally Minna and John stand there, and when she sees John, Anna holds her hands over her eyes and sobs. She knows she's failed there, and there is no forgiveness. If children count at all, if it's possible to have any consideration for them at all, she says, and pushes herself up onto her knees from the dirt floor. She swears through her teeth and waves her arms, scratches away, erases, wipes clean. And they pull back, the children--she scarcely has time to see Minna, and when her sight clears, she sees Jørgen who lies curled up with his back to her. The light is about to return, grayness filters down through the cracks. He doesn't have anything to say. He is too near, and she touches him and tugs at him gently, saying he has to get up now, they have to go now, they have to go home.

--What is it? he says.

--We have to go now, I say.

--Yes, but the dogs, what about the dogs?

He's sleepy and shakes himself under the sack. The revolver lies on the handkerchief next to him.

--They haven't been here since the day before yesterday.

--Yes, but it's light. We can't go when it's light.

I (Anna) look at him and remember a little of the old contempt, the old snarl.

--You said yourself that we should cut right through.

--Did I?

--I don't know but that's what we've done. So we should go now, too, when it's light.

Maybe it's the excitement, maybe it's because we have eaten too little, maybe it's because of what I've dreamed, I get sick again and he sees it and sits up and supports me, but won't go with me into the corner where I throw up.

You can't go when you're feeling like that, he says.

I nod while the gall trickles out of my mouth and the spit increases and increases amd I swallow and swallow and bay with my hand on my stomach. Potato eater, I a potato eater!

Shortly after, the attack passes, and I begin to collect my scraps and rags. Dior und die anderen Damen und Herren: Kaput! He looks at me as if he didn't want to go, but when he sees that it's serious, he sticks his weapon in under his shirt, tucks the corners into his pants and begins to button the jacket of his uniform. He'll be good on Kragskov Heath, no, no, no, he'll be good in Horsens Penetentiary because he can't be reformed.

The bells aren't chiming out there, but the skies aren't falling in, either, when he opens the lid over us, crawls out and gives me his hand. The weather's like Easter, clear, translucent April, day of battles, tactics, victories and defeats. We begin to walk north across the nursery's farthest field, find our way in between two willow hedgerows, turn to the right and can just make out the road to Schlesvig. The color we had gotten on the trip from Switzerland to here has paled considerably after a week in the cellar. We have only one direction now, but no plans. Anyway, I, at least, don't know what Jørgen has in mind, and I myself just have the feeling that from now on we can wander hand in hand (if he wants to) through the old Danish countryside, past the cathedral, past Duborg School, past lines of people with cognac bottles hidden under their seats, cameras in their bosoms and transistors up their asses. Behind the elm trees there is probably a bus, the wind is blowing, the last girls come dashing, and if I run quickly enough and shout loudly enough, they'll probably take me with them. Hi, girls, here comes Anna and her friend!

I ask if he knows where we should go, but he shakes his head and keeps on walking. When we near the road we can see that it's heavily travelled. That could be an advantage. When the police have a peak load on the highway, they don't have time to look for vagrants and assailants and women. The cars are lined up behind one another when we leave the lane between the hedges and come out on the asphalt side road leading to the main highway. The landscape is flat and open on every side. Over the horizon from the east comes a low-flying wave of jet planes right at us. At first they are wide dots, but they quickly become massive, fill up our field of vision, draw the intensity of their sound right up against us, at a thousand feet over the queue on the highway, where the cars quiver and rock under the pressure, approach in an apparent dive, and pass.

In the throwoff of sound and the turbulence of the slipstream, I put my head back and scream and scream, but everything is drowned out, and seen from the cars, I must look like a young woman watching the planes. Jørgen shakes me, shouting:

--It's Sunday! Sunday!

15

The sound of the airplane vanishes, and Jørgen speaks to me in his normal voice. But he says something that I haven't heard before. He points at the cars and says:
--We'll have to go around.
Yes, of course we have to go around. We can't just cut right through the cars, I know that, but what does he mean by go around? We should cut right through, right through each time. That's the agreement--it won't work otherwise. I didn't understand what he said before either: It's Sunday, Sunday! But maybe it's my old dream that's finally come true. Oh, yes, so it's happened then, and my feeling of *already seen* quivers in me like an echo. Even the line is a repetition-- it's always the entrance to the dream, the repetition or confirmation of a feeling one has always had, the nightmare's consummation, not for the first, but for the hundred and eleventh time. It is war, and it begins this way. I'm standing in a field open on all sides and the horizon is clear, but something is on its way. There's a sound that can't be heard, more nearly seen, a shimmer of the sun set for the last time. The landscape is desolate, the country is called Kov or kk or k or ngn or just gn, and you can't tell whether you are enemy or friend, whether you are one of the hated or loved. Something or someone is coming to attack, and I am no one, but still completely through inside and outside, Anna. The sound increases and the planes come. They creep forward on the horizon and they have but one target: me. Still they are distraught and completely impersonal. I say to myself: People are sitting in them, pilots, people wrapped in tubing and oxygen masks, cords and leather, but behind it all there are people, and since there's not a hole or a ditch nearby I have to wave and shout,

jump up and down, put my hands in front of my face and scream: Don't do it, don't do it, look at me, I'm alone, can't hide. But their anonymity is overwhelming, their singleness of purpose that of the robot. I watch the faces, the eyes above the oxygen masks, the eyes behind goggles, but they stare straight ahead, just keep on flying, keep on, and the image shifts, for now the planes steer into the cannon fire, into the heavy flak, and my heart is sucked upward, the terror *for their sake* sets in--I shout toward the thunder of the planes: Watch out, watch out, look where you're going! The shout never reaches them, the long fire-raking's morse code hammers into the fuselage, the men sit at their wheels and knobs with eyes pointed straight ahead, immovable. The speed of the planes becomes sluggish, stops, the colossi hover, burning, a second, hold themselves compulsively by the hair in a spasm of awe-inspiring, impersonal resolution, then they drop through and everything is extinguished in the dark.

I cling to Jørgen. He shakes me off and begins to walk. What does he mean by Sunday? Is that part of the old recurrent dream, too? Is that why I cowered in terror and thought that my parents' account of a play they had seen back then was so awful? They laughed and laughed while they said that in one scene you heard the word "Sunday" repeated from everywhere. It came out of the walls, down from the ceiling, in the windows, and later I heard my mother use it when my father lay down after lunch on Vibe Road: Sunday, Sunday, Sunday! What was wrong with Sunday, why was it so frightening, why wasn't it, like my Sundays, always good? I awoke and got up. It smelled of warmth and the curtains pulled the breeze into the house, the furniture was in its usual place, and there was nothing but security. I put on my clothes, tied my shoes, crept out into the entry and got the morning bread and milk. The newspaper lay on the mat. I put everything on the kitchen table, laid the newspaper beside it and went down the stairs and into the street. It was empty but not sinister. Everywhere people lay behind their curtains, sleeping. Whatever crises there may have been were over now. The children awoke naturally and got up everywhere and did the same things as me. The insomniacs had finally chafed themselves to rest. The magic number six was crossed--morning's first hours frightened the wolves away. I played alone until the others got up, and we drank our morning coffee together. It could never end. Yet it was a Sunday that I heard my first air raid sirens and a Sunday that my appendix was taken out. Sunday, Sunday, Sunday. He will have to explain it to me.

Dash after him down toward the cars, trying to hold my pants up. My stomach is lean and the ends of my hair are split. I want to go home to the hairdresser's. But it's closed today, Jørgen says. Get him by the shoulder and turn him toward me, while the people watch us, inquisitively. Have the gypsies come to town?

--You have to explain it to me, I say.

He shakes me off again.

--Stop it, he says.

I dig my nails in and he has to stop.

--Why did you say it's Sunday?

--It must be a show, he says.

--A show?

--Yes, an air show.

He shakes himself loose again and tramples up the bank to a Volkswagen. It can't be a police car, for they're a different color. The police Volkswagens in Germany are either green or white, the policemen wear either green coats or white coats, black or white hats, their clubs are white or black, and on their heads or on their hats they wear a rotating light that can be seen from far away. Sundays the police drive around with armed water cannons and spray up and down Unter den Linden. Once in a while they hit people on steps and in portals, and the stream from the water cannon hits very hard. Not so hard that it can break the arm of a dead man who comes driving along very slowly in a black convertible. Half his head is bashed in, and when the water gushes around it, tiny crusts of congealed blood are loosened and run down onto the floor of the car. The man gets up and shouts: Es ist nicht hier! Es ist gar nicht hier! Alles ist hier rein! Alles ist hier rein, sauber und nett. Wir sind im Osten. Es ist alles vorbei, alles vorüber. And the police turn on their blinking light and drive back to Kurfürstendamm, and we'll never get any farther because we have to go around.

He comes back and stands facing me. I look at my little man and want to touch his cheek. Now he has to go home to the fresh air camp and be fattened up. Now he has to be put out to grass. I say it to his teacher: It will do Jørgen Schwer good to have a few months in the country. I've followed him for a long time. His hemoglobin level isn't what it should be in a modern welfare state. He's nervous and unstable, and I'm sure you've noticed how at present he swings between forgetfulness and hysteria. Out to the woods and the beach with him. Peaceful surroundings and fresh air, loving supervision, gentle discipline and understanding will make him a new person. But there's no time to be lost.

--We can't get through.

--What do you mean?

--It's an air show in Schlesvig, and they're stopping the cars here and for the next eight kilometers. And there are too many policemen. He turns and walks toward the cars again.

--Jørgen, I shout, Jørgen!

He doesn't stop and I catch up with him between a Volkswagen and an Audi.

--Are you leaving me?

He tries to speak in a low voice and not show how excited he is. The scarecrow shows his teeth--his shoulders are shaking-- Andrew Aguecheek in battle dress has spittle at the corners of his mouth. Somewhere or other a radio plays "The Red River Valley." I touch his elbow.

--You're crazy, he says.

Yes, yes, I nod, happy, yes, yes.

He keeps on going but he doesn't know what to do in a queue of Sunday cars. There are no planes in the sky, the war is over, and they have only us to stare at. Gradually more and more car windows are rolled down. These people from Kiel and Neumünster and Hamburg haven't paid for their tickets. It's possible that they've thrown some coppers so that NATO's assembled Luftwaffe can make their balls shrink and their Carmen-curls flutter. But they haven't given me anything. They haven't applauded Anastasia out into the spotlight, but she stands there now, the old exhibitionist, and if nothing else is sensational, her costume is anyway. Hi, ho for the potato land, isn't that where aquavit comes from?

He begins walking again, wants to go down the slope, across the ditch, into the field. I hold onto him tightly and sing my old Irving Berlin number, "Let's Change Partners and Dance Again," and it goes swimmingly. The sausage people are wild with joy. They forget their party cards which are burning in their back pockets, forget Apfelstrudel and Sauerkraut in order to see die dummen Dänen dance the lanciers in the lost land. Their eyes are about to fall out of their heads in their amazement over anyone being capable of being so crazy, so eccentric, so touchingly funny and tragic at the same time. Their colpa and pena dances dressed in rags and tatters. There's a car hood to kneel on and the only

239

thing that's missing is our professional friends. Where is Roberto, the old whip-cracker? Where is the wop of an Odin, crowdaddy with a bird on each shoulder, where is my black wig so I can creep into his witch's snakeskin and find out what it really was she wanted of me? Inside the head, the head, the head under the hair, she could have whispered to me what kind of sinister plan they were brewing. Why they wanted my naked body on the radiator, what whipdaddy had up his sleeve for me. Oh, I would like to get inside of her, in under her little blue hat, into her stockings, which tighten and stick and grow and hold tight and don't flow over dikes and groynes and all the banks. I could dance now but something holds me back, and behind the glass right in front of me stare terrorstruck eyes, and I think Sunday, Sunday, Sunday-- here and on the other·side of the water, everywhere in queues, in cars, on the way out, on the way home, hands on a lovable wheel of Danish pastry, an air raid siren which observes the empty streets from a roof, silent, undaunted, the greased cells and ballbearings resting in secure assurance over the coming chances, the sound encapsulated and calm, solidified dreams of the later liberation, the unfolding another day, another Sunday.

The blows rain down on me, and when I open my eyes I see two motorcycles with antennae swinging on their way toward us in single file, wobbling and jolting on the shoulder of the road past the queue of cars. I wake and the dream continues in a new tone while we rush through the wet grass and hear the car horns behind us and a new wave of planes coming. They're coming from the south and this time they're helicoptors, Sikorskys, leaning forward like preying mantises, tilted, Romanesque churchtowers in the air, driven forward by rotating flyswatters. Our guest performance is finished, the elephants take over the circus ring.

We sit in a cemetery under a hedge of arbor vitae, each leaning

240

against a headstone. I have Anton Kiilian Hansen, homey, Jørgen: Ferdinand Heimbühl, strange, but known, anyway. It's very quiet here: the dead concentrate on the solemnity, turn over fatigued like patients in a hospital after a much-too-long holiday visiting hours. My travelling companion is mad at me, but he's too exhausted to say anything. I (Anna) want to talk with him. Want to say:

--Little father. It's us two. It's us two still and steadily. Thank you.

Or:

--Jørgen Schwer, brother and lover. Pretty soon we'll be back in the old country. What will we do then?

Or I could be completely matter-of-fact:

--On this joint excursion we've overstepped all the rules in the book, broken written as well as unwritten laws. We are sought across half, not to say the whole of Europe. I've scandalized my husband, destroyed my reputation, abandoned my children and my responsibilities, I've just skipped out and caused my parents sorrow and anxiety, and even if my brother Kjeld knows it's true, he refuses to believe it. He says straight out: I refuse to believe it, and behind his vest and the three hairs on his chest he knows in spite of everything that it's true and understands that that's the way it has to be.

Even though I can't keep up the matter-of-fact tone, my voice reminds me a little of Morten's. But I would like to talk about him, too. I could say to Jørgen:

--Do you remember Morten? He isn't an unfriendly man, and he isn't stupid, either. The only trouble with Morten is that *I* can't get him to exist. I know he's there. I can touch him, but I can neither get really mad at him nor really like him. He says something to me, and I react to it, both positively and negatively. I would like to follow his advice, and was just about to do it, but

241

finally I had to run anyway. I can't be in the same room with someone who isn't there. Afraid that it won't interest him, I don't say anything. The bees fly among the lavender, skip over the pansies with their false advertising, suck away on a digitalis with roots direct down into Anton Kiilian Hansen's heart. Anton Kiilian Hansen, who reminds me of Anton Hannibal Olsen, who stood in front of the roadsign and had to choose between "the right way" and "the wrong way." But I can say something, and I do.

--Do you think Christensen's all right?

He pulls his leg up under him and says with his dumb sneer:

--How the hell would I know?

--Do you think he's dead?

--Haven't the faintest idea.

--Doesn't it interest you at all?

He shrugs his shoulders.

--It interests me. He was a good fellow. I liked him a lot. He was nice.

The gravestone feels cold against my back. It x-rays my cheap epitaph with its scorn. I get up and look down at Jørgen. Feel my craziness ebb out. It's like after menstruation. First you're in a cage of glass, can see everything, hear everything, but can't touch anything and can't be reached. You would like to act in one way, but are forced to do something else. Words spoken to you strike the glass, curve away, arrive distorted. What you yourself say also hits the glass, is sent into unexpected fluctuations, becomes dissonant, reaches the recipient distorted. But one day the glass cage disappears, lifted off like a bell jar. You walk out, and mirrors are shattered left and right. Anna is master of her own truth. Smiling she looks down at her wild man sitting there with his legs tucked up, hand on forehead, hand on mouth, hand on ears. She speaks to her sealed-off ape, saying:

242

--I'm pregnant.

Suddenly everything falls together, and she feels the same trembling, giddy excitement, the same anxiety and expectation as the schoolgirl who catches the bride's bouquet outside the church and knows that it's her turn next, the next time she will be redeemed, embraced, receive revelations, be fertilized, filled, cry out, be stunned, buried, and freed. She steps outside the grave site and walks back and forth in the sun with her hands lifted over her head. He watches her stand in the baggy khaki uniform with her pants hanging around her hips and her hair matted. He sees her turn and lift her face toward the sun. She knows he's looking at her because she can feel his glance, but she doesn't know what he's thinking. Cut right through, Anna--weren't those the words? That's the way it should be. She puts her hands down and steps into the shadow under the yew trees. They have to think about going on. The shiver-worm now turning in her stomach or clinging tightly casts no shadow. So it's as good as not there. And the white dogged thought that's growing in his head she can't get out, either. With her specimen slide under her heart, Anna (she, I) understands that there's no answer to all these outbursts, that there can be no returning of these trump cards that can be hauled out at any opportunity: I'm dying, I'm pregnant, I'm drowning, I'm suffering, I'm falling apart, I'm losing my grip. No toughness is necessary to destroy this pathos, hoopla, a fashionable purse on a mountainside and the play is on. And now we have to go, home, home where the beech bower gives shade. I give him my hand and he lets himself be helped up. That makes the situation a little more difficult. He's damned unpredictable, like all spoiled people. The white dogged thought has become a question:

--Is it my child?

The remark is good enough to embroider in cross-stitch and hang up over the bed, girls. But it could open up the modern sober-mindedness in Schlesvig, too. While we walk out of the cemetery beside each other and the tower clock indicates that visiting hours are over and the dead can snore on, I take his hand and say yes. Ever since we came to the Stürmers' and lived as man and wife with snow on all the roofs, I haven't been very careful. In the first place my pills were gone, in the second, old wife that I am, I never gave any thought to the fact that one could get pregnant by a boy. These words were perhaps not completely in accordance with the Schlesvig sober-mindedness and weren't said in that way. But when it occurred to me that he thought there was a possibility that this turning mobile in my uterus could be made by American semen, I assured him again that it would be a fresh air kid. We travelled all day and all night along small roads to the north and east, and although it's a while before the light nights begin, the darkness feels thinner and more translucent here than where we're coming from. At daybreak I can smell the sea and stop for a moment. It's not like the water in the river moving mirrorlike over the lawn toward me, the water here is brackish, the smell dispersed and splintered, cut up from salt and rotten seaweed. The breeze is cold, and there is the sense of land *on the other side.* Over the shore's seaweed and the mouth and tar of the harbor flows a spiced scent of elder trees and budding apple blossoms. We are within the ferryland's radius, tut, tut, motorcycles, chimneys in red and white, Orphan Annie comes home.

I'm coming home, yes, and nothing has changed--maybe, at that, everything's more itself than I've ever seen before. It must be the time and the angle of approach that gives me the feeling. Since for I don't know how long, I've come to Copenhagen by plane. With my head compressed by the speed or the feeling of the turbines' supersonics, with the confirmation dinner's sixteen courses in my stomach and a little cart pushed forward filled with cognac and whiskey, I've gone through the rampway, the passport control, customs, the hall, the automatic doors to the taxi and have seen the cement of the airport road, the Four Winds, the Town Hall and Hotel Royal. Fine things, naturally, but strange.

Now I'm coming the way of the old trip, from the west. It's Tuesday and I'm walking. Even if the method isn't entirely the same as back when we cycled and went by train, the tempo is more suitable, anyway. Most of the houses along the road I haven't seen before, but they seem familiar because in a certain light the city always has the same atmosphere. I walk from the west and have the rising sun in my face. Even this early the rays are warm. I feel as if I've been here before.

I think of the homecomings back then, worn out with peering from the train, leaning up against the chimney stack of the Ålborg steamer with the wind in from the east with the flat sunbeams flickering in the backstays, but mostly I remember the random trips home from strange places in town, doors that open up at the end of stairs, the light that falls from an unexpected quarter, tobacco smoke that disappears, the taste of liquor, the morning chill. I think our difficult love was best during these mornings, even though we were tired and didn't get much out of it. We weren't very proficient, yet we slogged away proficiently enough, but how we walked. I don't know whether it's just my generation who've had to cycle and hike so much in order to satisfy their sexual desires. But it was that way in the fifties. You were always someplace or other where it couldn't be done. Or it could be done, but it was difficult to part afterwards and you never lived together. Out of bed, down from the sofa, on with the pants, and the seeing home. Everyone knows the seeing-home epoch in puberty--with us it stretched into eternity, and if one of the pair remained lying there egotistically, the other always had to go out onto the flagstone afterwards, up onto the bike, through the cold. It gave one first hand knowledge of the oddities of the city, it gave one first hand knowledge of the movements and appearance of the late-night people and the early-morning people. A very friendly people live in Copenhagen in the morning, and there are many animals that others don't know. I've seen a squirrel cut across Vestre Boulevard from Tivoli to the Town Hall Gardens at four o'clock in the morning, and I've said good morning to women delivering papers and milkmen in a clear and distinct voice as if the city were a hamlet and we were far out in the country. This warm solidarity in the cold is unusual, but it comes from a feeling of freemasonry, of being outsiders. Still more unusual was the way in which things, the houses, the trees, the chimneys, the weather vanes, the statues, imprinted their appearance. In the particular light it was as if every scene, every gable, every cornice said: Look, here I am. You've never seen me before. You see me now, and because the sun is shining wrong and you've run off the rails and slept with a man, you'll never forget me. Naturally, I've forgotten the cornices and the drainpipes and the houses with pale windows, but now they're there again and apparently nothing has changed. Two policemen with their hands behind their backs walk along Roskilde Road's right sidewalk, and when they are opposite me, I say good morning, and it doesn't seem as if they are surprised. Either at my greeting or my appearance. That's maybe the difference between back then and now, that a ragamuffin doesn't attract attention anymore. That a wild birdnested, redhaired witch at four o'clock in the morning can walk by the law unchallenged, greet them with a happy good morning and get an answer. Even a ragamuffin sought in various countries has a free pass in the morning when the houses mind their own business but nonetheless exhibit themselves in recondite significance. It can almost be called a step forward. Maybe I should relinquish the thought of the factory for longhaired people, maybe in spite of it all their contribution has changed opinion so that all of us can go around in peace here in Denmark, not only around sunrise, but all day long.

When we got so close to the harbor in Langballigan that I could see the masts of the pleasure craft, the clubhouse to the right, the customs hut in the middle, the red and green blinking of the harbor entrance lights, Jørgen stopped me with his arm and said I should stay where I was. That made me afraid. I don't know what I thought--yes, I thought a lot of things. First and foremost I thought: Here and no farther. Better ten thousand miles back, but here and no farther. Now the idiot will dump me. From here I'll be permitted to row home under my own power. I heard his primitive words and motive: he had to get home and talk with "connections," he couldn't get along without "contacts," but I also remember how honestly he had hissed when he explained to me that I was an idiot because I had prevented him from "going home." I looked at him and it was too cold and foolish to ask and argue, but I said to myself: Now this man's going out of your life, and you'll never see him again. That was too pretty a sentence for me to really cope with, and when it was followed by: There goes the father of your child, I really said something to him. I asked him right out where he was going, and because he didn't notice that my voice was shaking or thought that it was because of the cold, he answered factually and nicely as in our best times together. He had picked out a boat which he was sure he could start and steer without the keys. He pointed between the alder trees and I saw a high-rigged cabin cruiser moored with the stern toward the boat dock and the bow pointing directly toward the entrance of the harbor. It lay thirty meters from the customs office, and we'd have to run across an open stretch of at least a hundred meters to get down to it. It would be easier for one person to get down there without being seen, and as soon as he'd figured out the engine and

247

was ready to start it, he would signal me and then I could just run. Meanwhile, he'd loosen the moorings, and the moment I set foot on deck we would be out of the harbor and many sea miles on our way. I watched him all the time he talked and wanted to touch the tiny blotches of red excitement that appeared on his neck, but I controlled myself. Held my head coldly during the spring maneuvers--we aren't at the fresh air camp for nothing.

Jørgen sneaked down to the wharf along the dry-docked boats, ran the last bit of the way and climbed on board the cabin cruiser from the port side, which was turned away from the shut, morningquiet houses. I sat down in the grass and waited. I didn't think about anything in particular and maybe would have fallen asleep with the consciousness of a restored intimacy, but a sudden explosive rumbling from the newly started marine engine got me to my feet. I could see Jørgen run along the railing to reach the mooring at the buoy, but I didn't stop to watch, I ran at once and I yelled as loudly as I could that he should wait because it was impossible for me to stay behind on this side with everything I had run from, and I couldn't cross the last border without him. I ran recklessly and in full view past the overturned boats across the square down toward the quay, and I didn't stop when I saw him standing on the pilot's bridge with the revolver in his hand while the sound of the motor got louder and louder and the water between the stern of the boat and the wharf boiled up. I didn't stop because I couldn't and wouldn't stop, and I didn't see him raise the revolver and point it to my left, heard only one of its shots, from a new angle, at a new distance, different, more booming, then my shin cut insanely into the railing rope and I was thrown full force against the deck. The space between the revolver shot and the next shots was marked but brief. I heard the two bursts of the automatic weapons with my face pressed on the floorboards, I screamed from the pain in my legs and I screamed because I saw a shadow fall across me and disappear out over the side of the boat. In the middle of my scream I rose halfway up and in front of me on the cushion lay the revolver and I wanted to seize it, and just then the boat hit the crosswater outside the harbor entrance, and when I got to my feet again the entrance was more than twenty meters away and the two customs officials on the middle pier so far away that I couldn't reach them, nor could my insane, blubbering shout: Schweinhunde! Deutsche Schweinhunde!

That was yesterday, but now it's Tuesday and there aren't many of us at Valby Station. The police are certainly a little more accustomed to the eccentric than ordinary morning workers en route. Anyway, they stare at me more here, even though I've been to the toilet and tried to comb my hair. I really don't know why it should be exactly the city train now, but so it shall be. You don't take a taxi if you can't decide where you want to go. Only the rich do that, those who mount and say: Drive, no matter where, just drive! While I paid the woman with my Danish money, I figured out where I should go. I had thought of Vibe Road, but then I know the ride from Borups Allé and Godthåbs Road Station so well. I know the ride down Hillerød Street at the break of day ad nauseum, and I've had enough of memories. Nørrebro would have been reasonable, too, but the ride from there has always seemed to me uglier, less fashionable. I can't show up at my old parents' now. They would be ashamed or think I'd gone crazy. It's something else I can use now. Even though the sun has risen, you can still see the sunrise on the Langelinje.

The countdown to this compartment has been perfect. I sit down among new newspapers with trivial front pages among old countrymen with corresponding faces. It all hangs together, all of it, hangs together well. I am calm and safe--nothing bad can

can happen to you here. A man with a beret glances sidelong at me past his paper once in a while, and I smile at him. He doesn't smile back. When the runaway boat went agound south of Søby, I crawled out and waded ashore. The motor ran at full speed all the time and I didn't steer by markers or buoys, just away. No one followed me, apparently, and when the boat went off course because I misunderstood some markers--which before I hadn't paid any attention to--the boat slid up on the sand where the double screws kept on booming, as if they would push the whole island before them.

I slept two hours under a rowboat and woke to a powerful stink. Someone must have used the boat as a shelter against the wind while he relieved himself. The smell of human excrement brought me back to the East, but I got up and left, and on the road to Ærøskøbing I was picked up by a cattle truck that was going all the way to Ringsted. On both ferries I asked permission to stay in the truck because I was so tired.

The sun is higher in the sky, and a real sunrise is out of the question. I walk to the left from Østerport Station and down past the Swedish church. Spring is well in progress on the Citadel. The forsythia is still blooming, but it will soon be by. Later the laburnum and lilacs will come and in two weeks the beech will blossom. There's no one in the yachting harbor now, but I go around the point anyway and down by the cruise ship's mooring toward the harbor inlet itself. There's a Russian ship at the wharf--it's red all over. I think about how quickly you learn to adapt to new temperatures. I (Anna) am not cold even though my pants are thin and I'm sitting on bare stone. Want to think about a morning, early morning on Langelinje many years ago. No.

The revolver tastes cold and a little greasy when I put it in my mouth. It's repulsive to hold it between my lips, but, for all that, not unnatural to close my mouth because the barrel is so small. The hard bead of the sight at the tip of the barrel scrapes against my palate. It's the temperature of the weapon that is so disgusting. The cold and the taste. I think of Minna, but don't want to think of her anymore.

When the weapon has clicked twice, I realize that Jørgen Schwer can't count, either. I remove the choking point from my soft palate and the revolver disappears into the seawater with a faint rolling after the splash. My vomit wants to follow, but nothing will come. It has nothing to come from. It brings Minna back again. I say the name to myself: Minna, Minna, Minna. My little Minna, my little mini Anna. I come to think of Mini. I get up and begin to walk back toward the city. My brother must be up by now.

KLAUS RIFBJERG was born in Copenhagen in 1931. He attended Princeton University and the University of Copenhagen, taking his degree in English. He published his first collection of poems, *Getting Wind of Myself* in 1956 and two years later his first novel, *Chronic Innocence*. Since that time he has become the best known, most critically acclaimed, most controversial, and most prolific Danish writer. His output has been enormous (he has over 70 books to his credit) and he has demonstrated his literary skill in every genre -- fiction, poetry, the essay, journalism, film, radio plays, revues, and TV scripts. His work has been translated into numerous languages, including German, French, Dutch, Italian, Polish, Finnish, Roumanian, Czechoslovakian, and Bulgarian. His first selection of poetry in English was published by Curbstone Press in 1976. *Anna (I) Anna* is the first of his novels to appear in English.